From: Delphi@oracle.org
To: C_Evans@athena.edu
Re: professional gambler, Bethany James

Christine,

We're getting closer to naming our enemy. If we can just gain Salvatore Giambi's cooperation—or at least his information—we'll be that much closer to taking down the mastermind behind these plots against the academy. There is a certain piece of Giambi's past that will make him the perfect mark for one of my Oracle agents, Bethany James. She's taken on many identities in the world of professional gambling, and going undercover in Giambi's Monaco casinos will be nothing new for her.

Beth will bring us what we need at this stage of the game. She's the best player I know.

D.

Dear Reader,

Writing about an Athena agent who supports herself as a professional gambler has been great fun and has brought back fond memories. I learned how to play poker as a kid. Not from books or TV, but from the best, a friend of the family who made his living as a professional gambler. With us, it was nickels and dimes, but the lessons learned were invaluable.

I hope you enjoy the adventures of Bethany James, a consummate gambler who always works the odds, both at the table and in the streets.

Terry Watkins

Terry Watkins

STACKED DECK

ATHENA FORCE

Published by Silhouette Books

America's Publisher of Contemporary Romance

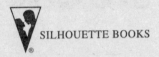

SILHOUETTE BOOKS

ISBN-13: 978-0-373-38976-6
ISBN-10:   0-373-38976-0

STACKED DECK

Visit Athena Force at www.eHarlequin.com

Printed in U.S.A.

This story is for Mike Tooley, the embodiment of a classy, full-time professional gambler, long before it became an "in" sport. He was not only a top card player, he was a philosopher in the fine arts of risk and chance. The object, he always said, wasn't to beat your opponent, it was to lure your opponent into beating themselves. In gambling, Mike was a true Tai Chi Master.

Chapter 1

Las Vegas, March

Bethany James, a twenty-eight-year-old Vegas poker phenom, stared at her quarry with a hunter's gaze as he riffled his chips, little columns neatly folding between his fingers. The tempo grew faster. It was one of his "tells."

"So you want to gamble," he said when she pushed her bet in. "Did you hit the river?"

"Jump in and find out."

She ignored the familiar buzz on her PDA for the fourth or fifth time as she studied her opponent's face, her unflinching stare boring into him like a surgeon's scalpel, cutting away the outer layer, seeing the tightened muscles beneath his expression of calm.

He was bluffing all the way and she was going to take him down.

"One way to find out."

When he was weak, he had the habit of putting his card protector, a small gold skeleton, down on his cards with authority, and he'd done that.

I've got you now, she thought. To needle him a little more, she said, "I should put the clock on you."

"I think you have fours with an over card."

"You wish."

The other three men, all under thirty years of age, had already been small-stacked and eliminated one at a time.

Truth, as her gambler father once said—quoting his hero, the great billionaire gambler Kerry Packer—is what is left when all the lies and secrets, those little "tells," have been revealed and your lie is the last lie standing. That is the moment when you take control of the game.

She waited for her opponent to play his mind games, knowing he was already looking to come over the top, maybe even go "all in" after she'd set him up by limping in with a small bet to look weak, enticing him into believing he could buy the pot with a bluff.

Through the window to the right of the dealer's head, over the empty flower box, beyond the patio of this estate on Sunrise Mountain, Beth stared for a moment to rest her tired eyes, her gaze lingering on the shimmering sea of orange that was the neon metropolis of Las Vegas.

Someone once said of her that she was just like the city she grew up in. A chameleon, a changeling, an impostor.

Yes, true. Survival demanded it.

"You checked on the opening bet. Played slow. What do you have?" he said in a low whisper.

He was searching, hoping to see something. All night she'd been building the fake tell for him to see. Three times she'd bluffed and when she did, she'd pulled her bottom lip in between her teeth and chewed lightly on it. If he picked that up, he would jump all over her.

She pulled her lip in and gnawed away.

Beth could see nearly all the casinos from where she sat and she was outlawed from just about every one of them. Because of her card counting days, she was forced to use disguises when she did attempt entry. Now she mostly played in high-stakes private games like this one.

"You didn't hit a set, did you?" he teased.

She didn't respond.

The city below was laced with traffic, like a vast tangle of white and red snakes, and in the darkening sky to the east planes stacked up like a string of bobbing Chinese lanterns as they descended on McCarran International Airport.

Her eyes rested, she returned her focus to the game.

This twenty-three-hour marathon of Texas Hold 'Em was nearing its denouement. She glanced to her left at the man she was heads-up with: black shaggy hair, an angled face and whiskey-colored eyes. She could smell blood, see it in his play, the faltering steps of a confused and tiring animal.

She knew her adversary was a member of a sophisticated cheating crew, but tonight he was freelancing.

The owner of this house was a friend of hers and knew something was going on between her and the man she was now heads-up with. The man was an addicted gambler who believed that, with or without cheating, he could take down anyone, especially a woman.

Beth knew a lot more about him than she had told her friend. She knew he needed a big score to service his debts.

She'd set the bait and her prey was ready to walk into the trap. Just you and me, babe.

She gave him a stone-cold stare and worked her lip.

The buy-in for this winner-take-all game had been fifty thousand. The quarter-mil take would pay the bills for a long time, but Beth had another use for her money.

She had two income streams, both intermittent. Playing cards for herself, and getting paid to bust cheating crews on behalf of those who'd been taken by them. But this particular game was strictly personal.

The man she was about to crush belonged to one of the largest and most sophisticated cheating crews working the international circuit, a crew that had started twenty years ago in Vegas. The one her father had once belonged to before he was murdered and dumped in a garbage bin sixteen years ago.

The crew was directed and financed by a secret backer who was either her father's killer, or knew that killer's identity. To find out who the backer was she had to flip one of his people. She'd chosen carefully.

She knew the one she'd chosen as the weak link was mortgaged to the hilt, his sources tapped out and in deep hock to loan sharks. He'd borrowed heavily for this last stand and she was going to snatch the prize away from him.

Once she had him at her mercy, she'd make him an offer he couldn't refuse.

He did as she expected and came over the top of her bet with an all-in push. If she followed him in and won, it would be over.

A dog without tricks, she thought, as she followed his all-in, much to his surprise and chagrin.

When she laid down her set, she said, "You're right, I do have a pair of fours, and one extra."

He was stunned. "You limped in, then slow-played when you had them from the get-go?" He seemed amazed and angered that someone would do that.

"It's called a winning tactic."

He stared at her cards, his face twisted in bitter fury mixed with that sick feeling all gamblers know so well. The shock of falling into total ruin.

"I've had crap all damn day," he protested, throwing his cards across the table.

"Maybe it's not the cards," she said. "Maybe it's how you play them."

She could see the rage in his eyes. He wanted to lunge across the table and grab her by the throat, but the other men in the room were *her* friends on the poker circuit, not his. He continued venting his anger verbally.

At that moment Beth got yet another buzz from her PDA, at least the fifth or sixth since the game had started. She'd been ignoring the outside world's attempts to contact her, but now that the game was over she reached in her black shoulder bag, glanced at the message and swore under her breath.

It was the last person on earth she wanted a message from right now—Delphi, her contact with Oracle.

She interrupted her opponent's verbal tirade. "Sorry, I'll have to catch your trash talk on another day."

In the wake of his swearing and the laughter from the other men at the table, Beth slipped out through the glass doors onto the balcony.

She read and reread the text message with consternation and disbelief. This was incredibly bad timing. She was being mission-tasked and Delphi wanted her at the Oracle town house in Virginia ASAP. In the past, she'd been assigned missions that were analysis-based, math and statistics being her area of expertise. This sounded very different. And agents were almost never summoned to the Virginia office.

Why now? Why today?

Using her thumbs like little pistons, she sent a message back requesting a replacement because she was involved in her own urgent business. She could have called Delphi and spoken to her, but not here.

A negative reply returned instantly. Code red. That meant critical and it meant now.

For the first time in her career, Bethany seriously considered the ramifications of refusing an assignment.

She knew if she was working directly for the Feds, NSA or CIA the problem would have been simple. Take the assignment or resign.

But Oracle agents worked for an intelligence agency that existed without mandate or congressional oversight. It didn't show up on any traditional radar, and Beth wasn't sure what the protocol was for refusing a mission.

I'm not going to Virginia, she thought. *Not now. I'll call in later, when I'm home.* She decided that if Allison Gracelyn was available, she'd talk to her. She'd understand. Allison worked with Oracle, too, and she was the one person who could get Bethany released from the assignment.

She went back inside. The men were drinking cognac and smoking cigars, except for her nemesis. He had made a hasty and bitter departure. She'd find him later with her proposition.

"Some of us are better losers than others," Manny Kirk, the owner of the house and a longtime friend said.

She nodded. "That's because you, unlike our friend, know you'll have a chance to get your money back."

The men laughed.

She added, "I'd love to stay and party, but I have some business that needs immediate attention."

There were a dozen or so "poker houses" owned by these guys and their friends scattered around Vegas. Games went on day and night. Partying for them wasn't about drugs and fast women; they were the nerds of the party world and preferred playing pool, video games and more poker on the Internet. These young hotshots in this new world of poker had the good life by the tail.

"I guess you want *the money*," Manny said.

She smiled. "That's why we live and breathe, is it not?"

In the end, unlike the big TV games where scantily clad casino girls brought out trays of money, this was much more subdued.

While the money was being retrieved from a safe, she called Curtis Sault, a bodyguard she employed whenever she was in a big game in Vegas. He'd dropped her off the previous day and now she was in need of a fast exit. The ex-Army Ranger turned professional bodyguard had been told, if she won, he'd be in for a substantial bonus.

She transferred the quarter mil to an expandable travel bag, thanked her host and the other players and then left. With the bag of loot slung over one shoulder, her purse over the other, she felt a little like a happy bank robber.

It was fully dark now when she spotted Curtis Sault roaring up the road in his vintage '58 Corvette. He pulled over the tricked-out red beauty and she dropped the bag on the floorboard and jumped in, settling in the red leather seat with its cool chrome trim. The bag sat between her feet.

Curtis did a one-eighty and they headed down the mountain. He glanced over at the bag. "Is that full of dirty laundry, or should I be congratulating you?"

"You should be smiling from ear to ear 'cause I just paid for your vacation in Costa Rica and then some."

"I'm liking the sound of that. You know what amazes me?"

"What?"

"These guys you play poker with don't get robbed, all the money they have around and no security."

She agreed. Many of the young guns of poker were so flush with cash that it had become commonplace to go into one of their houses and see it everywhere. Money was the new drug of choice.

Beth settled back, her mind preoccupied with how to handle backing out of the Oracle assignment.

They dropped quickly down past the Mormon church that stood on the side of Sunrise Mountain looking down on Vegas like a condemnation. It was her father who told her the Mormons provided the casinos with their most valuable employees, as they had long ago proven to be honest and trustworthy, a highly sought after quality in a casino.

Without warning, Curtis swerved and braked hard, the car's headlights framing a black car that was blocking the road. "What the hell's this?"

He brought the Vette to a skidding halt.

Two men on the far side of the black car raised their arms and extended from their hands the unmistakable glint of gun metal.

"Get down!" Curtis yelled.

He reached for the glove box, pulled out a weapon and at the same time started to back up. Bullets slammed through the windshield.

Another car pulled out of a side street behind them, its high beams flooding the Vette and blinding her when she turned to look.

The ambush was perfect. The trap doors closed at both ends. And when she looked at Curtis to see why he wasn't doing anything she saw blood on his face.

Chapter 2

"Get out, run!" Curtis said as he fired his weapon first one way, then another.

She snapped off her seat belt, grabbed the door handle, opened the door and he pushed her out onto the road.

The firing was from guns with silencers that made little spitting sounds. She rolled over the side of the embankment, her small shoulder bag tangling around her neck as bullets kicked dirt and rocks around her.

When she stopped rolling, she pushed herself up and started running. Glancing back as she ran, she saw Curtis get out of the car, still exchanging gunfire. He was trying to get away, but then he fell, face first onto the pavement.

A sickening feeling clenched her stomach.

Two men came after her, scampering down the hill, fanning out. Then she spotted a third running down the road.

The money was in the car. Why were they after her? Did they think she had the money in her shoulder bag?

Then the frightening thought raced into her mind that it wasn't the money. It was her they were after.

They wanted to kill her.

The houses along the hill were in uneven rows and the men were trying to cut off her escape routes.

She darted into what looked like a narrow lane between two large buildings, only to find that it was an alley that had been dead-ended by a high wall connecting the structures.

Trapped.

She turned and retreated the way she'd come in, but then heard someone running. Frantically she looked for a place to hide and found nothing. She tried a door but it was locked.

Everything slowed to a near halt. She felt the pulsing of her blood through her veins, the intense weight of the air, the granulated texture of the wall her hand brushed against, the push of the stones beneath the feet.

Her gut became a knot of cold, sickening fear.

In panic and desperation, Beth snatched up a large rock and waited at the entrance of the narrow alley.

It wasn't in her nature to die passively, trapped like a rabbit. Her reflexes and reactions had been honed in the tough backstreets of Vegas as the daughter of a down-and-out gambler, and later she'd been trained as a teen in martial arts and survival combat tactics at the Athena Academy.

She heard the gunman before she saw him, his breathing heavy, footsteps crunching gravel as he rounded the corner.

Beth crouched in the blackness, coiled tight as a cobra. She struck, driving up and swinging the rock with everything she had.

Startled, he had no defense other than to raise his hands a split second too late to shield his face.

The rock met skin, bone, teeth and nose with a sickening thud. Blood sprayed across her pink T-shirt, her neck and arms. The man went down hard and stayed there.

She yanked his weapon from his hand, then racked it to make sure a round was chambered as she ran. Curtis had trained her at a firing range, but firing at targets was one thing, firing at people, another. She'd never shot at someone before, but had often wondered what it would be like because she knew one day, when she caught up with the man she was hunting, it just might come to that. Would she hesitate, and because of that, be the one to end up dead? Curtis's words echoed in her mind: *When it's your life, you will fire.*

Her peripheral vision picked up a second man coming toward her twenty yards away.

Without hesitation, she took aim and fired right at him. The gun didn't buck much. The silencer seemed to barely make any sound. But it was effective.

Her pursuer vanished around the corner of a garage behind one of the tract homes and in that instant she knew the exhilarating power of a gun in all its deadly reality.

Beth darted in the opposite direction, cutting down a narrow path.

She caught a view of the third man as he tracked her from one street over, a blip of movement in the dark, sliding fast on her right as he tried to cut off her downhill escape.

She charged through one open backyard gate, then another, past a startled woman and her small white dogs barking with tiny fury in her wake.

Her pursuer cut across below her.

She tried to find another route, but already he was rising over a wall that separated two houses, the man moving with the agility of a gymnast.

She fired. He twisted awkwardly, landed with a yelp and

she didn't know if she'd hit him, or if he'd twisted an ankle. She didn't hang around to find out.

In that instant she thought she understood something about soldiers in combat. Bone-chilling fear can paralyze if you don't squash it quickly.

Sprinting toward another street that bled down the mountain, she came upon a young guy straddling a blue motorcycle, the engine rumbling as he talked to a girl on the curb.

They both glanced at Beth as she ran toward them, utterly unaware of the chaotic battle that had unfolded up the hill.

"I need your bike," Beth said. She'd dated an air force pilot on and off for two years and he'd introduced her to motorcycles. She'd owned a much beloved Harley for a while, but an accident and the increase in traffic had changed her mind about the joys of motorcycle riding in Vegas.

Maybe he didn't see the gun, didn't believe it, but in any case he told her to fuck off.

She was fully in the persona of the tough Vegas kid she'd once been. And her life was at stake. Beth pushed the astonished girl aside, and leveled the semiautomatic at the motorcyclist. "I said I need your motorcycle."

"Ron, get the hell off and give it to her," the girl said. "She's fucking crazy."

He abandoned his machine, hands up. "It's all yours. Don't shoot me."

Beth said, "You have a cell phone?"

He nodded.

"Then call the police and tell them somebody has been shot up on Peaceful Lane. Send an ambulance. Tell them there are three men with guns running around up there. I'll call in the location of your motorcycle in an hour. Sorry, but I have to get out of here."

She mounted the bike, heeled the kick stand and roared off into the Vegas night.

As she drove, the wind brushing across her face and the rumble of the engine on her legs, she tried to push the shock of what had just happened out of her mind so she could keep her focus on her driving. But the image of Curtis hitting the pavement, and not knowing if he was alive or dead, made her sick with apprehension.

Beth blew through traffic on Nellis Boulevard until she felt she was well away from trouble. Then she pulled into a strip mall and dialed 911 on her cell, just in case the couple freaked and didn't call the police. "There's been a shooting up on Peaceful Lane. A man's wounded or he may be dead."

She hung up before they could ask her anything. Then, trembling from all the madness, she called a detective. She knew most of the detectives in Vegas, but only trusted one man. He was the detective who had investigated her father's death and had never really let it get tossed into the cold case file. His voice was soothing in her ear.

"Detective Ayers? This is Bethany James."

"Hey, Beth what's up?"

She struggled not to sound hysterical as she told him what happened.

"Beth, where are you?"

"I borrowed a motorcycle from some guy to get away. He didn't volunteer it exactly. I'll call you later and tell you where it is. I can't explain anything right now. But my bodyguard was hit, Curtis Sault. I want to know how he is. Call me when you know something. I need to lay low until I find out who is trying to kill me."

"Beth, I need you to—"

Beth hung up. She didn't want to get involved with the police. Not until she had things figured out. She sat there thinking for a minute, staring at the flood of traffic on Nellis. Suddenly she knew what she was going to do. Get out of town, go to Virginia and straighten things out with Oracle even if that meant severing ties. Then she would come back here and deal with this.

She called the airport and made a reservation for the next flight out of Vegas that would get her to the Washington Dulles Airport in Virginia. She got a seat on the redeye.

She headed back out in traffic, turned south on Charleston heading for the freeway to McCarran International Airport.

Two hours later Beth, having learned that Curtis Sault had been taken to Sunrise Hospital and was in surgery, but expected to live, sat in a window seat as her flight took off from McCarran.

She was incredibly relieved. She didn't want tears in her eyes and the guy sitting next to her asking if she was all right. She wasn't in the mood for conversation.

She'd cleaned up in the ladies room inside McCarran and changed into a "What Happens in Vegas…" T-shirt and a pair of black sports pants with Las Vegas lettered across her butt in bright pink. She'd stopped at the first shop she'd come to inside the airport, having no choice but to change out of her dirty and blood-spattered clothes or she would never be allowed to board the plane. Now she looked like some kind of walking billboard, but at least she was blood-free.

The flight would get her into Dulles at six in the morning and she intended to stop somewhere for breakfast—she was starving—then go straight to Oracle headquarters and get this thing settled.

Beth tried to get a little sleep, but the catastrophe of

having an acquaintance shot wound her so tightly she stayed awake during the entire flight.

She was certain that because someone was trying to kill her and she was now mixed up with a homicide, Oracle would cut her loose from the mission without consequence and she could return to Vegas to deal with this situation. Convinced tonight's attack was connected to her search for her father's killer, she must be on the right track now, and couldn't afford any delays.

Allison Gracelyn was the only person Beth knew who was connected to Oracle. The organization did not advertise its existence in any way. Few knew about it at all. Fewer knew any of the people involved. Even the agents who were sent on assignments had little, if any, knowledge of other agents.

But Beth and Allison had a special bond. Both had lost parents to murder.

In Allison's case, it was her mother, founder of the Athena Academy, where Beth had gotten her education. Allison, of all people, would understand her current situation. She was also an Athena grad and was the person who had recruited Beth.

When Beth's father was killed she was twelve and had no other family to take her in. She became a ward of the state of Nevada. At some point she'd been given a battery of aptitude tests. The results, especially in math, brought her to the attention of a very special college prep school, Athena Academy for girls in Phoenix, Arizona. Allison was still very much involved in the school.

The academy had given Beth an education unlike anything offered in any other school in America. Besides a strong academics program she studied martial arts, learned horseback riding and analyzed war-game strategies, as well as languages and international political theory.

The school prepared her and the other girls for much more than just higher education. It prepared them to compete with men at the highest levels of whatever careers they chose.

For Beth, becoming an Oracle agent was the logical step for someone with her unique skills. As a professional card player, the legacy of her father, she played in high-stakes games all over the world.

Because of her card playing, Beth had unusual access to an entire strata of movers and shakers in the shadows of global finance. This was a big asset for Oracle and she hoped it might work in her favor now, allowing her to bow out of this mission, whatever it was, without souring the relationship.

It would be an immense loss if she had to cut her ties to Oracle, Allison and the academy, the only family she'd had since her father's death, but Beth was too close to learning the name of her father's killer, and nothing short of her own death would stop her from getting that information.

Chapter 3

When the plane landed, Beth headed for the nearest food kiosk. After a blueberry scone, one almost ripe banana, a bag of spicy tortilla chips and a large black coffee, she rented an Alero from Avis.

Once inside her car, she reminded herself what was at stake here, and rehearsed what she wanted to say to Allison. Other agents could be called in out of the cold to do this job. They really didn't need her. And she had something else to do that was, in her mind of far greater significance.

She had never quit anything important, let alone the most important organization she'd ever belonged to. Its code of silence and loyalty was unmatched. It was, to be sure, a lot tighter than the crumbling mafia code of *omerta*, or the sieve that was the CIA.

At eight-thirty in the morning, Beth drove the Alero through the security gate to the rear of the town house that served as Oracle's inconspicuous residential location.

The first time she'd been to Oracle's nerve center, she'd expected some huge building appropriate for a major intelligence operation. Instead it was an unassuming town house as befitting its very low profile.

Her arrival had already been cleared. The agency didn't like more than one at-large agent showing up at any given time. It was rare, in fact, to ever be invited here and that made this even more unusual.

Beth had never known Oracle's leader's identity, but she'd often wondered if Delphi was actually the code name for Allison Gracelyn. Whether or not Allison, also an employee of NSA, was Delphi she *was* one of the major powers in Oracle, and the one person Bethany wanted to deal with on a personal basis.

She entered the town house through the rear, her thumb print and a retina scan necessary to get in. She went into the kitchen where a woman sat at the table drinking coffee and talking on a cell phone.

Beth glanced at her, made a passing nod and headed upstairs. A young red-headed staffer told her that Allison was in a meeting and asked her to wait in Allison's office.

Beth made her way into the office. There was a desk, a laptop, a few photos of bucolic settings on the walls, a small refrigerator in one corner, a sofa against the far wall with matching chairs and an oak coffee table.

As she waited for her former classmate, she reflected on her years at Athena Academy at the base of the White Tank Mountains near Phoenix. They were some of the best years of her life.

Everyone who attended the academy was put in a particular group. Hers was Artemis, the Huntress in mythology. She often missed the camaraderie, the competition and the fun of those years, and it brought a smile to her face thinking about all the trouble her secret, "floating" card games had gotten her in.

And those famous words from one of her instructors: "Beth, are you trying to turn this academy into a Las Vegas casino?"

Beth was lost in her memories when she heard Allison out in the hall talking to someone.

Beth took a deep breath to calm down. She didn't want to just blurt out everything in a gush of emotion. Allison was the consummate professional and Beth wanted to keep her respect and the connection to Oracle.

Allison walked in carrying a laptop shoulder bag. She said, tongue-in-cheek, "Wow. The outfit is so—" she smiled ruefully and raised her eyebrows "—Vegas."

For her part, Allison looked great, her brilliant brown eyes smiling as she shook Beth's hand. She wore a tailored gray business suit, white blouse, short hair tucked neatly behind her ears, very little makeup, but the jade teardrop earrings gave the business look a feminine edge.

Allison motioned toward the sofa and matching chairs. They sat across from each other in the chairs.

Beth explained the outfit and filled Allison in on the incident in Vegas and the events leading up to it, and why, because of it, she couldn't take the mission.

"I'm convinced the men who came after me did so on the orders of the man who runs a cheating crew. It could be the crew my father once worked for."

Allison studied her intently for a moment, before saying, "The man you believe your father worked for when he was murdered?"

"Yes. I think he now realizes who I am and what I'm doing. I'm very close. I have to carry this through."

Allison nodded. "I absolutely understand the urgency of

your situation, but we really do need you for this operation." She smiled slightly, and rested her hands in her lap. "I really think you'll reconsider after you hear the details and the unusual set of circumstances surrounding this mission."

Beth shook her head, adamant and controlled. "There has to be somebody who can sub for me. I absolutely can't do it right now."

"Beth, you're not only assuming the hit team that tried to take you out is connected to the cheating crew you've been tracking, but you're convinced of it. However, you have no hard evidence to prove this, and you've been down this road before with other crews."

"I know. But I have a good feeling this time that I'm on the right track."

"But still no actual proof."

"Not yet. But I will."

"I can see that it's easy to fuse your own emotional vendetta with everything that happened."

"I don't think that's what I'm doing," Beth said, trying hard not to get defensive.

Allison sat back in her chair, folded her hands and tucked her legs to one side, then she sat forward again and straightened her back. All tells.

Beth knew she was in for a serious briefing.

"Beth, at the moment, every graduate of Athena Academy must be considered a target, as well as our students. There've been a few attempted kidnappings. We're all under attack. Since the school was founded it has had supporters and enemies, but there is one enemy in particular who has been there right from the beginning. We absolutely must track down this person. And for that we need your help."

"Am I the only one who can do this? I'm usually just given data analysis tasks. This sounds different."

"It is. Very different. And yes, you are the only one who can handle this, in my estimation. There are several reasons for this. The first being, we need your expertise in Monaco."

"Monaco?"

"Yes. There is a casino there, the Sapphire Star, owned by one Salvatore Giambi. He's the target. We suspect he was blackmailed by someone with a signature 'A' now known as Arachne. We want to know anything and everything you can discover about the blackmailer through Giambi's financial transactions over the years."

Monaco was so far from Vegas that Beth just couldn't do this, but still she asked, "The blackmailer is the person you think is the Athena Academy's enemy?"

"Yes. We think that is a very likely scenario. This goes all the way back to a jailbreak in Phoenix in 1968 and the attempted assassination of a female prisoner, known at the time as Weaver. She was about to stand trial for murder. My mother was the prosecuting attorney. Weaver was a suspected CIA assassin. She apparently believed my mother set up her boyfriend. Weaver was pregnant at the time. During her escape, her boyfriend was killed, and later she lost her baby. Weaver has since accumulated many aliases, one of them is Arachne. We suspect that Arachne is behind the attacks on Athena. We're hoping that Giambi will lead us closer to Weaver."

Beth still didn't see a reason for her role in this.

Allison continued, "Weaver was blackmailing my mother right up until her death. Blackmail is something she's very good at. We also believe she's been a freelance killer across the globe for a long time. She did so much work for the CIA and its clients over the years, heavy work during the Vietnam War, that she knows where all the bodies are buried. Which means, she has information of the kind that has allowed her to make a fortune blackmailing former clients."

Beth could feel the tension building in her neck. She tried to relax by sitting back in her chair and unclenching her hands. She'd had enough physical action to last her a long time, and really didn't want to get pushed into the underworld in Monaco.

"What we do know," Allison said, "is Arachne is called different names in different places around the world. In Russia she's known as Madame Web. We need to confirm our suspicion that Arachne is the same blackmailer Giambi has been paying for decades. What you're being asked to do is get into Giambi's financial universe and track down his blackmail payments to their source. This man has critical information and we need it."

"Why would you give me this assignment? It's not what I do, and it's a long way from Las Vegas."

"For a couple reasons." Allison untucked her legs, stood up and walked over to her desk.

She came back with a large white envelope. This time she sat on the sofa right next to Beth's chair. She put the envelope down on the coffee table. "We need you because you understand the people in the gaming world. Salvatore Giambi, like any casino boss, has always had his eye on the cheating crews to protect his own business. He's been around a long time and hasn't been hit by one of these crews in about thirty years or so. Whatever his source, whether it's the mob or some intelligence branch, we don't know, but we do know he's probably the most knowledgeable guy on the planet on this subject. That gives the two of you a bond of sorts. And his knowledge of the cheating crews was one of the reasons he was allowed to open a casino in Monaco. He protects the city from international cheating rings and the authorities allow him to run his casino."

Beth said, "The cheating crews that I know about are mostly out of Vegas."

"Giambi may not be located in Vegas now, but he was there for a time and he still has friends. He's invested heavily in Vegas. We've checked that out. And the casinos he's invested in, unlike all the rest, never get hit by the major crews. It's like they have a protective cloak against cheaters."

Now Allison had Beth's full attention. She sat straight up in her chair, leaning in close. A little jolt of excitement ran through her. "So you think Giambi might know something about the crew my father worked for."

Allison smiled. "If anyone does, it would be Giambi. The man's seventy-eight years old. He's been everywhere and knows just about everyone in the gaming world, on both sides of the table. Beth, I know what finding your father's killer means to you. When I realized we were going to go after Giambi, I thought of you immediately in spite of your lack of experience in physical missions. I'm extremely confident in you. We need somebody who can create the right kind of identity for this operation and you're the best at choosing the right identity for the game. And for you, this is a win-win. You help us and yourself at the same time. Though you aren't specifically trained for this kind of mission, you're exactly right for it."

Damn, she did it, Beth thought. She's got me.

She could see in Allison's eyes that she knew she had won. All of Beth's arguments fell mute. All the energy she'd built up preparing to go toe-to-toe with this woman, with the organization, collapsed.

Allison said, "Are you interested?"

"Of course. How could I refuse now? Who will I become?"

"A very wealthy, jet-setting widow and businesswoman."

"As of last night, I've become a little short of funds."

"Don't worry. We'll fund this operation. Your new accounts will have plenty of money in them. But don't lose it all."

Beth smiled. "I usually win. What's my new identity?"

"Anne Hurley, a rich widow with two major interests that happen to be Giambi's passion—Formula One racing and poker. You're going to arrive in Monaco with all the trimmings of a 'whale' who's looking for some action at the tables and also looking at the possibility of investing in Giambi's dream of fielding a Formula One team." Allison slid the envelope over to Beth. "You'll find your new passport, credit cards, driver's license, et cetera, inside this envelope."

"I know nothing about Formula One. Vegas is a NASCAR town."

Allison pulled an Apple laptop from her shoulder bag. "Everything you could possibly need to know is stored on this laptop." Allison handed the laptop to Beth. "You also have access to all the data we have on Giambi and his casino."

Allison continued, "Right now Giambi is rounding up investors. Before you make an appearance at his casino, your money will arrive ahead of you for deposit toward your gaming. And we'll see to it you have an established reputation, a past and the financial records to go with your new identity. Everything is being inserted into the digital universe. If he does a background check on you, and he will, you're going to come up as the ideal candidate for his needs. He's ambitious. He's even floated an idea to the mayor of Las Vegas about bringing Formula One there."

"Why would Vegas want Formula One?"

"Because it's the elite venue in racing, catering to the

international jet set. And it wouldn't impact NASCAR negatively. Their fan base is rock solid. Giambi seems to be trying to create a legacy. He's also looking into building a casino in Kestonia. He apparently believes that Eastern Europe could be the next Vegas. And he might be getting ready to leave Monaco in the near future. Prince Albert is trying to clean up Monaco's act. As Somerset Maugham once said, Monaco is 'a sunny place for shady people.'"

Beth nodded. "Sounds like a fit description for the old Vegas as well."

"Prince Albert wants any money laundering in the principality ended. He's trying to cooperate with the European Union banking regulations to get rid of illicit tax havens, and the presence of the *Cosa Nostra*. When and if this becomes a reality, Giambi will have to move his operations elsewhere."

Allison pulled out a photo from her laptop bag and handed it to Beth. "Giambi's Formula One driver, John David 'JD' Hawke. He's a bit of a bad boy who's been involved in some battles that got him suspended from Formula One. He's reinstated now, but needs a ride. He likes fast cars and hot women. A little mixing of pleasure with business might just fast-track your operation."

Beth stared at the photo of JD. He had it going on, no doubt. Right up to the cocky I-get-what-I-want smile, his blond cropped hair, smoky blue eyes and a slight dimple in his left cheek. She looked up at Allison and said facetiously, "Mixing pleasure and business dulls my edge."

"Getting close to JD will make your penetration of Giambi's computers and files easier. But it's your call."

"How close is JD to Giambi?"

"Very. Giambi has all but adopted JD Hawke. He's given him an apartment adjoining his sumptuous fifteen-thousand-foot Playboy-mansion style suite atop the casino. A lot of partying goes on up there."

"A real player." Beth stared at the picture for a moment longer then slipped it into the envelope.

"You should have everything you need, including the latest hacking software. If you're missing something, contact Delphi. You're leaving for Nice at five-thirty this evening. It's a short chopper-hop from there to Monaco. A villa has been rented in Monaco for your use. Take a couple days to prep. And enjoy the Mediterranean lifestyle."

Allison glanced at her watch, then stood up, saying, "I have a meeting."

Beth had one more question. "Just who is Delphi?"

Allison gave her a wry smile. "That's strictly need-to-know."

As they left the office, Allison said, "Oracle agents and Athena graduates have finally become a force in this town. The walls of the old boys' clubs have been breached. Some, of course, are fighting back. We still have a long way to go to achieve our final goals and we can't allow this current problem with Arachne to derail us."

Every Athena grad knew what those goals were. A woman in the White House and parity, or dominance, across the board.

Allison stopped and looked Beth in the eyes. "Good luck, Beth. I hope Salvatore Giambi gives up what we're looking for, and I hope you find what you're looking for as well."

"Thanks."

"I've made an appointment for you in thirty minutes with Randolph. He can help with a new look. He's very good."

She gave Beth Randolph's card, shook her hand and headed for the door to her office. Then she stopped and turned to Beth. "Oh, by the way, do you tango?"

The question caught Beth off guard. She hesitated for a moment, then said, "Yes, actually. I'm not great, but—"

"Good. Get yourself a tango outfit. Giambi loves to tango. I understand he's an excellent dancer."

It never failed, one hour with Allison and you walked out ready to give your all to the mission. The woman, Beth mused, would have made a fantastic no-limit poker player, but then those skills were also the same ones necessary for success on the big stage of politics and power.

As for Salvatore Giambi, he had suddenly become the most important person in the world to Beth. He was the key to protecting Athena, and he was the key, she hoped, to finding her father's killer.

On her way to her appointment with Randolph, Beth got a call from Detective Ayers informing her that Curtis was in stable condition. "He's going to survive, and we have one of the shooters in custody. He's not talking, but that's a temporary condition, I'm sure."

She told Ayers where she left the bike at McCarran, and thanked him for calling with the information about Curtis.

Beth didn't know what problems she would have to deal with in Vegas over the shooting and her leaving town, but they would have to wait until she got back.

"I'd like you to come into the office to answer a few questions," he said.

"I will," Beth promised. "But I have some important business to take care of first."

Relieved with the good news, Beth ended the call and wondered just what JD Hawke was up to at that exact moment, and what type of woman would get under his skin.

She had thirty minutes to figure it out.

Chapter 4

Beth quoted the movie lines with Grace Kelly's silky purr:

"'Hold them. Diamonds…the only thing in the world you can't resist. Then tell me you don't know what I'm talking about. Even in this light, I can tell where your eyes are looking.'"

Randolph, a short, plump, bald stylist, chuckled. "Believe me, honey, as wonderful as your assets are, they're not in my portfolio of thrills."

Beth laughed as she sat in Randolph's boutique in a trendy Washington D.C. neighborhood getting a makeover.

While he did his magic, she watched clips of Grace Kelly in *To Catch a Thief* on her PDA, mimicking the heroine's classy intonation. Grace was a woman's woman. Someone to emulate, to watch, to impersonate. Beth wondered just how much of it was an act. Was Grace Kelly the consummate actress on the silver screen *and* in real life?

" 'Ever had a better offer in your whole life? One with everything?' "

Randolph stopped fussing with her hair and looked at Beth in the mirror. "You're good. You sound just like her. She was a princess, wasn't she? Such class. And that hair, like spun platinum."

Randolph fitted yet another wig on Beth's head, this one honey-colored and shoulder-length. "How do you like this, darlin'? Hot and sexy? I think the color looks fab with your hazel eyes."

Beth twisted from side to side to get a better look in the mirror. "It's close, but I want it a little shorter."

Randolph slipped the honey wig off and replaced it with a blond, jaw-length bob.

"You're in a play, right?"

Beth decided to go with his guess. "Yes. Off, off Broadway. It's a spoof on Grace Kelly movies."

Beth had always loved morphing into an imaginary "other" ever since she was a child living a desperate life with her gambler father, bouncing from losing streak to losing streak. They were flotsam in the rapids of Las Vegas gaming, caught, injured, then tossed back into the current.

Her father, who had predicted he would end up buried in the desert, ended up dead in a Dumpster.

Her mother was only a figment of Beth's imagination, having fled before Beth could know her. So Beth created and recreated her life, her image, her history, shedding skin like a rattlesnake in August. It made her an accomplished actress on the world stage.

Beth tugged at the wig, getting it straight on her head. She liked this one. It gave off the right look—wealthy, without being too brash. Plus, it had just the right amount of retro to give her that elegant Grace Kelly look.

"Perfect," she said. "I want my hair lightened this exact shade of blond and cut in this style."

"Wish I could see you perform. I bet you're good."

"I'm a method actor, *dahlin'*," Beth purred. "I scare 'em and excite 'em at the same time."

Randolph laughed. "Ooh, you play rough."

"Sometimes, but I'm worth it."

He stepped back from the chair and gave her the once-over. "Yeah, I can see it. You've got that edge to you. Like you're hiding a tiger under a pink dress."

They both laughed.

As Randolph worked his magic on her, she thought about how crazy her life had been growing up in Vegas. As a kid, she never felt anger or hatred or even animosity toward her father. She had seen too much of his struggle, his love for her, his ambition—even in hopeless failure—to give her a better life. It was his purpose, his goal. And though he'd died when she was only twelve, without accomplishing that goal in the end, above all else, his love for her was the source of her great inner strength. Because he believed in her, she never doubted who she was beneath the disguises. She merely used them as a means to an end, not as an attempt to erase her true self.

The following day, wearing several thousand dollars' worth of designer clothes, shoes and obscenely expensive jewelry, carrying Louis Vuitton luggage filled with more of the same, Beth, aka Anne Hurley, rich widow, poker player, businesswoman and passionate lover of open wheel Formula One racing—and the tango—left Dulles International for the four-thousand-mile flight to Nice, France, followed by a seven-minute hop to Monaco by helicopter. She'd changed her voice, her walk and her attitude to fit her new persona. The next part of the metamorphosis was done at a fabulous villa Delphi had rented for her on a Monaco hillside above the Monte Carlo casino.

She spent much of the next forty-eight hours out on the patio working on her laptop, stopping once in a while to take in the breathtaking view of the French Riviera, while a soft breeze rising from the Mediterranean washed over her.

Periodically she'd look down at the yachts settled like a great flock of white birds on the deep blue sea, the steep hillside covered with pastel villas bathed in the golden sunlight and the endless blue sky above. What could be better, she wondered, than to be filthy rich in Monaco, playground for the rich and the royal?

With her near photographic memory and a capacity to focus for long periods of time, Beth could inculcate volumes of information quickly. To fake a background with success she needed the fine details, the particulars people in the profession paid attention to, the latest jargon.

She listened to dozens of CDs, watched DVDs, read bios of drivers and memorized the complete history of Formula One.

Through a tiny pair of binoculars she carried in her purse, she could see the Sapphire Star Casino on an adjacent hill. It had the look of old Europe to it. Understated. The home of her target: Salvatore Giambi.

We will meet soon, Mister Giambi, she thought. He'd been made aware of her arrival, and had been given advance notice that she was interested in investing in his racing team.

And she knew he was desperate for investors. Not just because of financial problems, but, according to the files she'd been reading, his marquee driver, JD Hawke, had a bad boy history that scared off would be investors. JD's on-track fights, off-track mouth, and daredevil driving had made him a pariah. Only his great talent, and Giambi's willingness to gamble, made a comeback possible.

On the fifteenth floor of the Sapphire Star Casino, Salvatore Giambi stormed into his office. He was in a sour mood.

His race driver, JD Hawke, was seated at Giambi's desk playing a video game on an open laptop.

"To hell with the prince! To hell with Monaco!" Giambi bellowed.

JD nodded without looking up. "What's going on?"

Giambi stared at him. "JD, when the hell is this Anne Hurley supposed to show up?"

As JD obviously crushed his cyber opponent, he held up his arms in complete victory and looked up, beaming. "I thought you said tonight."

Giambi stared at JD for a moment, wondering what the hell was so exciting about those damn games. "Can you do that somewhere else, I have work to do."

"Sure," JD said as he closed out and stood up.

"Let me know when she gets here." He walked toward his desk just as JD was leaving it. "How much did I say was transferred to her account with us? I forgot."

"An even million. If you took that Ginkgo biloba I bought you, your memory would improve."

"I hate pills."

"It's a vitamin."

"I don't care what you call it, it's still a pill."

"It's your choice, but I—"

"I don't have time for this." He waved JD's statement away. "She didn't want a comped room. What, my five-star hotel isn't good enough for her?"

"Apparently she's got friends to stay with," JD said, as he tried to leave.

"Don't get lost. I want you to meet this woman when she gets here."

JD tossed him a look. He didn't like being treated as if he was one of Giambi's assistants, but the way Giambi looked at it, the guy had nothing to do but train with weights, party all night with his friends and wait until he, Giambi, got him a seat in a race car. Nice life if you could get it. "You might as well do something besides play video games and party."

"Okay, *boss*," JD said, with that Tennessee drawl of his.

Giambi didn't particularly like the way JD called him "boss" like he was making fun of him. Like the way Paul Newman said it in that movie. What was it called? Shit! He couldn't remember, but it had something to do with prison.

JD left and Giambi settled in behind his desk. He was moving money as fast as he could out of Monaco and out of Europe. He knew he was being targeted by Prince Albert personally in this crusade against money laundering.

No respect.

And after all he'd done protecting the principality and the Grimaldi family over the years.

God he hated that Rainier and his beautiful princess were gone. Those were the days. When they were in power, Monaco was the greatest country on earth.

He blamed the Bush administration's war on terrorism more than the European Union for the present crackdown.

At the same time he was dodging the new regime, that bitch who was blackmailing him was demanding a bigger piece of his pie. Between her, the Monaco cleanup, and investors in his racing team suddenly getting scarce, Giambi felt the walls closing in. He was being forced to reach out to people he had never done business with and he didn't like it. You reach out, you don't know who you're gonna get.

That tended to kick his normal paranoia up a notch.

Now it was the time of the month, as with every month, that he had to wire the money to the biggest mistake of his life. One that was slowly bleeding him to death. He wanted be rid of her in the worst way, but he'd all but given up trying to kill her. Half the intelligence agencies in the world had been no more successful than he had.

He unlocked the drawer of his desk and pulled it out. The laptop came up into position. He opened up the secret account. The bitch seemed to know exactly what his take was each month and she made sure he handed the lion's share over to her. It was a double transfer from his bank in Monaco, through an intermediary, and eventually to her accounts in Puerto Isla. She changed numbers and destinations so often he'd begun to think she wasn't a person but an organization.

Hell, maybe she was dead and he was paying some rogue CIA group!

Giambi made the transfer, then made a call to check on the progress of a Greek shipping magnate's yacht, which was heading for Monaco. He was a billionaire with an interest in the proposal Giambi had made about building a casino in Kestonia. Giambi was talking up the small, Eastern European country as the next Vegas. It was also a place a man could work his money without worry. If Giambi could bring the Greek on board his casino venture, then get the rich widow to invest in his Formula One team, life might start looking good again.

He had a printout about this rich widow, Anne Hurley. Worth upwards of a hundred million dollars, she definitely could be the solution to some of his immediate problems. He wanted his race team up and running again, but it would take millions to accomplish that and he couldn't afford to go it alone.

Sometimes, and this was one of them, he'd just stop his mind. Just suddenly stare off into space at the truth. He was seventy-eight years old, and time was shooting by on a fast train to nowhere.

In those few seconds, when he stared that truth dead in the face, it scared him to the quick.

All those vitamins and longevity formulas he tried to down, all the care he took of his body by working out every damn day, none of that could erase the years.

And that reality pushed Giambi to get things done and get them done now. He still had ambitions, big ambitions.

If it weren't for that damn blackmailer, he'd be one of the truly big players. Steve Wynn and Donald Trump wouldn't have had anything on him. He'd have been as big as both combined. And as far as racing was concerned, Christ, he could have teamed up with Paul Newman in the Indy league and coaxed him over into Formula One.

One of these days, he promised himself, he was going to hunt that bitch down and put a bullet in her himself. At his age, he was beyond worrying about consequences.

His phone rang. It was the concierge in the lobby. "Anne Hurley just phoned and requested a limo," the rough voice said. Giambi didn't know which of his employees was speaking to him, he only knew that at that moment the guy deserved a raise.

"What time will she be here?"

"Around nine-thirty, sir."

"Let me know the minute she arrives."

"Will do."

He hung up, and downed three extra-strength Tums to neutralize some of the acid in his stomach. Then he walked over to his bar to pour himself a scotch and get a cigar.

I still have a good fifteen years, Giambi thought, and Ms. Hurley is going to help me enjoy every damn minute of it.

He lit his cigar and gazed out the window. "*Cool Hand Luke!* That was the name of that damn Paul Newman film. Ginkgo biloba my ass."

Chapter 5

While waiting for the limo, Beth checked her Judith Leiber bag to ensure that the cloner and tiny antenna were in the right pocket. This was her means to pick up a signal from a smart-card badge. She would catch the signal emitted from the badge and download the data onto her cloner, then later make the transfer to her computer. She had other B&E tools for getting in and out of secure places, and she'd been provided instructions, but not a lot of practice. Her main means of entry, she hoped, would be JD Hawke, once she figured out how to get some leverage with him.

The limo picked her up at 9:15 p.m. On the way to Giambi's place the limo passed Le Grand Casino on 1 Ave Princess Grace, then over to the Sun Casino on 12 Ave des Spelugues, and, of course, the Monte Carlo Sporting Club.

The playboys and playgirls of the moneyed world were out and about cruising in their Mercedes, BMWs and Ferraris.

Beth had had a great time here several years ago, gambling and dancing at Jimmy Z Dance, mingling with the trendsetters at this premier hot spot on the French Riviera.

When the limo pulled up in front of Sapphire Star, a dapper casino valet dressed in a red shirt, black vest and black pants opened her door.

"*C'est avec le grand plaisir* that we welcome you to the Sapphire Star Casino, Monaco."

She nodded as if her entire life was an entrance to sumptuous digs and servile attention. *"Merci beaucoup."*

She stepped out of the limo wearing a hot blue, butterfly-lace dress with black trim that hugged all the right places on her toned body; her bling bag dangled from her shoulder, and Manolo pumps on her feet gave a feminine look to her long, athletic legs.

Before she went two steps a gorgeous hunk of a man emerged from the casino wearing casual slacks, a tan shirt and a cream-colored leather sports jacket. Wow.

He headed toward her like a radar-guided, heat-seeking missile, and even though he was taller than she'd imagined, at least six feet, she recognized him instantly—JD Hawke. He walked with that cocky *Saturday Night Fever* Travolta strut, wide in the shoulders, narrow in the hips and every bit the cat on the prowl. Maybe mixing business and pleasure would be a nice advantage. Her body was already reacting to the guy, and she kind of liked how her heartbeat quickened as he strode toward her.

This Tennessee racecar driver, her initial target, looked like very delicious trouble. Bring it on.

She suppressed a grin.

She watched as he took her in from top to bottom, then locked eyes with her. "Miss Hurley, welcome to the Sapphire Star. I'm Mister Giambi's associate. He would like to invite you to have a drink with him." A warm smile followed his rich Southern drawl.

"Right now?"

"Yes, ma'am." He had an engaging smile, big and handsome enough to paint a blush on a teenage girl's face. She felt her own cheeks heat up after his intimate stare. C'mon, Beth, time to get a grip.

"Aren't you the racecar driver, John Davis Hawke?" She made sure there was just a touch of awe in her voice.

He nodded as they shook hands. "Yes, ma'am. But people generally call me JD. At least those who like me."

Beth smiled a slow smile back at him, then followed JD into the elegant, soft ambiance of Giambi's casino. She couldn't wait to meet the man who was able to establish a casino in Monaco, a major accomplishment in and of itself. Monaco was a very protective place and this ex-Boston Wise Guy was, apparently, part of that protection.

"If you want to play some poker," JD said as they stepped inside a private elevator, "we have a unique poker room for special guests."

"And what makes it unique?" She liked the smell of him, clean and fresh. As if he'd just taken a bath, a long, leisurely bath. A bath where he lounged in an oversized tub, his long finger beckoning her to join him. She liked the image. Too much. She forced the picture out of her mind.

"Let me show you."

She mentally shook herself as the elevator stopped on the fourth floor and the doors opened onto a piece of the old American West.

JD said, "This is a duplicate of the poker room underneath the famous Bird Cage Theater in Tombstone, Arizona."

"I've seen the original," Beth said. "That's where Wyatt Earp played poker and where he met his third wife."

JD gave her a glance. "You are exactly right."

They walked past the tiny poker room with its three tables nestled behind a railing. "Everything's to scale," JD said. "The exact lampshades and chairs, even right down to the bullet holes in the walls and cigarette burns on the tables."

Beth looked around at the surrounding closed doors. "I see you even have the rooms where the prostitutes served the needs of the clients. I presume they aren't in operation."

"Not exactly. These are private dining rooms for the players. Very private dining rooms."

Beth caught his eye and then glanced at the older men at the tables surrounded by a few women not much younger than Beth. "Some things never change," she said.

JD smiled, then laughed lightly. "Makes life more interesting, don't you agree?"

She found herself smiling. "Yes. There's something to be said for tradition."

"Yes, ma'am, there sure is."

They both smiled slyly at the same time, and instantly Beth knew this guy was going to be way too easy. And maybe just a little too much fun.

Several of the men at the tables wore ten-gallon cowboy hats. Beth said, as they walked around the outside of the railing, "If Vegas recreates everything that is classically European, why not return the favor with a little bit of the Old West in Monaco. Giambi is obviously a shrewd businessman."

"One of the best."

She noticed the players using the large, square Monaco-style chips. They were difficult to riffle, but Beth had mastered the technique and was anxious to hold those chips once again.

Soon enough, she thought.

They walked away from the tables and past a packed restaurant tucked behind a small piano bar. Beth decided to open a new conversation. "I've seen you race and you're one of the top-rated talents out there who doesn't currently have a ride."

He looked over at her, wounded pride showing on his face. "Hopefully I'll have one soon."

"Monaco Grand Prix is only a few weeks away. Any chance?"

With a note of bummed frustration, he said, "Not likely this year."

They encountered Giambi sitting alone at a back table of the piano bar. The casino owner rose when he spotted them and stretched his six-two frame, which appeared to have withstood gravity very well. He had a neat shock of white hair and excellent taste in clothes: dark, pin-striped suit, wingtip shoes and a tiny pink rose pinned to his lapel.

As if making an announcement, he said, "I'm Salvatore Giambi, proprietor of this fine establishment," and stuck out his hand to meet hers.

His hand felt warm, and his eyes were ice-chip gray with no sign of melt in them. She knew plenty of eyes like that in Vegas. They reminded her of tiny gun portals, the eyes of a man forever under siege.

They sat down at his table and chatted amicably for a minute or two about the weather and poker. JD kept quiet, his eyes rarely leaving her.

The waitress took her drink order, a green apple martini. When she left, Giambi got right to the point. "An intriguing rumor has reached me that you are looking to invest in a Formula One team. Any truth to that?"

"Quite a bit of truth." She made herself comfortable in her chair, knowing this might take a while.

They discussed his race team, who his other drivers might be, the cars he was building and his search for sponsors. Giambi seemed quick and sharp, despite his age.

By her second martini she was telling them about the Formula One race she'd seen right there in Monaco when she was six. She told lies with great conviction and flair, a talent that every good poker player must possess.

"I still have Alain Prost's autograph after he won that race. He set the record before the new chicane at one-thirty-eight kilometers. The lap record was a Ferrari, Michele Alboreto, over one forty-four. I actually got a ride in his car. Not very far, but it was one of the most exciting moments in my life."

The two men exchanged surreptitious glances.

When she was telling them about how she not only loved the races, but the endless work in designing and building cars, Giambi suggested she should have a look at his new race shop and the cars he was building.

She said, "I'd love a tour."

"JD will be happy to give you a tour anytime. Won't you, JD?" Giambi gazed over at JD.

JD looked a little startled, as if he hadn't been listening to what was being said. "Be my pleasure. Tomorrow I'll give you the grand tour. *L'excursion grande.*"

His Southern accent obliterated his attempt at French, and brought a smile to her face. Cute. Time for a test. "That's great, but the night is young for nocturnal creatures like me. Why waste it?"

"True," JD said, "but I'm afraid I already have plans for this evening, and I don't think I can get out of them."

She watched Giambi's head snap around. "If the lady wants to see the shop tonight, then tonight it is."

JD looked at Beth for salvation, but she decided that

Anne couldn't afford to give in to his gorgeous, pleading eyes. She said, "Then tonight it is." She was interested in seeing how Giambi would relate to JD's comment. It was a good time to start gathering tells.

JD glanced at his watch. "Maybe I could make a quick run to the Monte Carlo and—"

Giambi rose abruptly from his seat. "Excuse us a minute." He motioned for JD to follow him.

JD turned, gave her a shrug and walked off.

Beth sipped her drink then smiled at the sight of the old guy hustling his young stud driver out to the woodshed for an earful. The whole scene revealed a great deal.

Giambi had taken the bait and he seemed anxious. Maybe this little operation wouldn't take too long after all. She sat back to await the outcome of their *mano a mano*.

Giambi couldn't believe JD had tried to blow her off. When they were out of her earshot, he said, "What the hell's wrong with you?"

"You know I promised to meet some people from Hollywood, and I—"

"To hell with them. This woman has deep pockets. Did you not hear me earlier about taking care of this woman, Mister Southern Charm? She loves drivers. Her type always does."

"So, now I'm an escort service?" As soon as the words tumbled out of JD's mouth, Giambi could see JD was wishing he could take them back.

"I'll tell you what you are. You're a top-notch driver, unemployed, living free on the top floor of this establishment at my expense. A man whose future depends on my getting a racing team up and running. And that costs many millions, my friend."

He watched as JD stood a little straighter, visibly preparing to stand his ground. It was something Giambi liked about the man. "These people I'm meeting are potential investors. I'm trying to line things up."

"To hell with these Hollywood types. They're fickle. Look, right now I need you to find out if Anne Hurley is the real deal."

JD paused a moment, then said, "I thought you already ran a background on her."

"Electronic data can be faked and I don't have time to run hard verification on her. She might be who she says she is, but I need to know for certain. If she really knows racing, nobody better to find out than you."

JD's expression softened as he accepted the compliment. "I'm no detective."

"You'll know a false note when you hear it. Get close to her. Do what you have to do."

JD's lips curved up in a knowing smile. "Ah, you want me to seduce her."

"Like most men wouldn't give their left nut for a shot at something like that. This is your life we're talking about here. You want to drive a race car or a garbage truck?"

JD frowned, but nodded his acquiescence. "You know I don't like blowing people off when I've made arrangements with them."

"Call them and make your apologies. Then get in there and make this young woman happy."

JD nodded, his face showing he was back on track. "Fine, but I'm taking the Bugatti."

"Like hell you are."

"I'm taking the Bugatti. She's class, like you say. First class. So I'm taking a first-class automobile. She deserves a good ride. She's young, sexy, rich and looking to save our asses. Don't you agree?"

Giambi couldn't believe this kid. "You starting to enjoy the idea now?"

"The lady likes racing and gambling and I've got a feeling she likes guys about a third your age. The keys, please."

Giambi shook his head. He handed over the keys. "You better not scratch anything. And don't be racing. Every cop in France has you on their speed-demon list. You know that."

"I'll save it for the track," JD said, slipping the keys into his pocket.

Beautiful, smart young women are wasted on young guys, Giambi thought with a touch of resentment. Older men know a woman's value, know how to treat them. That was one of the many things he hated about getting old. Age was a nasty little thief. It robbed you a little each day. First one thing, than another, until you became an empty shell stripped of everything worth living for, then age killed you without dignity.

I have fifteen good years left, he told himself again.

It had been his mantra for years. He borrowed it from some big business guy. Maybe it was the one who once ran GE, but he couldn't remember the guy's name because he couldn't remember anybody's damn name.

On the way back to rejoin Anne Hurley, Giambi rested his hand on JD's shoulder. "Just so you understand something. I want nothing more in this world than to see you back on the race circuit. The troubles you've had in the past are over. A man with your talent has to be given a second chance and I'm doing everything in my power to get it for you. Just go along with the program."

"I'm with it. You know I am."

"And remember, I didn't survive all these years in this business by not knowing what has to be done. I like this woman. She's got brains behind the beauty and that can be a dangerous combination. You start thinking with the wrong head and before you know it, she'll run a game on you."

"She doesn't strike me as the game-playing type."

"That's just it. When they're good, you never see it coming."

"You suspect everybody of running a game on you?"

"They all would, if they could. I don't let 'em. Now go find out who the hell we're dealing with."

Giambi watched JD walk into the bar flipping the keys in his hand. As angry as he got at JD from time to time, he had to admit he loved the kid like a son. Cocky and wild as JD could be at times, he was talented.

Giambi wanted to see him fulfill that talent. Become the next Michael Schumacher. Unfulfilled talent was, in Giambi's opinion, about the greatest crime a person could commit in this life.

Chapter 6

Beth watched the two men as they stood toe-to-toe just outside the entrance to the piano bar. It appeared that Giambi was doing most of the talking and JD most of the listening, though there were some moments when the driver definitely held his own.

She hid her bemusement at the mixed expression on JD's face when he came back into the bar alone. He gave her the eyebrow shrug, as if to say it's not you, it's him.

The more she watched him, the better this race driver looked. He had a rugged handsomeness that appealed to her.

JD stared at her, spinning his keys around his finger. "You want to go for a ride?"

"Sure. I spent so much time in a race shop as a kid, if I don't see one from time to time I feel deprived."

"Well, let's take care of that. We don't want anyone feeling deprived. About anything."

Whatever other "plans" he'd had, he'd been forced to put them on the back burner. Things were definitely going her way, and she liked the powerful feeling it gave her. She liked to be in control of the situation. It made the task much easier.

As they headed out of the bar she said, "I'm also excited about seeing what could be my next big investment. I hope it's not interfering too much with your other plans."

"Not a problem," JD said. "You are my top priority at the moment." He actually sounded sincere.

"Whether you like it or not?"

He chuckled. "I don't think the night will be a complete loss."

She liked his tone and sense of humor. "I'll do my best."

Giambi had started talking to someone, but as they were passing he turned to her and said, "Have fun. JD, show the lady what we're all about."

Repeating the words she'd just used, he said, "I'll do my best." He exchanged a knowing glance with her.

She told Giambi that she'd see him later and they could continue their discussion.

"I look forward to it."

When they shook hands, Beth held his just a second beyond what would have been normal, throwing a smile at this repository of secrets. "I have a feeling we're going to be doing some business together."

"I believe we will," Giambi replied cheerfully. "Most definitely."

In the elevator Beth was still curious about the date that JD had given up for her. She needed to know if it was something that might potentially be a threat to her. "I hope I didn't mess up a date with your girlfriend."

"Haven't got one. It was just some people from Hollywood who wanted me to show them around. They'll be here for a few days so it's no problem."

No threat there.

"Scouting movie locations?"

"Actually, a couple of them are interested in investing in racing. And, maybe down the road, we can talk about coming up with a script."

"Starring JD Hawke?"

He shrugged. "I don't know if I'm much of an actor. Maybe a supporting role."

"You have a good look for the screen," Beth said, gazing into his eyes. "The strong, mischievous type." She gave him a warm smile.

"You still need to be able to act."

"You're kidding, right? How many movies have you seen lately?"

"Hey, don't knock Hollywood. I thought *The Matrix* was great."

"Too many special effects."

"Yeah, but Keanu Reeves is the king of the demon ride, which I do appreciate."

"What's that?"

"He likes to ride his motorcycle at night with no lights at high speeds. Nearly killed him a couple of times."

"Sounds more like a death wish ride."

"He's had a tragic life, but he doesn't let it make a wallflower out of him."

"More like a funeral bouquet, if he keeps that up. A lot of people have tragic lives—they don't deal with it by going on demon death rides."

He shrugged.

She smiled. Arguing with a racecar driver about risky

driving was something of an oxymoron. Besides, deep down inside, she was a little reckless with speed herself, but she didn't like to admit it openly.

When they exited the elevator into a small, private garage, she said, "I want to see the shop, but that's just an excuse."

"For what?"

"Getting to know you. If I'm investing in somebody, I want to know who they are. Not just by reputation, or from other people's opinions. Knowing people is how I do business."

He gave her a slow nod. "Okay. Sure. I'll do the best I can to give you what you want."

"Good." She aborted the sexual comebacks that immediately came to mind. "If you know a nice quiet bar where we could have a drink first, that would be great. We'll see the shop later. The night is young."

"There's a place on the way that's real nice."

They walked toward a group of cars.

"You don't have family in Formula One?" she asked.

JD shook his head. "They're all gear-heads. But I'm the rebel. My brother's in NASCAR, my dad, too. But I always had a thing about open wheel. Went from midgets right to the Indy Racing League and on to Formula One." He paused, then pointed. "We're taking this baby," JD said as they walked around a pillar and headed for a car that took Beth's breath away.

Beth stopped dead. "Oh, my God!"

"You like?"

Beth's knees went weak. "Are you kidding. A Bugatti isn't a *car.* It's the speed of light captured in metal."

She touched the hood with her fingers, gently, as if touching a work of art, an exotic sculpture. "I was at the London auction two years ago where one of these babies went for one-point-five million Euros. I came very close to buying it and have regretted not doing so ever since." In truth, she couldn't remember ever having seen this car before.

She stared for a moment at the world's most powerful sports car, the Bugatti Veyron. This one was a bright red metallic with a black pearl configuration. "It looks alive."

"Turn the key and you'll see some life. Maybe the finest road machine ever built," JD said. "Let's take her for a spin."

He flipped the keys in the air and snatched them with boyish glee.

She had the distinct impression Giambi didn't give up his prize possession often or easily. It told her a lot about how he felt about JD. Or her.

"You're the first person Giambi has ever let me take for a ride in his car. You're one special lady."

"I feel duly privileged."

JD watched her reaction to the Bugatti, enjoying how her eyes widened. He appreciated her understanding that this was no ordinary sports car.

He was equally impressed that she not only knew the car, but had nearly bought one. There was something else about her he couldn't put his finger on, but it was an attitude thing. Beneath all the sophisticated elegance of a super-rich widow was something wild, and he couldn't wait to get to know that aspect of her personality.

Anne Hurley didn't wait for him to open her door. Instead, she slid into the narrow passenger seat and eased herself into it. The Bugatti wasn't built for comfort, it was built for speed.

"This baby flies," JD said. "Only street car that gives me the same feel as a true racing machine."

"Anything that can go zero to sixty in two-point-four seconds better give you that racing feel."

"I take it you have a thing for speed?"

She gave him one of her little guttural laughs and said she actually craved speed. He liked that laugh, it had the sound of badness to it. As if underneath all the refinement, this was a lady to get down and real with.

Maybe, before this night was over, he was going to owe Salvatore a big thank-you.

"Ready?" he asked.

"Let's do it."

He turned the key in the ignition, and the roar of the engine vibrated throughout his body.

She turned to him. "God, it's almost as good as sex."

"Wait," he said. "It gets better." And drove out of the garage.

"Couple years. Actually I met him after I wrecked in San Marino."

She knew JD had lost his ride shortly after that incident and he was having trouble finding a new team.

He turned toward the Hotel Metropole then turned again toward the Monte Carlo Grand. Traffic prevented him from getting into any kind of speed as he shot past the Virage Du Portier and into the tunnel.

He said, "I've done around one-seventy in here. That's the top speed on the course." But the traffic prevented him from even going the speed limit.

"I saw you drive in Bahrain two years ago," Beth said, drawing on all the videos she had watched in her villa. "In my opinion, you weren't doing any illegal blocking. I totally disagreed with the black flag. They stole that race from you."

"I like the way you see things. They sure did steal my race. I owned it," JD said, anger creasing his brow. "Thank you. That idiot behind me acted like he was running NASCAR. He was trying to bump-draft me with an air cushion. I had to move out. It was purely a defensive maneuver on my part to keep control of the car."

Once out in the French countryside, he opened up the car. They were driving the roads of the Grand Prix now and she was loving it. Beth felt as if she were in a movie, or the actual race, taking in mile after mile of some of the best-known roads in the world. She let herself relax as JD took complete control of this fantastic machine. It was thrilling to watch his transformation, from Southern gentleman to a totally focused racer who loved the thrill of an open road and a grip on the steering wheel of a fast car. The smells of the night and the nearby ocean flowed over her from the open windows as they flew along the narrow streets. The Bugatti hugged the road as if it was on rails;

the G-forces, when he cornered and then opened it wide, were like taking off in a fighter jet.

Though the shifter in the Bugatti was nothing like the type on the wheel that was used in Formula One, JD shifted gears so smoothly she wouldn't have known except for the change in the whine of the engine.

He slowed, and glanced her way. "What do you think?"

"I think I need one of these," she purred. She wanted to tell him to keep going, continue driving the course until daylight, but she knew that was impossible. It was time to get down to business if she was ever going to find out the details behind Giambi's blackmailer and uncover his connection to her father. She was here in Monaco for a reason, and that reason didn't include racing around the countryside with an incredibly charming man in an obscenely expensive car…or did it?

He laughed, and for a crazy instant she thought he could hear her thoughts. She stiffened as he said, "It's really an amazing piece of machinery. Salvatore drives it like it's a damn golf cart."

She relaxed again, and sat up in the seat. "That's terrible for the engine."

"This car is a racehorse. It has to run."

"Absolutely. I couldn't agree more." They passed a small bar with people spilling out onto the sidewalk in front of it. "That place looks like fun. Can I buy you a drink?" Beth asked.

JD pulled in behind the bar. The small quaint town had cobblestone streets and dim street lighting. The place almost looked magical.

Before he could get out, she touched his arm and said, "JD, I'm a professional at reading people. I play poker with the best in the world. What are your instructions? Giambi didn't send you on this escort mission in the middle of the night without a purpose."

"I'm not sure what you mean."

She decided to put it right to him, get their situation clear. She said, "I'm sure you are. Look, it works both ways. You're supposed to either woo me, or check out if I'm really serious. You're on a mission. We're going in to have a drink and get to know each other. I like you. I know what kind of talent you are. I'm very familiar with your career and when I heard you might be coming back into it, and that you were with Giambi, a man with a shady past and financial issues, I decided to see what I could do. I have a lot of money and I want to invest it in a sure thing. So let's be honest with each other. Okay?"

"Okay," he said, but his eyes told a different story. His gaze had darted behind her for just an instant, and she immediately picked up the truth.

Beth smiled. *Well, JD, you're lying through your pretty bleached teeth, but I'll play along for a while.* "Great. I'm so glad we can be honest with each other."

At least she now knew how to read JD. So far, so good.

He escorted her in through the back door of the bar.

The bar was extremely noisy. Everyone inside was into a soccer match on the TV above the bar, so JD took her out onto the patio where they could have some privacy.

They ordered drinks and chatted about racing, then she jumped right back on him.

"So tell me. What are Salvatore Giambi's concerns?"

He took a sip of his vodka martini before answering. "I don't really know, other than he just wants you to get a good feel for what we're about. See the high-tech shop he's building. Get to know what you would be investing in. Which, of course, includes me."

"It's important we learn to trust each other," she said, trying once again to get him to open up to her. "I'm potentially investing in Giambi because of you, not him."

"So what's this all about?" JD sat back and studied her, his eyes burning into hers. His entire disposition had changed in a heartbeat. Gone was the smooth, cool Southerner. Now she was looking at a tough sell, but she'd already learned he was very susceptible to the Anne Hurley type, and she was all in.

She leaned on the table toward him, knowing her breasts were in full view. His gaze immediately dropped, and a rush of heat swept over her. She lingered in the moment, enjoying it, then sat back in her chair. "Like I said, I'm not interested in Salvatore Giambi."

"So what exactly is this about? You want me to leave Giambi for another team? Is that where we're headed here?" His voice was sharp, taught, defensive.

"Right now, he doesn't have a team. And he may not get one. What I'm interested in is you. With or without Giambi." She had his attention now. "It's the talent I'm looking at. I want to invest in Giambi not because I want to be a silent partner in his racing team. I know his financial woes. I know his precarious situation here in Monaco. Giambi might not last very long."

"What do you mean? You know something we don't know?" He moved in closer, sliding his chair up to the small round table.

"Yes. But right now you need to understand where I'm coming from. I have the money that it takes in this game. I have the desire and I'm going to be involved in buying, building and running a winning Formula One team. That's going to happen, period. It's not a question. And I want the best drivers in the world on my team. I think you're one of the very best talents there is. But you need the right people on your team and the right equipment."

"And Giambi's not the right guy?"

"That depends on his future. If he's got a financial problem, which he does, compounded with political problems, that changes things where he's concerned. So I have to know something about you."

"I'm an open book."

Another lie. She couldn't seem to get him to drop his act. She'd have to try a different tactic.

"What is your top priority?"

"What do you mean?"

"Is it loyalty to Salvatore Giambi, or is it your desire to get back into Formula One racing?"

"I'm a loyal kind of guy. He's done a lot for me and I wouldn't betray him, if that's what you're asking." He did a short fugue with his fingertips on the table. She couldn't make the tune out, but Beth finally felt as if the door had opened just a crack.

She said, "I'm not talking betrayal. If he couldn't make it work for you, would you walk to another offer?"

"If he couldn't make it work, then yes."

"Yes, what?"

"Look, I'm a racer. I'm not anything else. I don't want anything else. I want to race. I'll do what I need to do, within limits, of course, to get back into the game."

His eyes held her gaze. He was finally telling the truth. Gotcha!

"Good. We're beginning to understand one another."

For the next forty minutes and two more drinks, JD listened to Anne analyze the world of Formula One and how she intended to conquer it. The woman knew more about racing than he did. She knew every team, every driver and his results for the last ten years. He was amazed and highly impressed.

He found himself laughing with her, enjoying her enthusiasm, and really starting to like this rich widow's vision of his future.

At the same time, he was growing increasingly wary. As Giambi had said, and as JD well knew, the most dangerous woman is one who is both great-looking and smart. She was working hard to reel him in, but he wasn't going to be that easy.

When they left, she said, "You don't mind if I drive a short distance, do you?"

He started to hesitate, but she grabbed the keys right out of his hand. "You aren't going to deny me a thrill like driving a Bugatti Veyron are you?" She brushed up against him ever so slightly, but he felt the heat charge up his legs.

"Be my guest. Just take it slow. This baby can get away from you in a hurry."

They got in and he turned in his seat, pointing out the details of the car. A lot of females he knew, and a lot of males for that matter, couldn't drive stick, let alone handle a real beast like this one. He didn't want her launching it into a wall before they even got out of the parking lot.

Next thing he knew he was the one launched. He flew backward into his seat as if he'd been body slammed. And suddenly they were leaving town like they were escaping the front wave of a tsunami.

"Shit! Slow down," he yelled. "This thing has over a thousand horsepower. More than a Formula One race car. It's a lot to handle. You're gonna get us killed."

"Not if I can help it," she yelled back, laughing.

And she continued laughing as they jumped from zero to a hundred so fast it was like they'd been shot from a cannon.

And then, the full monster sixteen cylinders kicked in and she nearly lost it. She fishtailed coming around a turn, he grabbed the wheel and helped her get it straightened out, but she pushed his hand away.

She said, "Whoa, that's some beast under the hood. Damn, this feels good."

He was thinking, I'm in some kind of trouble here with this lady and I've got no clue what it is. Or, for that matter, who the hell she is, really.

JD had a feeling this was going to be a night to remember…if he lived through it.

Chapter 8

Beth was a bit shocked at the power of the car and at having nearly lost control. She slowed as they came over a rise. She'd driven fast cars before, including laps in a 600 horsepower NASCAR when a boyfriend bought her the Richard Petty Driving Experience for her birthday. But this was on the open road.

"I forgot… about the drinks. Hell of a thing when you're having fun behind the wheel. I love this car and I'd hate to wreck it, not to mention the damage I could have done to us."

"Giambi would hate it a lot more. This car is his pride and joy. I'm expendable."

She gave him a look. "You didn't think I could save it, did you?"

"Three or four drinks, I wasn't too sure."

"Me, either. Scared the hell out of me. It's like riding a mad bull."

They cruised through the countryside for a couple miles, chatting lightly, enjoying the night and each other's company. JD proved to be an easy guy to talk to, and he had a good sense of humor, jokes coming easily, banter smooth as silk in the summer wind.

He pointed as they approached an intersection of country roads, and said, "Take a right at the next one. The shop is out another couple miles."

She had a nice piece of straight road that fell into a valley and back up, like those that came out of the mountains into Vegas. She couldn't resist giving the car a little punch.

The balmy night, the French countryside, a superfast car, a few drinks and a great-looking guy by her side. Could a girl want anything more? She glanced over at JD.

Absolutely not.

"I have to tell you the French cops don't like this car or me much," he said. "I have a basketful of citations."

She slowed. "Instead of buying a driver, I'm beginning to wonder if I should have become one myself."

"Hey, everybody's looking for female drivers. NASCAR, Formula One, Indy."

"I think you have to start at about five to really be competitive, don't you?"

"In the womb would be better," he teased.

She laughed.

The race shop was about a mile from a small village not far from Nice. When Beth pulled in around two in the morning and parked behind the metal corrugated building, the place looked deserted.

She thought of that old saying that the quickest way to a man's heart is through his stomach. Maybe some men, but not JD. The quickest way to his heart was in a fast car, and they just happened to be sitting in one at that very moment.

It wouldn't be the first time she outsmarted some guy's heart, but she was very good at making sure she didn't scar the poor guy for life, or herself for that matter. She had a funny feeling that if there was a problem in this situation it wouldn't be with JD, it would be with her. Playing a guy was one thing. Getting involved on any other level was a big no-no. Taking her eyes off the road, or in this case the target, could get her in a lot of trouble.

But if she had to get a little randy with this guy to move him into her corner, well, so be it. She'd use the weapons at her disposal and think about the collateral damage later.

They sat in the car for a while, talking, joking. It felt a lot like a successful first date.

"To tell you the truth, you scared the hell out of me back there when you blew out of town," he said in a matter-of-fact voice.

"I scared the hell out of myself," she agreed. "You just touch the pedal and this thing takes off like you opened the barn door."

"You sure can drive, though," he said with a note of a admiration.

"Thanks. That's quite a compliment."

"It's the truth." And Beth could see that it was.

He was tapping his fingers again. Thinking. Considering. She was sure he was a little insecure about making the next move. He was, beneath all his cool Southern charm, a shy kind of guy. He almost made her feel a little guilty for setting him up so blatantly. But she was in a hurry. She had a mission to complete and if Giambi had the information about her father's killer she wanted to get it as fast as she could.

So, being the aggressive girl she was, and with the alcohol still on cruise control, she slipped a hand behind

JD's neck under his curly hair. "Thank you, JD." Then she moved her hand, embedding her fingers into his curls, and kissed him softly on the mouth. Being a little drunk aided and abetted the whole seduction process. Not that kissing him was anything but pure pleasure.

"Let's go inside and see what you've got." She said it sexy and hot…maybe with a little too much purpose. She had to be careful. She didn't want him to catch on.

She had decided long ago that it was so much easier making a move on a guy when she was playing a role. Were she herself, Bethany James, she knew she wouldn't do this. But she was a hot, globe-trotting, race-groupie widow worth millions. This kind of chick took what she wanted, so Anne wasn't doing anything that wasn't expected. Right?

JD kissed her again, this time hard, pulling her in tight, but she restrained him, not wanting to get into anything heavy just yet. At least not in the parking lot, in a very uncomfortable, but beautiful car.

Beth slipped away from the Tennessee dude and stepped out of the car.

She felt he was being rapidly drawn into her scenario. She'd paid his ego major compliments and now she felt he was ready to get totally honest with her. But she was just a little bit cautious. Behind that racing-stud, super-jock demeanor was no hick. He might like to play that role, but he hadn't hooked up with Giambi out of blind faith. He knew exactly what he wanted, and how to get it.

A driver who washed out early because of his temper and some unfortunate circumstances, who can't find a ride with the usual run of teams and sponsors, had to play it smart if he ever wanted to get back in.

JD might be able to hide his true character from most

people, but she was an expert at seeing the real person behind the persona. JD was pure focused intelligence.

"Look," she said, clasping his arm with hers as they walked toward the back door. "I'm not out for you to dump Giambi. I'm willing to work with him if his troubles aren't too much to handle. But I need to know—what, exactly, was your mission tonight?"

"He wanted me to make sure you are who you say your are. That's only natural. Both of you wanting to check each other out."

"Seems fair."

"He's paranoid these days. Under a lot of pressure."

"I understand. I can take that pressure off of him. And I can give you some information. Your boss isn't being paranoid for no reason."

"I know there's something else going on with him, but he keeps that kind of thing to himself."

"How far did he want you to go with me? Did he want you to seduce me? Get me into bed?"

"Just a minute ago, I'd say that was your plan, not mine."

Beth knew he had her. "Okay, I admit it. Seduction might have been part of my plan to get to know you better." She laughed. "As jobs go, maybe that wouldn't have been so terrible for either one of us."

"Seducing women for Giambi or anybody else isn't my thing, Anne."

"In your case it might be inadvertent. Some men can't do it if they try, others can't avoid it."

"I told him I wasn't much for that kind of thing. If he wants a seducing detective, he should have hired one."

She didn't know if she believed him. He was sweet, but that was probably part of his appeal. No better mask to hide behind.

"Magnum, P.I.," she said.

He turned to her. "That's right. Where's Tom Selleck when you need him?"

"Probably taking care of his grandkids."

They laughed and chatted about the show, both agreeing they had watched it because of the Ferrari.

They were connecting now, and she had his full attention. She could tell she had him wondering what her deal was going to look like. He was looking right into her eyes and that was where she wanted him.

Beth said, "I'm sure you know that I've taken a good hard look at Giambi's assets, and his past business dealings. I wouldn't normally get anywhere near him. I could buy and sell about half the teams in Formula One. If Prince Philip kicks him out of Monaco, it could make it very difficult for him, especially in Formula One."

"Is that going to happen?"

"It might. And that will only make the hole you've been in that much deeper. On the other hand, if we can get him to clean up his act in a hurry, or to sell his casino and move into racing as a full-time enterprise, I think I can smooth the transition and protect him at the same time. And, of course, you. But I also know that Giambi thinks of you almost as a son. That gives you influence. That's why you and I have to trust each other and work together. In the end, one way or another, I want to see you with a ride and I want to be involved. That's the bottom line."

Her persuasion wasn't in the words. It was in her demeanor, her look, the intensity of her projected honesty. Poker was all about the art of hiding the lie behind the lie. Words meant nothing. It was all in the eyes, and the ability to lie with the eyes was a talent few possessed. It was the reason Beth hated to play poker with people who wore sunglasses.

Deception was her trade. Her livelihood. Her father said only a truly good lawyer or a pathological liar was the equal of a winning poker player.

JD had stopped talking. She could tell he was thinking hard about something. She wished he would tell her what was on his mind.

She began to ramble about Monaco, comparing it with other hot spots. Entertaining him so he focused on her rather than whatever else he'd been thinking about.

He opened the back door to the race shop with a key and ushered her inside as he hit the switch for the florescent lights that washed the blackness with intense white. A vast space opened up before her.

He took her on a tour of the high-tech facility that he explained was in the process of being fine-tuned, talking about a sheet-metal fab, computer programs that would help design the chassis and a welding shop.

Then he walked her over to the main attraction. Three open-wheel racing cars in various stages of deconstruction.

Beth said, as she ran her fingers across one of the cars, "Is there any machine as sleek and beautiful as an open-wheel race car?"

"I don't think so," JD answered.

They walked around the cars in silence. Beth was having fun on her private tour. She loved peeking under hoods, and imagining herself behind the wheel. Part of it was, of course, an act, but part of it was real. And that part was growing stronger all the time.

She followed him around as he explained the machine tools, the art of car rebuilding. He had a strategy already worked out for how he wanted to approach the next season.

He'd been watching drivers from McLaren, Williams and Ferrari, the big three who had won all but two world championships since 1984, and Michael Schumacher, who took two titles with Benetton.

"The costs now are astronomic," he said. "Some independent teams just can't hack it anymore. They can't stay competitive. Prost and Arrows had to withdraw a few years back because of costs. That's what we want to avoid. That's why Giambi wants to bring in some major partners. The sponsors won't come around until we get a big showing. But to get to that point costs a ton of money."

"I know. That's why I'm here." She smiled.

He looked over at her and nodded, deadpan.

When she'd seen enough and they were getting ready to leave, she decided to get the evening going again.

He turned out the lights and opened the door to go out.

She put a hand on his arm and said, "I might be getting into a long-term relationship with Giambi racing. That means you and I will be seeing a lot of one another. Just don't forget that I want to help him in order to help you." She felt herself beginning to lose the distinction between Anne and Beth.

He was standing very close to her now in the doorway. She could all but feel the hard lines of his body. Her legs had a little tingle in them.

"Yeah, that's what you say and I sure want to believe it. But you're getting in bed with Giambi, so to speak, in spite of how risky he is."

"So to speak," she said thinking, if there's somebody I'm going to bed with, it won't be a seventy-eight-year-old man.

She was standing close to JD now. Too close. His breath soft on her face. For all their talk about seduction and business, none of that seemed to matter at the moment. He moved in even closer, his body barely touching hers. Her heartbeat shook her entire body. She looked up at him, her mouth slightly open, inviting him to take a shot.

He did.

It was a kiss that started slow, but grew in boldness, in hunger, and she was now back up against the wall, his hands moving around her body, hers on his butt, the side of his legs, his chest, stomach.

She pushed him away. "I thought we agreed, this is business and you brought me here strictly to see *your* equipment," she whispered.

"We did, but I like your equipment better."

When he had her dress pulled down and was going after her breasts like a dehydrated desert wanderer falling into a pool of fresh water she knew she had to make him back off.

But then, she changed her mind and let him play a little longer. It was too pleasant to interrupt. This Tennessee boy knew his way around a woman and now she was wondering who was seducing whom.

He kept murmuring about her beauty and all that nice, sweet, hot stuff a girl liked to hear. She began to get seriously warmed up and knew this could get completely out of control. Even though she'd known it might come to this, she still wasn't convinced it was a good idea.

Still, she let him linger a while longer, running her hands through his silky hair as he kissed, licked, fondled and nibbled. Nothing like the hands of a man who knows what he's about, she thought in an erotic fog.

Then, about the time she knew he was getting the best of her, dragging her down a little too deep for her own good, she began to gently, but firmly, insist on getting this thing under control.

"Too fast," she said.

"You like speed."

"Not in all things."

This was good because now she was testing not only herself—she really wanted to let this go wherever it might take them—but him. She wanted to see how he handled getting black flagged before the finish line.

He was cool and gently backed off.

That could mean that he was a controllable guy. Or, he had all the women he could want at his beck and call and if he lost one here or there, what did it matter when a replacement was around the next corner. Or, maybe he was just a decent guy.

But now she didn't know where this thing they'd started was going. It had been a long time since her last lover. Maybe too long.

This is business, she reminded herself. Potentially deadly business if they ever found out who she really was, but seducing him, her modus operandi, was undermined by her growing attachment. It was a conflict she needed to resolve.

She regained her composure, and refitted her dress.

"I'm here to get you a ride," she said. "We can't do this."

They kissed again. Long and luxuriously.

"Whatever you say," he said when he pulled back, still holding her in his arms. But they remained where they were.

"We need to go," she said.

"Okay."

But they continued to kiss.

"We really should go," he said.

"Whatever you say."

But he kissed her again.

"I mean, like maybe now," she suggested.

"Fine. Right now."

And once again they kissed.

Somebody had to break this off first, she thought, but she felt so very comfortable against his body, kissing him, touching him. He was simply too good to give up. Reason had blown out the window with that first kiss, and now she was acting on raw emotion and loving every moment of it.

Suddenly, there was a noise outside.

In that instant, all romance vanished as shockingly as if a bucket of ice water had been poured on her.

JD tucked his shirt back in his pants and opened the back door. Beth followed close behind.

The silhouette of a man ducking behind some large shipping containers, back-dropped against the faint moon, caught her eye. For a moment she wasn't sure what she'd seen.

"Expecting company?" she whispered.

"Nobody comes out here this late."

The sound of the crunch of gravel drew closer.

A car with its headlights out stopped up on the hill a few yards away. They watched it. Nothing happened for a moment. Then two men got out, also silhouetted in the pale moonlight.

"Hey, this is private property," JD yelled in belligerent French.

The men started down the hill at them as if they had serious business to take care of.

"I don't think they're here for a good cause," Beth said. "We need to get the hell out of here. Now."

"They're the ones leaving," JD said defiantly. "Let me see what's going on. You stay here."

When he started to walk toward the men, who were now moving more quickly, she grabbed him. "Not a good idea. I think they have bad intentions. And I saw somebody in back of those shipping containers. I don't know what's going on, but let's leave."

"Relax. I can handle myself."

"I think they have guns, JD. I don't like guns. Get me the hell out of here, dammit."

She turned toward the car and as she did, one of the men yelled, "There they are!"

A bullet slammed into the corrugated wall, making a tinny sound that cracked through the night.

Beth kicked off her heels and sprinted toward the Bugatti, JD right beside her.

Another man, who appeared from around the building on the far side, ran right into them. For the second time in less than four days she found herself facing men with guns who wanted to kill her and she didn't like it any better now than the first time.

Chapter 9

JD grabbed the man's gun hand, spun him around and slammed him into the shipping containers.

Beth launched a barefooted kick that hit the attacker in the hip. Unfortunately, her kick had little impact as he and JD struggled for control of the gun.

Beth reached for the nearest weapon, a three-foot-long two-by-four leaning against a container. She brought it down on the man's arm like an axe. The man yelped out in pain, and his gun dropped in the gravel. JD got in a couple solid punches to the man's face and the guy staggered backward.

Beth hit the guy again with her two-by-four, this time in the back of the legs and he went down, hard. JD grabbed the gun and her and sprinted to the Bugatti, bullets slapping into the building and containers as they ran.

JD had the key in the ignition and the car moving before she could close her door.

She grabbed the gun from his lap, lowered the window, checked the action to make sure a round was seated and the safety off, then fired a few shots back at the men still standing in the gravel parking lot.

JD rammed the gear home and they took off like a rocket. She saw the two men running back to their car on the hill. One of them stopped and fired at them.

Beth fired three quick shots in his general direction, forcing him to suspend his firing and look for cover.

"Friends of yours?" Beth yelled as JD drove around a building and headed for the feeder road.

"If they are, I never want to meet my enemies."

"What the hell are you into?"

"Me? You knew those guys were trouble from the beginning. You also know how to use a gun. And how to fight. Something's wrong with this picture, Ms. Anne Hurley," JD said as he danced the Bugatti around several small industrial buildings. "Who are you?"

"Just drive," she snapped. She'd have to think of something fast, come up with another identity, but she couldn't focus on that when men with guns were still trying to kill her.

"Where'd they go?" JD peered out of the rearview mirror.

"I don't know," Beth said, turning in her seat, adrenaline pushing through her veins so fast she thought her head would explode.

"I don't see them," he said. "Maybe they couldn't keep up."

The road JD took to get out of the area was different than the one they'd come in on. This one was blocked by a bulldozer and some construction equipment. JD turned the wheel and drove up a hill over some rough ground.

When they hit the tarmac JD went into overdrive and the Bugatti's surge forced Beth to pay more attention to holding herself in place than looking for bad guys.

"Uh-oh," JD announced. "Trouble straight ahead."

The other car had gotten ahead of them somehow. It jumped out on the road and JD had to swerve left, jump the brim, then wrestle his car back on the tarmac. More shots were fired and this time they hit the Bugatti with solid thunks.

The other car turned and was right on their tail.

"Jesus! What the hell are they driving?" Beth asked.

"I don't know, but whatever it is, there's sure a lot of power under that hood."

Whatever they were driving, it was very fast and had only dropped back a few hundred yards. Now, with the road swinging in sharp turns, JD couldn't milk the power he had at his disposal.

Suddenly, she remembered kicking off her shoes. "Shit!"

"What?"

"Nothing."

"What? Tell me."

"Those were Jimmy Choos."

"You know one of the guys in the car?"

"Me? No. I don't know those guys."

"Then who's this Jimmy Choo?"

"My shoes. He designed my shoes and I left them back there in the parking lot. I liked those shoes."

"You're upset about your shoes?"

"They weren't just shoes, they were designer shoes. There's a big difference."

He gave her a quick glance and a shake of the head. "Great. People are trying to kill us, bullets thick as ticks on a coon hound and you're worried about your shoes?"

She could tell he was really scared and all the syrupy sugar and spice she'd heard earlier in his voice had hardened and cooled.

"They went perfectly with this dress," she said. Though it did occur to her that even thinking about them was probably carrying her new rich-widow image a bit too far.

JD wheeled the car down the narrow lane into a tiny village. Nobody was out on the street. A good thing as they flew over the cobblestones at an insane speed. A car that is mostly engine isn't very comfortable on cobblestones.

She didn't have her seat belt on because she needed to be able to lean out the side window to fire if their chasers caught up. She took a couple of hard knocks and it felt as if her insides were in a blender.

Finally they were back on flat road and there was nothing behind them. JD slowed down to around sixty.

"You're as bad as Giambi," JD said.

"How's that?"

"He has a closet full of shoes. You two are meant to be a team."

He slammed up a hill, picking up speed as he went.

She searched again for headlights behind them but saw none. "I think we lost them." She sighed, thankful they were safe inside this fantastic automobile. But it did bother her that the other car had been able to keep up. Who were they, and why all the shooting?

"If this car can't outrun them they have something I never heard of. C'mon, humor me. You won't tell me why somebody is trying to kill us, and you're stressing about lost shoes?"

"Those shoes are classics, and besides, they cost a lot of money."

"You're rich. You can buy a hundred pairs of shoes."

"We'll talk about that later."

She chuckled dryly and shrugged. Truth was, she'd never really been a big shoe girl, until she slipped on those

Jimmy Choos. There was just something about them, and now she was hooked. Being Anne was having an effect.

"What's that mean?"

"Just get us somewhere safe where we can talk." After that attack, she knew she had to get real with him a lot sooner than she'd expected.

"And for your information, those shoes were not just shoes," she said in their defense. "Certain shoes are like this car. There's simply nothing else quite like them."

He gave her a baffled glance, hoping, she thought, to see that she was just kidding. She was. Sort of.

As they drove through twists and turns on the mountain roads she paid some attention to how incredibly easily he handled this car, even after being shot at. The man was a total professional behind the wheel and nothing shook his focus, not even bullets.

Then, after a while, when it appeared they were completely out of danger, he slowed and pulled off the road.

"What are you doing?"

"I want to see how many bullet holes there are in the car. Giambi is going to have a heart attack."

"Now might not be such a good time."

He ignored her and got out to walk behind the car.

She got out, too, and went back to suggest that maybe they should get moving. He was squatting, touching one of the bullet holes, shaking his head and swearing.

"He's going to be really pissed," JD said, straightening up.

"Better they shot up the car than the driver, right?"

"Depends on who you ask. Salvatore would rather see me riddled with bullets than this baby."

She smiled.

JD said, "This is a rare model. Those idiots don't know who they're messing with."

"Or maybe they do," she offered.

They both heard it before they saw it. The other car. The driver had turned his lights out and was coming fast down the grade about half a mile back, visible in the moonlight.

Now they saw it was a black Ferrari.

"Shit!" JD shouted.

"You want to maybe get back behind the wheel and get us the hell out of here? We can look at the damage later. If there is a later."

He seemed a little surprised and dazed that the other car had continued the chase. He didn't move, but instead stared in the other car's direction. "They can't really believe they can catch us."

"It's a Ferrari."

"We're still faster."

The Ferrari came screaming down the hill through the rustic countryside in their direction at an astoundingly high rate of speed. Beth was getting scared now.

"That may be, but not when we're standing still. Can we please get the hell out of here?"

They raced to the open doors of the Bugatti and jumped in. JD was swearing nonstop now. The car was half a mile behind, but it was coming at them full tilt.

"Make sure that seat belt is tight," JD warned.

She belted herself in and grabbed on to her own seat for extra support. The windup of the engine shuddered every cell in her body. The zero to sixty in two-point-five seconds was enough to nail her to the seat as if she was taking off in a space-bound rocket.

The Ferrari was losing ground, but still coming as hard as it could.

"Persistent bastard," JD grumbled.

"How's the gas?"

"It'll get us home."

Then they had to slow for a truck and the Ferrari gained on them. She picked the gun up off the floor just in case.

"You a cop or agent of some kind?"

"No. An ex-soldier taught me at a gun range in Las Vegas."

"Boyfriend?"

"No. Just a friend."

She checked the clip. Eight bullets counting the one in the chamber. The gun was a SIG Sauer P-226. "This is a nice gun."

"You like guns?"

"When people are trying to kill me, it's nice to have one around."

JD said wearily, "We're running through the damn French countryside turning it into a war zone. Where the hell are the gendarmerie? In the U.S. every donut shop for a hundred square miles would be cleared out. Highway patrol, local fuzz, SWAT in tanks, choppers. Here, thirty miles from Nice, nothing."

"Maybe they have less crime here than in the States."

He pulled out his cell phone. She immediately panicked, wondering who he wanted to call.

"What are you doing?" she asked.

"Calling Giambi. If we can't get cops he can get an army of his personal badasses out here in a hurry. He's got a chopper up on the roof of his casino. He may be seventy-eight, but he's old school. Somebody shot up his car, he's going to be madder than a nest of smoked-out hornets."

She grabbed for the cell phone and they nearly crashed. No way was she letting him call Giambi about this. Not yet. She needed JD on her side first.

"What the hell are you doing?"

She didn't get his phone, but she'd managed to stop him from making the call.

"Just drive. Keep it under the speed limit, find some country roads and get off this main highway. We need to have a chat." She knew she sounded harsh, but she couldn't let him make that call.

"To hell with you. I'm not taking orders, Anne, or whoever you are."

He sped up and they shot through a canopy of poplar trees whose branches overhung the road.

"My place is near the Monte Carlo," she said. "We can go there. Nobody knows about it."

"We're going to the casino. We're protected there."

"No."

"Why not? That's the safest place in Monaco."

"We're going to have a talk first."

"What's going on?" He downshifted as they hit a series of turns. "What do I have to know?"

"Don't ask questions going a hundred miles an hour on a country road."

"To hell with this. I'm calling Giambi."

He tried again to make the call, driving with one hand as he worked his cell phone.

She grabbed the phone and when he moved to take it back, the car hit something in the road, maybe a pothole or some road debris. Whatever it was, it threw the line of the car violently to the left.

JD fought the wheel as they broke through a fence and lurched across a mound that sent them airborne.

At the speed they were traveling, once the car launched there was no way to save it.

Horrified, Beth let out a low moan as they bounced off the hill and took out another section of fence, hit a large rock and careened to the side. Beth asked him if he had it, but she could see there was no way he could control what was happening.

He didn't reply.

They flew downhill, glanced off a tree and then rolled over and over until they came to a sudden and violent halt in the middle of a grove of trees.

Chapter 10

They were crushed together in the stillness, Beth on top of JD, the car on its left side, engine still running. She didn't know how badly she was hurt and she was half afraid to find out. They were still inside the car. She asked wearily, "You aren't dead, are you?"

"No. Not yet."

She moved her arm, then a leg. Limbs intact. She was still a little stunned from having hit her head on something.

"JD?"

"Yeah."

"Can you move?"

"I don't know. You?"

"I think so. Nothing seems broken. Shit!"

"What?"

"I think I smell—"

"Yeah, gas. Let me turn off the engine. I'm not dying inside a burning car."

He pushed his hand under her arm and turned off the engine. He was jammed in tight and she could see a trickle of blood from a cut above his eye. She hoped that was his only injury.

"See if you can open the door. It's heavy. Push straight up," he said.

The door was above her and the full weight of it was enormous. She couldn't do it. The window was partially open, but not enough so they could get out.

"I'd turn the engine on to see if the window might open, but I don't want to chance it with the leaking gas."

The harder she pushed, the more her shoulder and hips squeezed down on him. He was wedged under the wheel and against the door and she could hear him grunting with pain with every move she made.

"I'm sorry, but I can't budge it."

She imagined fire. Then their pursuers showing up and watching them burn alive with smiles on their faces. If she was going to die, she would at least like to know who had caused it.

She began to panic. She hated being confined. When she was a little girl she'd gotten trapped inside a dark closet once and had waited most of the night for her father to return and let her out. She never forgot how scared she was that the house might catch on fire while she wasn't able to get out. This was the same feeling, only the potential for fire was much more real.

She had to get out. Now.

"Think of something. Those guys could show up any moment, or this car could explode."

"Let's turn you," JD said. "So your back is on my chest. We need to get your legs free so you can use them. That'll give you the strength and leverage you need to push that door open."

His voice calmed her. She focused on that, falling into the warmth and steadiness she heard there.

She turned so that her back rested on his chest. Then she pulled her legs up until her knees were tight against her stomach.

He helped her the best he could, pushing here, pulling there until she was able to get turned around completely.

Now her head was next to his. They were virtually laminated together, a couple of sardines in a flammable can.

He reached up, got his hand on the door lever and pulled to get the locking gear in the open position. "Okay."

She grabbed the shift with one hand, the back of the seat with the other, then, knees still against her chest, she placed her feet on the door. She positioned one foot just a little above the other. The first time she tried to push, her right foot exploded in pain.

"Dammit!" she grumbled.

"What?"

"My foot." It now throbbed.

"Don't use it. Let me see if I can get my leg around you."

He worked his right leg between her and the seat. "Okay, pull your right foot down."

"When I say go, we drive everything we have into the door. If it doesn't budge, back off and we'll do it again. Ready?"

"Yes."

"On three."

He counted down and at three she drove her left foot, he his right, in an explosive move. There was a creaking of metal against metal and some movement.

"It's going to open. One more time on three," he told her. She could hear calm determination in his voice, and it soothed her fears. Her complete attention was now on opening that door.

"One. Two. Three." She counted with him.

This time the door sprung open.

He held the door until she could get herself off of him and through the opening. She pushed herself up the rest of the way, then crawled out and sat on the door frame.

He was able to work his way out from beneath the steering column, and she helped him with her free hand, the other holding the door while he worked his way out.

He slid to the ground.

She let the door close and then turned so he could help her down so she didn't have to put too much pressure on her foot.

When she touched the ground she let out a sigh of relief, shivered, then regained her strength. She was glad to be out of the car.

They stood for a moment in the dark silence of the woods, looking up the hill at the torn fence.

She turned back to the car. "What were you saying about those bullet holes?"

He tilted his head. "Nobody likes a smart-ass."

She smiled, and realized that her bottom lip was cut. It stung, and she pulled it in and ran her tongue over it. She could feel the swelling and taste the blood.

"You okay?"

"It's nothing compared to what could have happened. How about you?"

"I'm all right. Been in worse crashes than this."

"I'm sorry, I am. But I didn't want you to make that call."

He pulled his shirt up and wiped the blood from his face.

"This car is a wreck," he said, gazing back at the Bugatti. He shook his head.

"It's just a car."

"Giambi's gonna have a heart attack. It's his pride and joy. He won it from—"

"He has insurance, doesn't he?"

"I imagine." JD turned to her. "Okay, maybe now is a good time to tell me what—"

He stopped. A car pulled up to the spot where they'd gone through the fence above. It was a good fifty yards or so away and in the dark the men probably couldn't see them. Beth heard them talking, looking at something with a flashlight. Probably the tire tracks.

She whispered. "I think it's the same guys."

There were two men at the top of the hill looking down toward them.

"Don't they ever give up?"

"Let's get out of here," Beth urged, tugging on his arm for support. "Where's the gun?"

"Should be in the car, unless it fell out in the roll. Your window was open, mine only part way."

The men headed toward them.

Beth reached into the car and grabbed her purse, then looked for the gun. "I can't find it," she whispered.

"It's in there somewhere. Let me look."

He stuck his upper body in and started looking around.

"They're too close," she said grabbing him by the belt. "We need to get out of here. It probably fell out."

They ran deeper into the woods. Her foot hurt like hell, but certain death was a great pain reliever. They continued for about half a mile along a narrow stream.

JD stopped there, one hand up, motioning her to be silent. Then he said, "This way."

She followed him into a ravine and up the other side. He seemed to have some idea what he was doing, where he was going.

Her foot hurt with each step, but she had no choice but to ignore the pain. It eventually slowed her down and JD had to help her over some dead trees.

He motioned for her to follow him across a second narrow stream and started back the way they'd come.

She stopped him and whispered, "What are you doing?"

"I'm a Tennessee mountain boy, remember? I know how to move around in the country. I hunted before I knew how to ride a bicycle. Just stay with me."

Instead of running away from their pursuers, he'd circled back, keeping in the tree line.

Then he found a good hiding place. It was a thick clump of mixed bush and trees and some deadfall.

They crawled into a tight place and got comfortable. To her it seemed very risky. If found, they had no chance at all. On the other hand, they might easily be found out in the open. She acceded to JD's decision to hunker down and wait.

"These bastards are probably after Giambi," JD whispered as they sat shoulder to shoulder.

"Why do you think that?"

"Some hit team sees us drive out of his private garage in a car only he drives. They think it's him."

"They didn't see it wasn't him at the bar?"

"Maybe they held back and waited."

"It doesn't matter what they started out to do," she said. "Right now their intentions are pretty clear."

She didn't say that this was round number two for her this week, or that it could be they were after her, which would mean Giambi had discovered her ruse.

Voices filtered down to them from along the hillside, but nothing came of them. When they heard the voices again they were off in the distance. Beth hoped the men were giving up the hunt.

"Let's get out of here."

JD turned and said, "You didn't answer me. Who in the hell are you?"

She didn't have time to answer that question. At least not yet. "We should get out of here while we can."

Though he was obviously curious, JD agreed with her. They headed around the side of the hill in the opposite direction of their pursuers. Beth leaned on JD for support. The valleys were lush. A river gleamed in the moonlight like a strip of mercury running through the ravine. There was a village embedded in the distant hillside.

They headed out of the trees and across a field. Her feet were taking a beating now on the rocky soil. She so wished she hadn't kicked off her shoes. She made a vow to herself that no matter what, from now on her shoes were staying on her feet.

The world of farms was already awake for the day, lights on in some of the farmhouses. Country life. In Vegas, at this time of morning, half the city would still be in full swing.

She was a total mess now, her dress ripped and dirty, blood matted on the side of her head from another cut, her feet bruised and cut from the rocky terrain.

"You know this area?" she asked.

"Not really, but there are villages scattered all around these hills."

She sat down on a rock to check her feet. She shivered from the early morning chill.

He took off his jacket. "Put this on. It's cold."

"That's okay. I'm fine."

"I have a T-shirt and a long-sleeved shirt over that. Take the jacket."

She took the jacket and thanked him.

They both glanced back into the predawn darkness, but

saw no signs of the men. They started up again, but at a slower pace.

He stopped her at one point. "You're going to cut your feet all to hell and you won't be able to walk at all."

"You going to give me your shoes?"

"A little big for you. I'm going to make you some shoes."

He took off his shoes and socks. Then he took the jacket from her and with a pocket knife he cut away some of the leather around the bottom. He made little pads. He then cut strips of the inner lining.

He told her to put her foot up on his leg. He attached the leather to the bottom of her foot and tied it with the lining, then he slipped his sock over the whole thing to hold it together. He took the other foot. His hands were gentle and firm and he concentrated intensely on the task.

"They're not your Jimmy Choos, but they're a hell of a lot better than nothing."

"Thank you."

"My pleasure."

"You've done this before?"

"Not exactly like this. When you grow up in the mountains of Tennessee you learn to make something out of nothing and I now live with Giambi, the son of a family of shoemakers from way back. He would be proud. If it's not handmade, he won't wear it."

"This jacket you ruined for me isn't nothing."

"It's replaceable. You're feet aren't."

Never in her life, at least not since her father's death, had a man been so caring toward her. She really didn't know how to react to such kindness.

He put her leg down and looked up at her. For a moment, it was as if he could see right through her, and she didn't like the feeling. It made her uneasy for having to lie to him.

"Try them out," he said, beaming at his invention.

She stood. After walking a couple miles on her bare feet, they felt great. "A thousand percent better."

"Good."

"Thank you. Again," she said, and gave him a gentle kiss.

"I'll take more of that later," he offered. "Now we just need to keep going."

JD stared at Anne—or whoever she was—in the moonlight. Her dress ruined and dirty and bloody. Her shoulder scraped. Her lip, cut. His makeshift shoes on her feet. She looked like a refugee from a natural disaster. She was a natural disaster. But, for all that, she looked incredibly beautiful. How that was possible he didn't know, figuring he must still be a little drunk. She'd come into his life half a dozen hours ago and now men with guns were trying to kill him. This woman had pretty much destroyed his plans. Giambi would never forgive him for wrecking his car, so JD's dreams of getting back in a race car were pretty much over. Just when he'd gotten his explosive temper under control, found a backer, this femme fatale waltzes into his life.

He shook his head and a frown tightened his face as he looked around. JD had other thoughts going through his mind. Like, why didn't she let him call Giambi in the first place? And what kind of rich widow acts like she walked off a James Bond film set?

They moved through another grove of trees and skirted along the bank until they found a place to cross the stream.

Whatever she was, he admired how she handled herself. Never showed panic or hysteria. Always seemed to be under control. But after what they'd just been through he didn't believe anything she'd said now. Giambi was right. Everything they'd gotten off the Internet was probably made up.

At any rate, the party was over. The sexy, rich widow was not what she said she was. Not when she handled herself like a damn ninja.

He had no time to third-degree her.

She grabbed him. "What?"

"We wait here a little. Then cut over that field and get into the next valley," he said.

"That would put us out in the open."

"Yes. But the roads are pretty far. If we're spotted, we can make a run for it." He had no time for games anymore. He wanted to get back and try to explain things to Giambi before the man heard about his car on the local news.

"I think it would be better—"

"Look, I'm cutting across here and getting back to the casinos. You can do what you want." He knew his tone was harsh, but she was messing up his life and he couldn't allow that to happen. He loved racing more than his next breath, and nothing and no one was going to get in his way, even if she was the finest woman he'd ever met. There were plenty of women out there. Women who didn't lie…at least not as much as this one.

She followed right behind him, but he refused to look back.

When he reached a hill he finally stopped next to some trees to turn around. Not for her. He didn't care one lick about her. Well, maybe he did care, a little, but he wasn't about to let that stop him now.

He had a long field of vision, and couldn't see anyone coming from any direction.

She was still right behind him. He had to hand it to her, even with that bad foot, she managed to keep up. "Okay, I think we're good here. At least for a while. Now, tell me something that I can believe."

"We'll discuss that at a more appropriate time. I want to get back to Monaco."

"Not until I get some answers."

He was tired of being pushed off. "You're cool under pressure. Maybe too cool. You know how to shoot, and you know how to survive. That makes you more than some grieving widow with a few bucks in the bank. I want answers before we take one more step."

She put a finger on his lips. "Okay. With two conditions."

"Conditions?"

"First, call Giambi," she said, pulling a cell phone out of her bag.

"I thought you didn't want me to call him. That's why we crashed the damn car."

"That was then, this is now. He needs to know something happened. Don't tell him much. Just that somebody came after us, shot at us, we crashed and then ran away on foot. If somebody finds the car and the police run the plates they'll be calling him and he's going to be really pissed." It was risky, but she believed she had a hold on JD, that he was ready to accept the need to work with her.

"You're not telling me anything that I don't already know."

"But we can't go back there yet. Please trust me on this. It isn't safe. Just tell him we're staying with a friend of yours. Or mine. That you have no idea what this is about. Tell him where the car is and leave it at that. If he starts grilling you, tell him you aren't in a situation where you can talk. Tell him you'll call him later with the details."

JD stared at her. He didn't want to trust her, after all he didn't even know who she was. But there was something about her…. Something about how she looked at him, how she spoke, that made him want to give her another chance.

He took the phone and dialed Giambi's private line.

The call went right to the message box. JD told him what Anne had said, and added the car's location and told Giambi how sorry JD was about the accident.

"I've had some rough dates, but this beats 'em all," he said as he returned her phone. "What's condition two?"

"A nap."

Chapter 11

They were still nowhere, but Beth simply couldn't walk another step. Daylight had captured another morning, and it was way past her bedtime. She lay down in the tall grass, slipped her tiny bag under her head and sucked in a deep yawn.

"A nap?"

"Yes."

Beth closed her eyes, but her mind was spinning. She knew how close she was to losing this whole operation. Somehow she had to prevent that from happening. Yes, she needed rest, but more than that, she needed time to think. How could she get things to move even faster? How could she get JD securely on her side? Who were those men chasing them? And if Giambi was the key both to Athena's problem and her father's killer, Beth was getting into his computers and files no matter what she had to do.

She needed a believable story, one that Giambi would not question. If he was as paranoid as JD said, then she had to make sure it wasn't *her* he should be worried about.

If she played this right, the thing with the Bugatti could work in her favor. But for that she needed a damn good story.

No matter how wired you were, how much adrenaline had flowed, how frightening or strenuous the circumstances, eventually you hit a wall. That's how Beth felt now. She needed to rest. JD was up and alert, but she just couldn't stay awake one more moment.

Not long ago she'd been in Las Vegas running from a gunman. Then booking a flight to Virginia, the absorption of a mass of information, the change in identity. The flight to Monaco. Meeting Giambi. JD. The drive. His kiss. The escape from more gunmen. A nasty crash. Walking endlessly through unfamiliar countryside. And now sleep. Deep, much-needed sleep. Even ten minutes of sleep seemed not only desirable, but necessary and unavoidable.

Her last image before she slipped away was of JD Hawke staring at the sky, lost in thoughts. He was probably thinking terrible things about her…too bad. Changing his mind about her would take a miracle, and she was fresh out.

JD stared at the approach of morning over the tranquil countryside, a time of day he didn't often see, unless he was on his way home from a party. The events of the night had sobered him in a profound way. He knew he was in the middle of something that was going to change the course of his life and he had no control over it. Not even any knowledge of what it was.

He turned and looked back at Anne. How she could sleep was beyond him. Unless this kind of danger wasn't so unusual for her. He, on the other hand, was so wired up from being shot at he could have run the rest of the way over the hills and down into Monaco.

He argued with himself about calling somebody in spite of her obvious desire that he not do so. The only thing holding him back was not knowing who she was or what was going on.

The sun rose slowly as he paced and worried over each car that passed. Finally daylight flooded the hills with a warm, buttery yellow glow.

He sat down and waited for her to wake, staring at her with curiosity and interest as she slept. A ray of light pierced some branches behind her and set her pale blond hair on fire. She was dirty, and badly bruised. He gently brushed a lock of hair from her face, and wondered who the real woman was behind this facade. He took a hard long look at her, and found that his emotions were somewhat shocking.

Even a little depressing.

He found her—in some strange way—even more attractive than she'd been last night, before all this started. How was that possible? He figured he saw fifty great-looking women in a single day in Monaco, minimum. A hundred every night. Yet this woman had a strange effect on him. If he were an artist, he'd paint her just as she was. Or if he were a photographer, he would snap her picture with just the right exposure to capture her beauty.

He liked how she breathed, the soft rhythm of it. He liked the curve of her mouth, the nose that wasn't quite perfect. The long, fine whiteness of her neck.

He laughed out loud. A laugh heavy with sarcasm. He felt like a doomed guy from a noir flick, blissfully waiting for his world to come crashing down.

JD stood up and paced, watching the road for that black Ferrari, shifting back and forth on his feet, wishing he had some gum to chew, or some coffee to drink, and food. A nice hot breakfast. His stomach growled from the power of the suggestion.

From time to time he stopped and looked at her. She was trouble. Big trouble. Right now, at this point in his life, trouble was the last thing he needed.

This night had put his career into the wall and he was damn well going to find out why. If somebody wanted Giambi dead, how was Anne connected to that?

JD didn't like mysteries. Especially ones where he was involved.

About an hour later, she finally she opened her eyes and said, "Good morning."

He didn't know exactly how to reply to that. It seemed so friendly. So natural. As if she'd just awakened in her own bed after a long night's sleep.

He nodded.

"How big is your apartment?" she asked.

"It's big. Why?"

"You're going to have a guest."

He stared at her. Under other circumstances, that might have sounded like a great idea. But not today. "Who might that be?"

"Me. I'm your new girlfriend. Your rich widow squeeze."

"If our first date is any indication of our future, I think I'll break up with you right now."

"You were pretty excited about me a few hours ago."

"That was before people started shooting at me."

"When I explain things to you, you'll be more than happy to have me as your girlfriend. But—"

"I know, you can't tell me anything now. I'm supposed to wait until you feel like letting me in out of the dark."

"Yes. When we get to my villa it'll all become clear."

She got up, tugged on her dirty dress to get it into a more favorable position and walked off. He saw her take something out of her purse. It was a PDA. She began to text a message to someone.

Maybe she was some kind of undercover agent. At least then he could make some sense out of all of this. Maybe she was here to take Giambi down. Maybe *she* had been the target last night.

He didn't like that idea at all. But the more he thought about it, the more it made an odd kind of sense. She shows up just when Giambi needs her, papers and money in place. Then she courts *him*, saying he's the reason she's in Monaco.

She was going to use him to get to Giambi.

When Beth finished texting a message to Allison Gracelyn, she saw JD staring at the road, bouncing from foot to foot, restless, chomping at the bit.

She needed to have a nice long talk with him, convince him where his best interest lay. The hit attempt might have been on Giambi. It was Giambi's car and those guys might have assumed he was in it. But why were they after the man?

She didn't have the slightest idea. Giambi stayed very clean, for a gambling man.

Could the cheating crew from Vegas have followed her to Monaco?

She immediately dismissed that idea as preposterous.

She walked back to JD. As they traveled along the highway a small pickup truck approached from the west.

JD asked, "You owe money anywhere?"

"No."

"Serious enemies?"

"Not that I know of. There are people who probably don't like me for one reason or another, but nothing that would make them hire a team of killers to come after me," she lied. A necessary part of her job with Oracle. "How many people in Monaco drive a Bugatti?"

"There might be one or two others."

"Anyone attempt to hit Giambi in the recent past?"

"No. He's generally well-guarded. He takes security seriously. Men like him have plenty of enemies."

"It's possible then," she said, "that you were right. The would-be killers saw the car leave the garage late at night. Nobody else drives that car. They couldn't see us with the tinted windows. They followed us to the shop. It's dark. We went inside. They waited and when we came out all hell broke loose. We saw them so we needed to be killed. Only we got away."

"Right. What else could it be?"

She didn't want to answer his loaded question so she focused on the lone truck nearing where they stood, next to the road in a copse of trees.

"Let me handle this," Beth said. "If he's looking to pick me up, you should act like you can hardly walk. I don't want him to get suspicious, like we're highway robbers or something."

She walked out, limping. She handed JD the jacket and waved to the truck driver. He pulled up and stopped. Beth was so happy, she was nearly giddy with excitement.

"Vous gens dans accident?"

Beth spoke in French, telling him they had been assaulted, their car stolen, but that they hadn't reported it yet because of her father.

"Why. You are afraid of your father?" the stocky driver asked in French.

"Yes. He's got a very bad temper," she replied.

"Ah, fathers. I am one myself."

"I hope you don't have such a bad temper as mine."

"I hope not."

"He was," she said, "the kind that might just have somebody killed."

"Then maybe I should go away from you quickly."

"I'd much rather you were more heroic and helped me get to Nice, where my friends will ensure my safety."

He considered that for a moment. Glancing from time to time over to JD as if to consider the risks.

She motioned to JD, and he walked toward the truck.

The driver nodded and told them to get in. He didn't ask any more questions. He was a weathered guy, aging fast. He wore a fedora and suspenders over his blue shirt.

It was a really lovely morning, sunny, bright, the sky with only a few scattered clouds. She stared at the countryside while the driver and JD talked about soccer, racing, the French Open. Men had the same conversations everywhere in the world. Sports. They loved sports the way women loved clothes. Music was said to be the universal language, but she believed it took third place to sports and clothes.

Their conversation gave her a chance to consider her next step. This little operation that she had hoped would go quickly was now a very big mess. Now she had to salvage it.

Courage, as Hemingway once said, was grace under pressure. She didn't know how much grace was involved, but she was happy to report to herself that, having survived two major encounters, she could handle herself very well, thank you very much. And JD, for all his complaining about wanting to know who and what she was, had showed her a lot of courage. If things were going to go downhill, he was somebody she wanted at her side.

Chapter 12

Salvatore Giambi sat on his balcony having breakfast and thinking about all his mounting problems. He felt a lot like a man sitting on the beach watching the water recede and wondering how big the wave was going to be when the wall of water came crashing down on him.

Casinos were nothing if not an endless stream of problems.

He dropped a shot of Kahlúa into his coffee, then settled in his favorite deck chair to listen to his phone messages.

The fourth one was from JD. Some bizarre story about somebody trying to kill him and Anne Hurley, crashing the car, running off into the countryside.

"What the hell is this?" he said out loud, angry at the crap he was listening to. His Bugatti had been wrecked? Was this some kind of joke? Had to be, he thought. That damn JD was having some fun with him.

When he tried to call JD he got his message box. He tried three more times.

Nothing.

He decided the man was probably sleeping. With any luck, he was sleeping with Anne Hurley.

Giambi used the walkie-talkie function on his cell phone and ordered one of his many minions to go check JD's apartment.

Ten minutes later, Giambi got a call. "He's not there, sir," the male voice said. "I don't think Mister JD has been back all night."

Giambi figured JD and the lady were in a hotel somewhere. Could be anywhere. Hell, maybe they drove up to Paris. Nothing for Giambi to do but wait until he showed up. Giambi loved JD as he would a son, but he trusted JD because of the racer's self-interest. Giambi was JD's last best hope of getting back into racing.

He played the message again. It didn't sound like JD was drunk. The voice sounded strained.

The idea that the Bugatti had been shot up and crashed, that JD and Anne were hiding somewhere irritated Giambi to the core.

Then another thought slipped in, maybe they had been kidnapped and this was only the first call. The next would be a ransom call. Or, maybe this was an elaborate set-up. Anne Hurley was going to ask him to come and fetch JD. He'd walked right into a trap of some kind.

Giambi played it again. The message didn't sound like the cool JD he'd come to know and trust. It sounded like some guy under a great deal of stress, but then gunfire and a crash would do that to any man…if he was telling the truth.

Right off Giambi leaped to the worst conclusions. That was his habit and he was good at digging out the truth.

He called his security chief. "Get up here, now."

"Yes, sir, but first—"

"Just get up here. We have a problem."

When Vincenzio Leoni showed up a few minutes later Giambi had him listen to the tape a couple of times.

"Well, what do you think?" Giambi asked. He could hear the tension mounting in his own voice.

"Doesn't sound like JD. I don't know what to think. I haven't heard any news on the Bugatti."

"It doesn't sound right to me," Giambi said. "It's not like him to joke about my car. Listen to what he says and to how he says it."

He played it again.

Vincenzio scratched his head and nodded. "He doesn't sound right. Definitely sounds like he's under stress. He knows that car is your pride and joy."

"Maybe somebody grabbed them."

"Could be." Vincenzio adjusted himself as he seemed to do whenever he was faced with a problem. It was a habit that irritated Giambi.

Giambi thought about his car being wrecked. JD being gone, and that woman having something to do with it. "Get somebody out to the crash site and check this thing out. I'd rather we be the ones to find my car."

"Could be the woman's involved. In her background, though, nothing suggests it."

"Maybe it's not a real background."

"We did a global search."

"I keep telling you, you can't trust the Internet."

The whole evening came back to Giambi and it suddenly painted a scenario that he didn't like. "Goddamn. She kept insisting on going out to our garage last night. Never gave a real reason. I thought…hell I don't know what I thought."

"If it was a kidnapping," Vincenzio offered, "you'd have gotten a ransom demand. Maybe that's not what happened at all."

"What are you talking about?"

"Somebody follows the car. It's your car. Nobody else in Monaco drives that color Bugatti."

"A hit. They thought I was driving!"

"Could be. They shot the car up. They wouldn't do that if it was a kidnap and ransom. You only do that when you're trying to kill somebody," Vincenzio insisted. "Maybe the shooter thought you were driving."

Giambi hadn't been awake long enough or had enough coffee to think straight. But now, with Vincenzio spelling it out, he could see things clearly.

"And then this shooter finds JD instead. He and Anne Hurley get away, and they're hiding out now, somewhere they think is safe."

"It's the best theory we've got right now," Vincenzio said. "I'm thinking it's a botched hit."

Giambi lit another cigar and poured another shot of Kahlúa in his coffee while his security chief took care of sending somebody to find the car. The police would be all over this if Vincenzio couldn't get to the Bugatti first.

Giambi's stress was escalating and it wasn't even noon yet.

"Get everybody on this. If there's a contract out on me I want to know where it's coming from. I'm gonna find out and when I do, I'll hang the bastards head-first off the bow of my boat, throw some chum in the water and let the fucking sharks eat their faces. I'll stick their heads in a bucket of scorpions first to get things warmed up."

He came up with about twenty ways to torture and kill the imagined kidnappers.

"What if it's the woman behind this?" Vincenzio asked.

Giambi backed up and stared at the man. "You think she's in this?"

"I wouldn't rule it out."

"What would the game be?"

"Money. Revenge. Who knows?"

Giambi thought about this for a moment. "I'm not ruling anything out."

Giambi hated to think that Anne Hurley might be involved. He liked her and he didn't want to have to torture and kill someone so fine as her. He'd have her killed and be done with it. Still, he didn't like that modern women were getting more and more into traditionally male crimes. It just didn't seem right. If women got as bad as men the world would be finished. That's how he saw it.

"I hope it's not her," he said.

"Maybe she's too good to be true."

In Giambi's experience, he didn't believe he'd ever met a man who didn't have some crime in his past. But he liked to think there were still virgins and pure females…somewhere.

Ten minutes later the bad news got just a little worse. A farmer had found the car and the police were at the scene.

Giambi phoned Vincenzio. "Let's get out there. I want it towed to the shop. Tell the police I'm on my way. Get my chopper ready," Giambi ordered. Vincenzio hadn't even gotten out of the casino yet.

"It's your pilot's day off."

"Well, cancel it. If somebody is gunning for me, I'm flying overhead. Right now, until further notice, nobody has days off."

He began listing all the enemies he had, or ones he might have acquired lately. One of the big problems with still being in Monaco when the Prince had pushed out the *Cosa Nostra* and other "unsavory" elements, was that people might think Giambi was playing both sides of the street. Helping the prince and, thereby, helping himself. Not true, but the thought could be enough to put a contract out on him.

And there were other people with other reasons. Even the damn head of the Monaco police could have set it up, for all he knew.

"You can't trust anybody in this miserable, backstabbing world," Giambi stated. If he had a philosophy in life, that was it.

Chapter 13

When the truck driver dropped them off on a side street near the middle of Nice on the Rue Rossini, saying it was only a block from the Boulevard Victor Hugo, he wished them well.

"Fathers," he said, "can be tough customers where daughters are concerned. I know. I have five girls myself. They add years to your life, then take them away after about age eight."

He laughed, waved and drove off.

Beth said, "I need a Starbucks. You know where I can find one?"

"This is France. The French like their shot of espresso, a *petit noir* or *noisette* with a Gauloise cigarette first thing in the morning. You ask for a standardized American coffee and you could end up under the guillotine for treason against French culture."

Caffeine, when it came down to it, was caffeine, Beth

mused. She'd gladly accept a *petit noir* at the first coffee shop they came to.

The early morning denizens of the city acted like her and JD's disheveled appearance was just another example of a night gone bad. Or good, she thought, depending on how you looked at a young couple who had apparently spent their evening in the woods.

They both cleaned up as best they could in the communal bathroom, drank their coffee and ate croissants, two each, then went looking for a car rental agency.

They took a taxi to Côte D'Azur Airport and JD rented a Peugeot. They had stopped talking long ago. Morning and the harsh realities of being tired and hunted left little energy or desire for conversation. And JD had, thankfully, stopped asking questions.

Beth stared out the window as he drove back to Monaco. All she wanted was a shower and a bed, and some time to think about how to handle Giambi.

Half an hour later they slipped down the winding road into Monaco, the wind blowing in her hair. She told him where her villa was. They drove in silence toward the hills above the Monte Carlo.

Her villa loomed straight ahead. "Turn in here," she told him. "That's my place, but drive past it first. I want to see if I have any visitors."

"You expect any?"

"You never know."

They sat outside about two blocks away just watching the place. People were coming and going, but nothing looked out of the ordinary.

"Let's go in."

He pulled in front of the villa, parked and they went in.

"I'm going to take a shower, eat a real breakfast, then sit down and tell you everything you need to know about what is really going on."

He gave her a look.

"I'll be out in no time, then the bathroom's all yours."

"Can't wait," he said with a sardonic smile.

She headed in to take a shower.

But then he said, "You know, on second thought, it might be a good idea for me to go on back to the casino. Make sure Giambi isn't going crazy."

Beth stopped and turned to him. "After all we've been through, after all your questions, you don't want to hear what I have to say?"

"Maybe I don't think you're ever going to tell me anything I can believe."

She walked back to him. "Judge it when it happens. You leave now, it'll never happen. There are fresh coffee beans and a grinder. Eggs and toast. I'll be out in fifteen minutes."

"What happens if some of these uninvited friends show up? You have any guns in the house?"

"No. Warn me and then run like hell."

Beth turned and limped down the hall. Her foot was feeling a little better, but she couldn't wait to get out of her dress and soak under the water. She wondered if she should have invited him into her shower, all that steam and soap might have made for an interesting morning. Of course, if she did that, she might just have to tell him the truth about herself, and the truth wasn't something she was ready to tell.

JD stared at Anne Hurley until she vanished into the bathroom. This is just great, he thought. He felt himself sinking into a really bad frame of mind.

Little Miss No Answer.

All he knew for sure about her and about last night was that he was in some deep shit and he had no idea what it was. Or how to get out of it.

He paced, something he'd gotten used to doing during the last twelve hours, and glanced down the hall in the direction she'd taken. Imagining her in the shower, plotting whatever it was she had come here to do.

He couldn't see anybody wanting to kill *him*, so it had to be her or Giambi the hit men were after. Giambi had sensed something was wrong with her right from the beginning. He must have known it the first second he laid eyes on her. That's why he didn't trust the background check. This woman had big trouble written all over her.

One way or another, he intended to find out her story before they left her villa.

When he heard the shower running, he slipped down the hall and into her bedroom. He rifled through her drawers, through her purse, looking at her ID, passport, driver's license. All of it said she was Anne Hurley. And all of it looked new.

He looked hard at the driver's license. She was, according to it, in the third year. Yet the hair style, the look, was now. This stuff could all be fake, he thought. Everything about her could be fake.

The closet contained nothing but clothes. He felt everything that had a pocket. Nothing, but the clothes were all new. Some still had the tags.

He shook his head, realizing he was thinking more like Giambi every day. Maybe paranoia was contagious.

When he was about to leave the room, he glanced at the mirror on the far wall and, from that angle, the mirror reflected the bathroom and the shower with its glass door and walls.

He could see her there, surrounded by steam, her hands

working her hair, face turned up to the water. Naked. He felt a jolt in his groin.

When she turned away, her back to him, he lingered, his anger mixed now with an unbidden erection.

Get your shit together, dude, he told himself. Not like you don't see naked women on a regular basis. She's nothing but a hot piece of misery.

JD swore all the way down the hall, using every choice phrase he could think of.

He was filthy and probably stank like a junkyard dog. He looked at the pool out her back doors. He wanted to jump in, but he wasn't going to chance it. No matter what she said about this place being safe someone might be waiting for him out there.

Suddenly he felt tired. He needed sleep but that would have to wait. More coffee. Maybe some eggs.

He got up and went into the kitchen. He rounded up the coffee beans, a grinder and set about getting his caffeine going. Then he pulled the eggs out and set them on the table, along with butter and muffins.

He went down the hall and into her bedroom again.

"How do you want your eggs?" he yelled over the rushing water.

"Scrambled light will be fine. I'll be out in a few minutes."

He had a hard time being as angry with her as he knew he should be. As he went back to the kitchen, he mocked himself for his attitude.

JD focused on breakfast. There were times when he envied those guys who could focus all their energy on whatever task they were pursuing. He couldn't remember a time, since he was eleven or twelve, that he wasn't getting distracted by some female. Some were worse than others. But this was a cat of a different stripe. There wasn't anyone to compare with Anne Hurley, or whoever the hell she was.

He knew, with a touch of truth, that, were Mama Wese alive to meet Anne Hurley, she'd have liked her. One strong woman to another. Mama Wese as the kids had always called her, butchering her actual name—Louise—had been feisty as a hornet, hard as hickory when her dander was up. Nobody tangled with her and walked away without regretting the encounter. But to JD, when he behaved, she was soft as new cotton and warm as the morning sun.

Anne Hurley was that kind of woman.

You're an idiot, he told himself, shaking his head. The woman in that shower is taking you down and all you can think of is how you'd like to get it on with her. C'mon, moron, wake up. All this work to get back in the race and this had to happen.

He cracked another egg and dropped it in a bowl.

Chapter 14

Beth, lost in the luxury of the shower's pulsations, was thinking that somehow the near disaster of the night had to be turned into a positive. She just had to make an adjustment in her strategy. And she had to be careful about getting involved with JD beyond what the assignment demanded of her.

Sobering thoughts tumbled through her mind about her dad, Giambi's blackmailer and the threat to the Athena Academy.

The hit attempt added yet another layer of worries. With the police in Vegas all over the attempt on her life, it was unlikely the two events were connected. She doubted anyone could have followed her movements and her change of identity then arranged a hit attempt in such a short time. Yet the possibility of a connection still gnawed at her. It was way out of the realm of probability, but she couldn't absolutely rule it out, either. It was too dedicated an attempt. But who had been the actual target?

Even though all of that was going through her mind as she showered, on another level she was trying every which way to sabotage her growing interest in JD. Playing him was one thing, getting involved with him was another. He was a potential interference to her goals and she had to play the game with him without emotion.

She never had been very good at keeping her emotions in check.

A half hour later, she walked into her living room wearing white shorts and a lavender shirt. The cause of half of her worries sat on a kitchen bar stool, looking tired but still awake.

"I feel so much better. It's all yours. I left some towels on a hook behind the door."

"Thanks."

He served her a plate of scrambled eggs and a muffin. The eggs were a little dry, but she was thankful for the food.

"Looks great. Thanks."

"No problem."

He left to take a shower while she ate, alone.

Before she took her last bite, JD emerged wearing nothing but a white towel. She put her fork down and watched as he walked across the room. She found herself staring at this race driver as if he were some sort of god.

"Now," he said, raking his hand through his wet hair, "are you going to be straight with me?"

She took a sip of coffee for strength. "Yes. As much as I can be."

JD sat down on the white sofa. "So, let's start with your real name. What is it?"

"That's not important. What is important is that I'm here because Giambi has something I'm after."

"Not the racing team, or the driver."

"No." She could at least be honest about that.

"Then his suspicions about you were well-founded?"

"It's what keeps him alive, his suspicions."

"The way you went after that shooter, all that martial arts stuff. Your facility with a gun. Shooting like you've been doing that all your life. Cool, giving orders. Who do you work for?"

"What you need to worry about isn't who I work for, but what I'm actually doing, because it's going to have an impact on your future."

"Why is it such a big secret?"

"Because it has to be."

JD stared off into space for a moment, then turned and gave her a dead-serious look. "This better be good. Otherwise I'm done with you."

"And doing what?"

"I'm going somewhere safe. Then I'm calling Giambi and letting him know you're a fake."

"This is a two-way street you and I are on," she explained. "I know a lot more about you and Giambi than you can imagine. And there's a quid pro quo."

"Which is?"

"Don't play games with me. Trusting me will serve your long-term purpose. And I need to trust you."

Good, she thought. Now we're putting this relationship into perspective. This little thing they had going on between them was a means to an end and she told herself repeatedly to keep it that way.

She continued, "Let's understand each other. You're a racecar driver with a bad temper and a messed up past, trying to get back in the game with the help of a gangster. I'm here to see to it that particular gangster stays alive and gives me some information I need. You can help me and in return I can help you get back behind the wheel."

He stared at her, lips clenched skeptically. He shook his head as if he couldn't believe his miserable luck. His stare morphed into a glare. "I didn't know he was mobbed up. I knew he had a past and he's Italian and all that, but he insists he's not a gangster."

"Whatever he is, he's very close to being kicked out of Monaco and that is the least of his problems. I really think those guys were after him and not us."

"Are you part of his problems?"

"Maybe the solution to his problems. I'm not in Monaco on vacation or to buy in to a race team. I'm here on an operation. There are only so many things I'm at liberty to tell you. As much for your own good as mine."

"Why exactly are you here?"

"To get some vital information from Giambi that he wouldn't necessarily be willing to give me. And I need you to help me get it."

"What kind of information?"

"Somebody's blackmailing him. Has been for a long time. Did you know about that?" She stood up, walked over and sat next to him on the sofa.

"No. I don't know anything about it. You're telling me somebody is stupid enough to blackmail a guy like Giambi?"

"Yes."

"Hell, when he picks up the phone, he can have a dozen hit men at his disposal."

"I know. He's had them at his disposal in the past. And one of those hit men may be the origin of his blackmailer. Why do you think he's out begging for investors? That casino not only generates a ton of legitimate profit, but Giambi also runs millions in laundered money through there. He takes his own cut. Yet he's always on the verge of financial ruin. Doesn't that seem a little odd to you?"

He thought about that for a moment. "I guess I never gave it much thought. It costs a fortune to build and run a racing team. Having investors, sponsors, is just how it's done."

"You need to pay more attention to Giambi's reality."

"Why do you care if he's being blackmailed? Just who do you represent? You CIA or what?"

"Let's just say I'm part of an investigation. We're not after Giambi. But his past intersected with someone we are very interested in finding. We're after the people, or person, who's blackmailing him. When we find out what we want to know, if you cooperate, we can make sure you come out of this with your career ambitions in tact. Did you know about his money laundering?"

"No. Like I said, I don't know anything about his financial activities."

"When, and if, any of the bad news about these activities gets into the public arena he's going to have major problems getting established in Eastern Europe, or anywhere else. And your dreams of getting back into Formula One will be over."

"I'll find someone else. Those guys from Hollywood—"

"They can't back you. Not enough cash, and no sponsor will want you because you're connected to Giambi. Face it. If he goes down in flames, you'll crash and burn with him."

JD leaned his head back on the sofa and stared at the ceiling. "You're saying I'm finished. No way out?"

"There's one way out. If you help me get into his private files."

He turned and looked at her. Sincerity on his face. "I was your target right from the beginning, wasn't I?"

"Yes."

"So when he finds out, I'm dead. Or when you get what you want, maybe then I'm dead."

"No. Nothing like that." She stood up and sat in a floral chair across from him.

"C'mon. We're being honest here, right? I'm just a means to your end. Any way you look at it, in the end I'm a dead man. Whether it's the guys who were chasing us, you and whoever you work for, or Giambi and his henchmen—I'm finished."

"That's not how I work. You'll be protected. In fact, the only way you can come out of this is with my protection."

"Why am I less than excited about all of this?"

"You're in it now and there's no way out but for you to trust me. We saved each other last night. We had to trust each other with our lives. I'd say that's a good start."

"Couldn't you have chosen somebody else? He's got all kinds of people close to him."

"No. Giambi treats you like a son. He's the king and you live in his castle. You were the perfect choice."

"He might treat me like a son, but he trusts no one."

JD focused his attention out the window. She didn't know if he was buying her story, but at this point, he was her only hope.

"You have access like nobody else. A guy like Giambi doesn't trust many people. Only those he has a tight hold on, or who have a powerful incentive to be loyal. You have a powerful incentive. As far as he knows, without him, you're going nowhere."

He turned back to Beth. "You say you want to know who's blackmailing him. Who would care, other than Giambi himself?" He shook his head. "I don't get any of this."

"It's not important that you understand, just that you

help me. I'll tell you what you need to know, when the time comes. Until then, you're just going to have to trust me."

Her cell phone rang. She didn't recognize the number that flashed on the tiny screen. She showed it to JD.

"It's Giambi," he said.

"You answer it. I'll put it on speaker phone. Just stick to the story. We were chased. We crashed, but got away and now we're back."

JD followed her instruction.

"Okay, but where are you now?" Giambi asked when JD had finished his story.

"I'm with Anne here in Monaco."

"Well, I'm at the shop looking at my car," Giambi bellowed. "It's totaled. A complete goddamn wreck."

"They catch the people who chased us?"

"No. Nobody caught anybody. I was worried somebody might have kidnapped the both of you."

"No," Beth said. "JD held them off. We're banged-up a little, but that's all. It was scary."

"I imagine it was. We'll find them. Don't worry about that."

"I hope so," Beth urged. "They were some evil men."

"They cost me one of my prized cars. It's a damn mess."

He went on about the condition of his car, then wanted to know the details of the chase, but Beth cut him off. "We'll talk about it later. Are the police involved?"

"Yes. They're with me now and I have to fill out a report."

"Keep us out of it if you can."

Giambi hesitated for a moment. "Somebody was driving the damn thing."

"You could tell them it was stolen."

"I could," he said slowly.

"Good. Let's leave it that way for now. I really don't need the bad press."

"No, I suppose you don't."

She motioned for JD to hang up.

"Okay, then," JD said. "I'll see you in a little while."

Giambi tried to say something, but JD cut him off and disconnected. "Nobody talks to Giambi that way. He'll be calling back."

"We're not going to answer. He'll be out there for a while filling out the report, fretting about his car, right?"

"Most likely. Why?"

"We need to go to the casino. I'm moving in with you, remember?"

"What are you talking about?"

"We had a hot night and became fast lovers."

"You make me wonder if you're not a little crazy. And I still have no idea who you are, or what you're really after. I have no way to know if I can trust you. I'm just as much in the dark as ever. If all you're doing is trying to find out who's blackmailing him, why wouldn't he want to know? And if he does know who it is, why wouldn't he want you, or whoever you're connected to, involved?"

"Many reasons. My knowing would put him in jeopardy with the blackmailer."

"And my role in all of this?"

"I assume he has a private office?"

"Yes."

"I need to get in there."

"Nobody gets in his office unless he's in there, except me, on rare occasions."

She retrieved her tattered bag from the previous night and pulled out the cloner and antenna. "This tiny antenna and cloner activate and pick up the signal from a card reader. When I was sitting next to Giambi in the piano bar, I downloaded the info from his card. Does he use it to get into his office?"

"Yes, but now I'm totally screwed," he said, agitated.

"Not necessarily."

"Giambi will turn on me. When that man turns on somebody, it doesn't matter if that somebody is a relative or a best friend. He'll take care of business." JD grimaced. "Somehow I don't see myself coming out of this mess alive, no matter what you say."

"I promise you, you'll be fine."

JD hesitated for a moment, thinking. Then he asked, "Are you working for somebody trying to take over the casino? The Greek?"

"No. I've told you enough already."

"So, I'm just supposed to play along."

"Yes. You really don't have a choice."

"What if I cut out? Catch the first plane out of Nice and go back home."

"Not an option. If you run, Giambi will be convinced you betrayed him. He'll send somebody after you. You won't live long enough to grab a taxi out of the airport."

"You're going to break into his office, into his personal computer. With my help. I don't see that as a plan with longevity."

"JD. I'm sorry for your situation. But you have to trust me when I say I'm going to get you free of what's going on here. Giambi's my real target, not you. It's your only play."

His look was sober and less than friendly. "You are going to get me killed." He grimaced and shook his head despondently. "But before you do I'm going to jump in that pool of yours and try to cool down."

"Go ahead. I'll pack."

He stared at her for a moment. Then, shaking his head and frowning, he slid off the sofa and walked to the French doors leading out to her secluded pool.

He had his back to her when he dropped the towel. He stood there naked, staring out across the rooftops below. Then he slowly turned, and dove into the pool.

She sat on her chair staring at him, her mind in a kind of daze. The image of him standing there had not yet faded.

She fetched two towels from the hall closet and walked out as he was doing laps. Putting the towels down, she intended to quickly leave.

She didn't. And she blamed her lingering, voyeuristic interest on her sleep deprivation.

"I brought you…towels. I'm going to pack."

"Great pool," he said while treading water in the middle of the pool.

She tried to focus on his face. For some reason she decided to sit down at the edge of the pool and put her feet in the water. He swam over. "How's that foot?"

"Sore. I need to soak it in Epsom salts."

He took her foot and began to massage it with a soft, firm gentleness that tingled up through her legs. "That feels good," she purred.

She was finding it impossible not to look at him because, well, he was right there at the shallow end. The water came up to his stomach and for some reason she felt a little light-headed….

"You have great feet," he said.

"That's not a fetish, is it?"

"Never was before, but it's working on me."

She laughed.

Somewhere in her mind this was a silly game, or maybe

it was a serious move to ensure his loyalty, or maybe she wasn't exactly sure what this was.

He was staring at her now as he massaged her foot and her leg—and whatever else he could get his hands on. She was staring into his eyes and she was pretty sure now that her intention to not let this go anywhere had died as soon as she walked out there with the towels. Did it really matter? If JD was going to play her amour, then there should be enough reality to make the illusion work.

She was way into sleep deficit territory and he was doing something to her legs that was getting her excited way beyond her control.

I should get the hell up and go pack, she thought. Even as his hands moved up her leg, even as he started something she knew she should stop. But his hands were so delicious on her body that stopping him was just not going to happen. She became fascinated by the way he could massage her calf, the way he could play around with the underside of her knee and make it tingle like that.

Then she was simply out of control.

Those magic hands were up her thighs, kneading, and when they were up under her shorts, and he was then pulling those shorts off, she could barely raise her hips to assist him.

In that blissful moment, she knew she had lost to whatever this bad boy racecar driver was going to do because she was already having orgasmic spasms before he even finished the massage.

Apparently, somewhere in his life, John David Hawke had run into a copy of the *Kama Sutra,* and he had mastered all the right moves.

Chapter 15

In front of his shop, Giambi, flanked by bodyguards, glanced over at the wrecked Bugatti twenty feet away. The totaled car was still on the car hauler, surrounded by police with notebooks, two French detectives and Giambi's personal security team. He was sickened at the sight of his prized possession.

Staring at the shoes that had been found in the dirt, he said, to no one in particular, "What the hell happened here?"

He held the shoes in his hand like they were precious Fabergé eggs. He knew shoes. These were top of the line.

"Expensive?" Vincenzio asked, walking over from where he'd been talking to an officer. The suit jacket he wore was cheap and not hanging properly on his thick torso.

"What?"

"The shoes?"

"Hell, yes, they're expensive."

"They hers?"

The question hung in the air for a moment. Giambi watched a cop put a small marker down on the ground where another bullet casing was found.

Giambi turned the shoes over, and looked at the workmanship. Excellent. His father would have greatly appreciated the craftsmanship. What Giambi had appreciated, along with the shoes, was Anne Hurley's saucy strut in them as she came toward him as if she was on a runway. Most men might watch the movement of her breasts, or the flash of leg, her expression and attitude, but for Giambi his first glance went straight down to her feet, to the pumps. The son of Calzolaio, an Italian shoemaker who was also the son of a shoemaker. The love of shoes was in his bloodline. Had he not had an early falling out with his father, he had no doubt what business he would be in today.

"Would have been a lot easier," he said out loud.

"What?" Vincenzio asked.

"Nothing. You don't leave a pair of shoes like these behind unless there's a damn good reason."

Vincenzio nodded as if heavy, solemn thoughts were churning around in that brain of his. "Unless you're running and somebody is shooting at you."

Yes. That's what JD had told him. They'd run from the shooters. But something looked wrong with the whole scene. Giambi just stood there, staring down at the ground. Taking it all in.

"Her shoes are here, in the shop. The bullet casings are all around. There are bullet impact marks on the building. Shooting was going on here and way the hell over there." He pointed to where the casings had been found some distance away. "Makes no sense. Okay, so she's running. But from where to where?"

"The detective thinks there might have been a scuffle."

"JD didn't mention that."

Giambi tried to envision how a pretty lady and JD got in to this knock-down-drag-out battle and somehow got away and then crashed a car nobody could catch.

And they survived.

No, he thought. Something's wrong.

A dozen scenarios rambled around in Giambi's agitated mind and none of them were very good.

The last twelve hours had brought Beth closer to this stranger than to any man she'd ever been involved with. It was unnerving. JD was no longer just a means to an end.

On the way to the Sapphire Star, he talked openly and freely about his past, his family and how he became a Formula One driver. If she was going to depend on him, work with him, sleep with him, she needed to know things no dossier, however thorough, could provide. And now that they were on his own turf, he seemed more relaxed and ready to admit to almost anything she threw his way. "I was the guy who wanted to do things differently. We were a contentious family. Racing families in the South aren't running 'shine on Thunder Road like back in my grand-pappy's day, but the personalities are still pretty much the same. Mountain people like to settle things with their fists and sometimes their shotguns."

The more he talked the more she saw common denominators between them. They both grew up in rough circumstances and learned early how to deal with a hardscrabble existence. They both had big dreams and ambitions kick in about the same age. Both had ambitious fathers who hadn't fulfilled their own dreams.

Then it was her turn. They sat on tan cushy sofas looking

at a view of the entire hillside, sipping iced tea with plenty of lemon. Just the way Beth liked it. The doors and windows were open, letting in the cool breeze off the azure sea. He wanted to know something personal about her. Something real, he said. Something that had nothing to do with the operation.

And because he'd shared so much without really knowing who she was, she found herself telling him the second reason she was in Monaco. "My father was a professional gambler, but he ended up working for a cheating crew. It started in Vegas and eventually got around to other cities, like Atlantic City. But as the poker craze took hold, he wanted to go legit. Become nothing but a straight player. A family man. But this crew he worked for didn't buy in to that. He couldn't leave. He knew too much. He quit and a week later he was dead. Dumped in the garbage like trash."

She told him about the day the police came to the shabby hotel where'd they'd been living. How they took her to the morgue with this lady from social services to ID her father.

"I didn't think they let twelve-year-old kids do that," JD said.

"Nobody else to do it, I guess."

"I have to admit something," JD offered. "What you've been telling me just now is probably the first thing I've really believed about you."

She smiled. "I was an orphan for a long time, but never a rich widow. I've been a card player since probably before I could walk. I'm often employed by people who've been cheated. Or by casinos who want to bust cheating crews."

"What about this other thing you're involved in. The blackmailer."

"That I can't tell you anything about and it's much better,

for your sake as well as mine, that we keep it that way. Ignorance is bliss when you're dealing with this sort of thing."

"You mean, when somebody hangs me off a fifty-story building by my feet and wants to know something, I'll have nothing to tell them?"

"They'd drop you either way."

They laughed easily with each other.

Beneath the talk about their pasts their eyes were having another conversation. In the afterglow of the kind of all-out intimacy they'd shared poolside, she was taking a step back to check out the nature of the thing that was her new relationship. Was it good or bad? Temporary passion, or did it have the potential to be something more?

She couldn't answer that question.

She was good at quick character assessments. At least insofar as superficial traits. But JD was on another level. She always believed if you get involved you need to look for all the pitfalls or you'll fall into one of them. She was sure it was as true for him. He wasn't callow. He had substance. And she liked him. Maybe too much. What that meant was the big unknown. Romance on the job was both inconvenient and dangerous.

She'd told him they had to cool the passion for a while, but after this was over, maybe they could take up where they left off. Take a little vacation together. Have some fun. He was up for that.

She thought she'd read him. Then she'd discovered there was a lot more to him than she'd anticipated. He was complicated. He raced cars, had a checkered past, came out of the whiskey-running stock of the mountains of Tennessee and made love in ways that should be illegal.

She had needed his lovemaking in a bigger way than she'd realized. So if you're gonna slut around, she told herself with bemused self-tolerance, do it with somebody worth the price of a candle. This guy was well worth a whole warehouse full.

Giambi was arguing with a detective about who had jurisdiction over his car, when his cell phone rang. It was his butler, Jason, telling him that JD and Anne Hurley had returned to the hotel, and she had moved in.

"Moved in. Moved in where?"

"Into JD's suite. I asked if they needed anything, and JD said they wanted me to go down to the market and get a few things. I was holding off until you returned, sir, but it's been a couple hours, and Miss Hurley just phoned to see if I had returned with their things."

"Go ahead. I'll be coming back soon and I may need you."

After Giambi hung up he was more confused and incensed than ever, so he took out his handkerchief, sat down on a wooden stool inside his now empty garage and began cleaning Anne's shoes.

The leather was as smooth and fine as any he'd ever seen. The quality of the overlay and gluing, perfection. Women understood jewelry, fine clothes and shoes. Most men were barbarians. They didn't care about the finer things in life.

Vincenzio broke Giambi's trance. "The police want to take your car."

"No," he said, concentrating on his shoes.

"They say they're gonna take it. It's a piece of a crime scene."

Giambi moved the shoes close to his mouth and blew gently to remove fine particles of lint still attached to the leather, then slowly dragged his handkerchief across the top to remove what the eye couldn't see. When he had finished, he tucked his handkerchief in his back pocket and stood.

"Let's get out of here. I need to have a little talk with my racing hero and his new roommate," Giambi said. "To hell with my car."

Chapter 16

Beth unpacked in the guest bedroom with its heavily mirrored, Roman motif, and wondered how many girls JD had entertained in his plush digs.

With the butler gone, and Giambi still at the shop, it was time to make her first foray into Giambi's inner sanctum.

It had taken a while, after the episode at the pool, for her to find her brain again. She was eager to get back to work.

She walked out of her bedroom to find JD asleep on the sofa.

It was a shame to wake him, but she couldn't afford to overlook this opportunity to get into Giambi's office.

Gently, she stroked his thick hair and kissed his cheek. He opened his eyes, and smiled up at her. He looked just like a sweet little boy. She kissed him again.

"That's nice," he sighed. "Are you ready to go, or can we just stay here?" He pulled her closer.

"Love to, but—"

"I know. I know. You're on a mission."

"Yeah," she said, standing.

"How's the room?" he asked, sitting up, then slipping on his sandals.

"Fine. A bit much with all those mirrors, but it's very convenient."

"My room's much better. Sauna. King-size bed. You are more than welcome."

"It's all business right now."

"What happens if your reader deal won't work? He changes his badges frequently."

"There are other ways. No silent alarms?"

"I'm pretty sure there aren't. He doesn't trust his own security enough to want them to know anything about his private quarters. He's very tight about that."

"It's what you don't know that worries me."

She was happy they'd been able to get rid of Giambi's butler. He would have been a big problem. When they'd first gotten up to Giambi's suite they'd encountered him right away, the second they'd gotten out of the private elevator. Like he was waiting for them. She didn't like him right off.

Jason was a piece of work, dressed formally, he had all the stiffness of a true butler, but the eyes of an assassin. He called JD sir, and she was madame. It took her about two seconds to see he was as big an impostor as she was.

Jason had surveyed her luggage before taking it and said, "Will madame be staying?"

"Yes. In my room," JD had said.

Jason had raised his eyebrows.

"And we need you to go to the market and get a few things, if you would be so kind," Beth had asked and handed him a long list of items, hoping it would keep him busy for quite some time. Jason hadn't liked the idea, but acquiesced. Trained but not indoctrinated fully to his new calling.

Keep an eye on this boy, Beth told herself. He's too heavy in the shoulders and hard in the eyes to be a true butler. More of the bodyguard type.

Beth felt much more comfortable now that she had JD firmly in her pocket.

"You're sure there are no hidden security cameras to worry about? Ones maybe recording just for his use or for his security team?"

"The office is off his bedroom in his private suite. With Jason, his private elevator and security allowing no one access to this floor, I don't think so. If he feels secure anywhere, it's here."

"He doesn't trust his own security?"

"He trusts them the least because they can hurt him the most. He's a careful man. And a private one. Once he's in his room, he can come and go as he pleases and nobody really knows about it. Except Jason, of course."

"What about this butler? He looks like he's more than just somebody serving drinks and getting clothes pressed."

"Yeah. Eagle eyes and elephant ears. He's definitely one to watch out for. He's very loyal. I think because Sal takes care of Jason's family back in Italy or something, but I'm not sure."

"Giambi have a desktop computer or laptop?"

"Both."

"I need to get into his office. Now."

Breaking in to Giambi's private suite was easier than Beth had anticipated. He hadn't changed his code after all.

She and JD made their way across the Vegas-style suite. It was one as plush as any she'd ever seen, from the piano and four or five sitting areas, to space for a band, a grotto pool that was a duplicate of the one in Hugh Hefner's place, the paintings and frescos and Greek and Roman motifs.

JD showed her where Giambi could enter and leave if he wanted to use the side door to the emergency exit stairs, without his staff knowing.

"What's with the caves in the pool?"

"Well, Giambi always liked the Hugh Hefner lifestyle. Silk robes, fine cigars, healthy appetite for pretty girls. He was at Hef's mansion a couple times. Liked the grotto pool. Little love caves, that sort of thing. His office is behind it. There's a way we can go into the love caves, exit from the other side and into the office without Jason knowing about it. He pretty much stays in the kitchen area. His apartment is behind the kitchen. Watch this," JD said. He went over to a power box. The lights around the pool suddenly vanished, replaced by a moon and stars and mood lighting.

"Nice."

He led her down to a door in the back. "Maids are supervised by Jason. They only come in here when Giambi isn't around."

Unlike the rest of his sumptuous suite, the office was small and sparse.

"It's his panic room," JD said. "You could hole up in here and survive just about anything. Fireproof, bullet- and bombproof. This is both office and vault. You throw the bolts on the door and nobody gets in. You have communications with the world. And that—" he pointed to a ladder that led to a roof hatch "—leads to the chopper in case you want to get the hell out fast."

"I see the desktop. Where's the laptop?"

"Top drawer."

She tried to open the top drawer of the desk. "It's locked."

"Shit. That's a problem. Hopefully what you're looking for is on the desk. Maybe the laptop is just a backup."

She'd have to go with that theory for now. She set up her own laptop, then inserted the first flash drive in Giambi's computer and went to work hacking in.

"What kind of program is that?"

"This is called a brute force attack. It's very good and much faster than most programs out there. It can crack any encryption he might have. Still could take a while, though. What's different about this particular program is that it not only locates every file and throws encryption breaks at them in the event they're on multiple protection schemes, it compacts and prepares them for a rapid download. If he didn't have the right firewalls set up, I could have everything sent directly to my laptop, but from the looks of things, he's well protected."

"How long will it take?"

"We'll be in and out in a matter of minutes. I just need to get in, then insert some spyware. I'll be able to access his files from my laptop."

Now, twenty minutes after the butler had left, Beth told JD to call him to add something to the list, delaying him from returning until she had gotten her programs running and, hopefully, some results.

When JD hung up, he nodded to Beth. "He's just pulling into the parking lot of the first market. The list will force him to go to at least three different places. It will keep him busy for an hour, maybe more."

With any luck Giambi was still dealing with the police out at his shop and would be there for a while longer.

JD watched her work. She inserted a series of flash drives into one of the ports then booted up and began running a program.

He had a lot going through his mind. What worried him most about her was, well, just about everything. He believed her Vegas story and knew enough about the place to know that anyone who grew up in Vegas knew the dark side of human nature and how to deal with it.

And he liked her. Liked her a lot.

He'd spent much of his life under the control of other people. But never women. This was the first time he'd ever experienced anything like what he felt for her and he didn't know what to make of it. She had him by the short hairs in every way and not knowing what was really going on made him both vulnerable and pretty much tied to whatever she had in mind.

Somehow, this agent, bent over the computer, working feverishly to break its codes, was a fast current that had caught him up and would dump him on the rocks whenever she chose.

"I feel like I'm in a James Bond movie," JD announced.

She glanced up. "Which Bond is your favorite?"

"The old Bond. Sean Connery. Which one do you like?"

"Pierce Brosnan. Very sexy man."

"Nobody touches the original."

"Whatever you say, but Pierce is my hero."

He wandered around the office, gazing at photos, picking up artwork. He was getting bored, and a little worried about this taking so long. He really didn't want to get caught.

When his cell went off he thought it was Jason wanting to know about something on the list. It wasn't.

"It's Giambi," he whispered as if the man could hear and see him.

"Better answer it. See what he wants."

"Hello."

"Where the hell are you?"

JD's throat tightened, and he coughed it clear. "I'm relaxing. Having a drink in my room. Are you at the shop?"

"Anne Hurley's there with you, isn't she?"

"Um, yes. She's here." He looked over at her and shrugged. "She's decided to stay in my suite for a while. I assume that's okay with you?"

Silence.

"We need to talk. I'm on my way up."

JD stood up straight. "Where are you?" He mouthed to Beth that Giambi was in the building.

Beth's heart raced, as she tried to hurry things up on the laptop. *Shit!* she mouthed back.

"In the garage."

The phone went dead. JD turned to Beth. "Christ. He's on his way up."

"Damn. I'm not done yet."

"Well, get done. We have to get out of here."

"It takes time. I need to set up a back door into his system and I need to break down his codes and that can take some time."

"Too late. We'll have to break in again."

She closed out, gathered her things and they got out of there and ran to JD's suite in time to open the door just as Giambi emerged from the elevator, her shoes in hand.

"My shoes!" she said, making a beeline for Giambi. "You're my hero." He handed them to her. "I thought for sure we drove over them, but they're perfect. Thank you." She gave him a quick hug, but Giambi didn't reciprocate. Instead, he looked at the two of them like they were a couple of escaped convicts with bad intentions, then turned and walked away.

Beth knew she had her work cut out for her if she was ever going to win his favor back.

Chapter 17

Beth knew this would be a critical moment in her relationship with Giambi. She had to make him buy in to their story. She couldn't let his suspicions get the best of him.

"Let me handle him," she said, as she and JD walked to Giambi's suite later that evening. They were both dressed in their casual best, with Beth wearing the Jimmy Choos Giambi had rescued.

"Believe me," JD said, "you can have him. Good luck."

JD knocked on Giambi's door, and Jason opened it, wearing a scowl. Apparently he still hadn't recovered from the market-hopping trip they'd sent him on that afternoon.

They walked in and were escorted to the living room.

Giambi came in five minutes later looking angry, walking fast, a tight frown on his face, with two men who looked like a couple of well-trained bulldogs flanking his sides.

"Vincenzio and Letta," JD said under his breath.

"His arm-breakers?"

"Yep." JD stretched his arms as if he was preparing for the worst.

Beth immediately took control of the situation. "I want to thank you again for returning my shoes." She twisted her left foot to let him see she was wearing them. Her right foot still ached, especially stuffed inside her shoe, but she was going for effect.

"Yes. I'm happy I could return them to you."

His eyes were narrow, severe, his shoulders tight, lips pursed. She noticed for the first time, in the bright light of day, the liver spots, the loose neck skin, the excessive eyebrow hair. He was an aging man. Yet, for all of that, he was still elegant, still ramrod straight. Imposing.

Giambi turned to JD as if he was going to start in on him, but Beth interrupted the onslaught. "I was frightened out of my mind," she cooed, clasping her hands together for effect. "I thought for sure those men were going to kill us. I've never been shot at before. It's just horrifying. You see it in movies and on TV, but you don't have any idea how terrifying it can be."

"I'm sure it was pretty awful," Giambi said, with just the slightest hint of concern.

"Oh, you would not believe how scared I was."

"I can only imagine."

She caught the cynicism in his voice, but went right on as if he had said something kind. "And then we crashed down that mountain and the car was on its side, and JD knew just what to do, but those men were coming down to kill us. We had to get out. I thought I was going to die right there. But then when we crawled out of the wreckage, they were shooting at us again. I wanted to cry, but JD wouldn't let me. He told me to be strong, so I was and fortunately we got away without any bloodshed. They hunted us in the woods for hours. It was horrible." Beth sat down on a chair and covered her face with her hands.

Then she grabbed JD's arm, and looked up at Giambi. "This Tennessee mountain boy here fooled them. Instead of running away, we circled back and hid. They walked right past us like revenuers walking past moonshiners."

She thought that was an apt bit of dramatic description, but Giambi's frown remained. She'd have to work harder for his sympathy. "Would you mind telling your men to leave us. Some of this is a little embarrassing."

JD threw her a look, asking *what's this all about,* but she never dropped her suffering character for a moment.

Giambi waved off his men. They retreated into another part of the suite.

She smiled, then, pulling out her best acting skills, made a little shake of her entire body, as if she'd been hit by a blast of cold air. "I was so scared I literally peed my pants," she whispered.

Giambi softened and said, "I'm sure it must have been a terrible experience."

"It was the worst moment of my life. I don't know who they were or what they wanted. Do you?"

"No, but we'll find them, don't worry about that. I have contacts all over Europe who know just how to find these people."

She told him how they hiked over all those hills, her bare feet getting cut up and sore. How JD made her a pair of moccasins using pieces of leather and his socks. "It was genius."

"He's a man of many skills," Giambi said, gazing over at JD, a touch of sarcasm on the edge of his words.

Then she said, "I'm really sorry about the Bugatti. Such

a beautiful car. So much power. Hopefully it can be restored to it's original condition."

"I'm not so sure that's possible," Giambi muttered. She could tell that even the mere mention of his baby made him angry.

"Will it be sent back to the factory, or can your shop handle it?"

"We can build anything from top to bottom if we have to. They'll do the best they can." He looked down at her shoes. "They're quality. I'm happy I could save them for you." His tone was heavy.

"I had to kick them off to run to the car when those men showed up at the shop," she said. "I never ran so fast in my life. JD got us out of there in a hurry. It was like a scene right out of a movie. People shooting guns, bullets ricocheting off the containers."

Giambi lit a cigar and studied them intently before speaking. "JD did good. Real good. If you don't mind, I'd like to have a word with him. The police will want to talk to him and we need to keep our stories tight. You won't be mentioned at all."

"I appreciate that," Beth said.

He looked from her to JD, then back to her. "Jason said you moved into JD's apartment."

"Yes. He has an extra bedroom and I thought it would be convenient. Hopefully, that's okay with you."

"You make your moves quickly."

"It makes it much easier for us to discuss our business arrangements. And to be honest, I'd be too afraid to be anywhere else. This looks like the most secure place outside of the royal palace."

With a touch of understanding, Giambi said, "Your sense of safety, and the fact of it, is of course very important. If you're considering investing in a team you might as well get to know the driver."

Beth smiled. "I owe JD my life. We're going to get along fine. Just fine." She smiled over at JD.

Then Giambi got a call. "Excuse me, but I need to take this." He turned to JD. "Meet me out on my patio in ten minutes."

Giambi started to leave, but hesitated. He said, "Jason was out doing some errands for you?"

JD nodded. "Some things Anne needed."

Giambi nodded.

Beth watched Giambi march off across his vast living room in the direction of the gourmet kitchen, speaking to somebody on his cell as he went.

"You're good," JD said, once Giambi was out of earshot. "Hollywood's really missing something."

"I don't know that he bought it," she said. "He's got a look in his eye that tells me he's not completely satisfied with the script."

"I'm going to find out."

"Just stick to the story. It's true enough. Just leave out the rest of it."

"You don't want me to tell him that you're the hottest thing under the sun since Mount Vesuvius?"

That got a chuckle from her.

"I know how he works. He's going to run a hard background on you for sure this time. Your cover won't last long."

"That's why I need to get back into his office."

"He's throwing a huge Formula One party tomorrow tonight. Maybe there'll be a chance then."

While he was talking to Jason, who had called him from the kitchen, Giambi was watching JD and Beth talk on the other side of the room. From where he stood on his patio he had a clear view of them. What the hell were they up to? He wasn't buying her scared-little-girl routine.

"So, what did they want you to pick up at the market?" Giambi asked.

"She wanted salts for her foot, ointment for her bruises. She was very particular about brands. I had to go to three different shops."

"You could have sent somebody else."

"JD seemed to want me to go so no mistakes were made. He was in a hurry. I thought he was worried about her, that she was giving him a problem."

"How'd she look when she came in. Frightened or nervous or what?"

"Not really either. Not that I could see. He had on messed-up clothes like he'd been dragged around in a ditch, but she was all cleaned up and looking just fine."

"Yeah, okay. You get everything she wanted?"

"Yes, sir."

"Fine," he said and disconnected.

Giambi called Vincenzio and told him to deepen the background check on Anne Hurley. "Check her out thoroughly. Blanket coverage. Call people who would know her. Hire detective agencies every damn place we can find an address for her or an association of any kind. I want to know who the hell she really is. I want to know who deflowered her. Who her relatives are. What her grade school teacher thinks of her. Get on it and get me results. I want to know more about her than her own mother knows."

Giambi poured himself a drink from his bar on the patio. This girl was big trouble. The kind he didn't know the origin of. If there was a hit out on him, that contract all by itself was big enough. But now this woman compounded his troubles.

The problem with having many enemies was not knowing in which direction to look.

He turned and stared out over his balcony. He had a view of the prince's regal quarters on the hill. He fixed on it with malice. "Your royal high-ass, you better not be the one playing games."

He waved at JD to join him on the patio. His anger and blood pressure were spiking and he had to calm himself down.

Damn human race, he thought. Liars, traitors, blackmailers, assassins. Who the hell could you trust in this world?

Chapter 18

"Do what you can to calm him down," Beth told JD. "We have to get this guy focused on anyone but us."

"I'll try. But when he gets excited it's hard to have a conversation with him."

"How are we going to get the desk key?"

"I don't know," JD said with a shrug. "He keeps his keys on the gold chain you see on his belt."

"He must have a spare."

"He's one of those guys who knows where everything is. It goes missing—"

"I don't need the key, just an impression." She opened her purse and pulled out a small plastic container. She snapped it open and showed him how to take a key mold.

"You came prepared."

Giambi called him this time, on JD's spare cell phone. "I gotta go. He's on the warpath."

"Good luck. Stick to the story."

"Hey," he said, putting a hand behind her neck. "It was a strange first date, but one I'm not going to forget anytime soon."

She kissed him and then pushed him in Giambi's direction. "While you're talking to him I'll go in his room and see if I can find another set of keys," she whispered.

"Jason's here, lurking around somewhere. Don't let him catch you," he warned.

"Is there a way to know where he might be?"

"No."

"Is there a way to lock down the elevator so he has to call?"

"Yeah, but that's also on Giambi's key ring."

"Can you see the elevator from the balcony."

"Yes," he muttered.

"Then just warn me. Hit my cell phone number on your cell. I programmed it in this afternoon. Number five."

He nodded and squeezed her hand. "Be careful."

"You, too."

Beth gave him time to get past the grotto pool, then she headed for Giambi's bedroom.

JD crossed the twenty yards or so to the balcony. Giambi, when he was really pissed and paranoid, could get ugly and he needed to cool down the old man and occupy his attention to give Anne enough time.

He walked out onto the balcony, glanced at Giambi, then went to the bar and poured himself a cup of coffee. He glanced back into the suite and saw Anne dart past the grotto and disappear down the hall toward Giambi's room.

"I sent you out there to find out about Anne Hurley and this is what happens?"

"I did what you sent me out there to do. Somebody trying to kill us wasn't part of the plan."

He sat down across from Giambi, swinging his chair so he had a view back inside.

"Yeah, what you did was get laid and wreck my car. Maybe everything happened just the way you said, and maybe not."

"You think I'm lying to you?"

"I don't know anything. That's the problem. Middle of the night somebody attacks you at the shop. Bullet casings all over the place. Shoes in the dirt. The car ends up wrecked miles away and you two show up the next day. Sounds like you had one hell of a night." Giambi took a drag on his cigar and let the smoke out slowly, watching it as it swirled through the air and then vanished in the moonlight.

"Salvatore, what happened, happened. There was nothing I could do about it." JD felt a wave of nausea sweep over him. He didn't like how Giambi looked, almost evil.

"I'm not saying it didn't happen that way. But I'm trying to imagine how you got away. How they didn't kill you or her. If she's kicking her shoes off to run, then somebody is already there, am I right? So how is it you got away?"

"Use your imagination. It's the middle of the night. We saw them coming. When somebody takes a shot you'd be surprised how fast you can run to get in a car and get the hell out of there. It adds up. I think they were coming after you and were surprised it wasn't you. That's what I think happened."

Giambi seemed to ponder that, no doubt looking for holes, something to pounce on. He asked, "JD, you have enemies that I should know about?"

"None that want to kill me."

"Maybe they wanted to kidnap you?"

"Who the hell would want to kidnap me? To extort money from you? That's ridiculous. You have the means to hunt down and kill anybody you want to. Nobody would do that."

"What about Anne Hurley? Rich widow like that, maybe somebody was coming for her?"

JD shrugged. "I don't know that much about her so I can't say if she has enemies or not. You'll have to ask her."

"I intend to. But I want you to tell me about last night."

"She told you what happened."

"I want details."

"It's like we said." He told Giambi about the bar, the ride to the shop. The attack and how they got away. He left out the part about kissing her while still inside the shop. "That's all there is. If you're looking for something else, you won't find it. She seems to be exactly who she says she is." He was out-and-out lying now, and somehow he found it real easy to do. Especially after their tryst in the pool. Everything had come easy since then, even his willingness to help her in her crazy scheme.

JD continued, "And the whole thing traumatized the hell out of her. She didn't particularly want to get involved with the police. Neither did I. She was scared and so was I."

"She better now?"

"Yeah. She believes they were after you or they wanted to steal the car and got pissed when we took off so they loaded it up with bullets."

"And she's fine with either of those scenarios?"

"I think so, but she needs to be convinced you can deal with the aftermath."

"Convinced how?"

JD thought he had him now. That Giambi actually wanted to help the terrified widow get back her confidence. Anne would be proud of him.

"That's up to you. All I know is this lady is loaded and she is really in to this whole racing venture. She's got some great ideas. Really interesting stuff that agrees with your ideas about how Formula One and NASCAR can work together in ways nobody has considered before. All these drivers from Formula One switching over to NASCAR. This idea of getting a race in Vegas on the heels of the NASCAR. Dual advertising. She's full of terrific ideas. We need to team up with her."

"You didn't get back to me when I called you this morning. Why?"

"I didn't have my phone, and besides we were busy."

"Busy, how?"

"Hey, you aren't *that* old. Boy saves girl's life. Maybe she thinks he deserves—"

"Those details I don't need."

"You asked."

"I better not find out this is something involving you and somebody you're into for something. You best be telling me the truth, JD. If I find out later you owed somebody money, or screwed somebody's wife, or whatever, our deal is off. I can get fifty guys like you. Just remember that. So if it's one of those deals, you get straight with me right now, dammit."

When JD said nothing, Giambi stood. "I gotta go check the arrangements for the party I'm throwing, but I'd like to talk to her for a few minutes."

"Listen." JD sat forward in his chair. No matter what Anne said, JD didn't want to lose Giambi's support, at least not until he was sure that Anne could come through for him. "I don't want you thinking I'm pulling anything over on you. There's nothing strange going on."

"You involved with drugs?"

"C'mon, Salvatore, you know me better than that. I couldn't drive if I were using."

"Well, hell. There's a lot of drugs going on at those parties you attend. I don't know everything you do."

"I'm going to risk my future by getting into drugs. Is that what you think?"

"Human behavior is unpredictable. I never think I know anybody well enough to predict what they're gonna do tomorrow."

"That's a sad way to be." JD shook his head.

"Yeah, well maybe it is and maybe it's the smart way to be."

"You live in a dark world."

Giambi sat back down and leaned forward, eyes intense. "Hey, look out beyond yourself sometime. You think that world out there is full of sunshine and roses? It's dark and getting darker every day. You just spent the night running from some kind of hit team. You think that's not dark?"

JD had him worked up again and that meant he could stretch this conversation longer. Give Anne more time. Giambi loved to argue.

"You sent me on a mission to find out who she was," JD said, sitting back in his chair, then sipping on his coffee. "Well, that's what I did. And she's ready to bring some big money into this deal, so you should be happy. Every damn day isn't five to midnight. You need to put some batteries in your clock and get it running. The sun does shine sometimes."

"If the target wasn't you or Anne, then it was me. For that I should be spending time in the sunshine? I don't think so. I'll take the cover the night affords me."

"They didn't succeed, did they?"

"They killed my car."

"You'd rather I was dead?"

He held out both hands as if he were weighing the thought, like it was a real hard choice. "You … the Bugatti.

You … the Bugatti. About even I'd say." He emitted a dry, sarcastic chuckle.

"Thanks. At least I know where I stand."

"Hey, I loved that car." Giambi reached out and slapped JD on the shoulder.

"I know. Look, there's nothing to worry about. I got her wrapped around my little finger." JD wished that were true, but it sure felt good to say it out loud. "She's looking for the excitement of hooking up with a race car driver that she can help make a winner. You've seen the type. Hell, you were once involved—"

"Don't. I don't want to hear it," Giambi warned. "How big of a piece of this does she want?"

"That's between you and Anne. We didn't talk about the specifics."

Giambi was lightening up, and the knot in JD's stomach had vanished. He took in a deep breath and let it out.

"You got something with this lady that's different than your usual deal?"

"I had a great time with her. She's on fire."

"You watch you don't get burned." Giambi patted JD's arm as if he was really concerned about this issue. "I want her to join me at my table tomorrow night. Both of you."

"Thanks. We'll be there."

"You invited your Hollywood crowd?"

"Yes. It's going to be fun. Look, I trust you," JD said. "I want you to trust me a little. Have faith. We've got big plans and I think Anne can help make them even bigger."

"Your story proves out, I'll apologize and never distrust you again. Until then, let's just stay business associates because that's about all I'm in the mood for right now."

"I'll take that for now. You aren't showing a little jealousy, are you?"

"What?"

"I see how you look at her. She's the whole package."

"No. I might be jealous of your age, but that's about it. You're a hotshot, but you aren't that grand."

JD saw the light of the elevator. He got up to fill his coffee cup and walked over to the bar. He hit number five on his cell and hoped that Anne hurried out of there as soon as her phone rang.

Giambi got up when he heard the elevator open. "Don't be sending Jason on errands. He's got his hands full with my party tomorrow night."

"Never again."

Jason exited the elevator and headed straight for Giambi's bedroom. Anne was seated in the living room, as if she'd been there the whole time.

JD let out a long, heavy sigh.

Chapter 19

Beth shut the door behind JD when he walked into their suite. "I looked everywhere that I could without messing things up. No keys."

"What now?"

"I'm thinking I need to get him in the grotto pool in his swimming trunks. Does he ever go in?"

"Sure. All the time. Nothing the man likes better than being in the grotto pool with a beautiful young female. It's the Hugh Hefner thing kicking in. And he's just a touch jealous that you and I are an item. I think he wishes he hadn't set us up."

"Good. If we can get him in the pool, you're going to have to get into his room and get an impression of the key he carries."

JD nodded. They headed toward the living room.

"How'd your conversation go?"

"He's all upset—" he flopped down in one of the living room chairs "—about everything. This is just another mess to deal with. I don't know if he believes the story or not, but I suspect he's going to really check you out now."

"We need to move fast."

"He wants to meet with you. He wants to know your business plans vis-à-vis the racing team. And he wants to hear some of your ideas. I warmed him up on those. You have bruises you want to soak. I'll tell him you want to meet him in the grotto pool. You can talk there."

"Good. What do you think about Jason?"

"He's going to be very busy. Most of the time he'll be down in the ballroom supervising the set-up for tomorrow's party."

"Giambi really didn't believe you? Most of what we told him was the truth."

"He's had things happen to him in the past. He's about as skeptical of human behavior as you can be outside of a mental hospital. And in his world, there's a lot of justification."

"What bothered him the most? I'll try and ease his mind."

"You in a bikini will ease his mind."

"Did he say specifically what's bothering him?"

"The pattern of the bullet casings. Where the shoes were and where the car was parked. He's the kind of guy who puts that all together and wonders how the hell we managed to escape. He hasn't seen you in action. So he's wondering just how it all went down. Like I said, he's a very skeptical guy."

She was sitting close and he reached over, grabbed her hand and pulled her onto his lap.

"What are you doing?"

"I'm just checking things out."

"You're supposed to go set this up."

"I will. We have a little time."

"For what?"

"To make sure these bruises of yours are okay. That's one reason the grotto is the best place to meet him."

"My bruises are fine." She grabbed one hand and moved it out from under her blouse only to have to deal with another and then it was like he had three or four hands. She was laughing, but she slid over to the other side of the sofa. They had work to do, and no time for anything else. At least not at the moment. "I need you to tell him I want to talk to him in his pool."

JD made the call, but she could tell he wasn't happy about it. When he hung up he said, "He'll meet you there in twenty minutes. I know you'll handle him with no problem. Just remember that he's been at this for a long time. He can read a person about as well as anyone I've ever met."

"So can I," Beth said. "You just get an impression of that desk key. I'll handle Giambi. Once I have the key, I'm going to need to be able to get away from the party."

JD nodded. "He's going to have potential investors at the party. He planned on showing a film compilation of my greatest racing moments in his ballroom theater after dinner and dancing—he's a big tango man."

"What about Jason? Will he be there all the time?"

"He'll be serving drinks." JD pulled his laptop over from the coffee table along with a controller and began playing a game. "He's always at Giambi's beck and call when he's entertaining. There's a good chance you can slip out. Get a headache. Have to go back to take some pills or something. Or maybe just sneak out. If he notices, I can tell him you went to get something. It's the only chance you'll get. Things are bad right now. At night, if he sleeps more than four hours I'd be surprised. And Jason is all over the place. On top of that, Giambi has been in his office a lot. I think he's looking at moving all of his assets out of Monaco unless the climate changes real soon. So the party will be about your only chance."

She nodded. "Okay. The party it is."

"What happens if you can't get in the office or you can't break the codes to get into his programs?"

"That can't happen."

"But if it does?"

"If we can't do it one way, we'll have to do it another."

"Meaning what?"

"Meaning I'll deal with that if it happens. I came here to get some information and I'm not leaving without it."

She had to work Giambi, get him to buy into what she was going to tell him. Then she had to work a little on his jealousy—if, in fact, that was the case with the man.

"Of all the groupies and jet-setting playgirls in all the world, I end up having a crush on the girl who's gonna bring down this house. Is that a bad joke or what?"

"For the grandson of a whiskey runner you're doing okay. You didn't expect a normal life, did you?"

She watched him maneuver the action on the game. A lot of shooting and running.

"No. I expected a great life. Full of victory laps."

She looked at him, smiled and winked. "You'll get those laps."

"Like my grandma used to say, a wink is like a nod to a dead horse."

"That one of your Tennessee sayings?"

"Yep. By the way. You aren't alone. You have a competitor."

"Who?"

"A Greek billionaire. His yacht should be pulling in here maybe tomorrow or the next day. Giambi wants you to meet the guy. Help persuade him to come aboard. He's the big money behind the casino in Kestonia. If he can get the Greek behind him, he's thinking of becoming the Steve Wynn of Eastern Europe."

"Giambi's almost eighty. These are long-range plans. I admire that, but I don't know if I'd invest in it."

"Like Giambi says, eighty is the new sixty. He works out, eats power foods. Takes vitamins, most of the time. Thinks he's going to be good for at least another fifteen years. He and the Greek are about the same age."

"More power to them." Then she gave him a little nip on the lips. "You're definitely trainable."

"Bond material?"

"Well, that's yet to be determined. But so far, so good."

"I think he's going to put something on the table tomorrow night at dinner. He expects that you're ready to make a deal."

"Does playing those games help you as a driver?"

"I think it does. It takes great hand and eye coordination. Games make good practice for drivers and fighter pilots. Want to play with me, little girl? It's *Grand Theft Auto*. I'd say you know a little about that."

She smiled and nodded. "A little, but you know much more. Teach me everything."

"It would be my pleasure," he said and handed her a cordless controller.

Not exactly what she had in mind, but under the circumstances, it was probably the right move.

When she reached the grotto pool, Giambi was already in the water, sitting on the formed-in pool seats that were along the side. He had drinks prepared on the floating table and he was smoking a cigar.

She walked toward him with a smile. "How's the water?"

"Great."

She gave him plenty of time to check out her walk and her body as she kicked off the flip-flops and dropped her silky robe.

She stepped slowly into the water, then cruised over to him and took a seat right next to him. The water felt divine, and the twilight view only added to the sensation. "Very nice," she muttered. The man knew comfort.

"You do justice to a bikini," Giambi said as he handed her a pink martini.

"Thank you. A lady never hears too many compliments."

Giambi checked out the bruise on her shoulder. "You might want to have some X rays. You might have a cracked bone somewhere and don't know it."

"I think I'm okay. If something was cracked, I'd feel more pain than I do. But if it flares up, I definitely will. Thanks for the concern."

Giambi said, "You mind the cigar?"

"Enjoy. I like the smell of a good cigar. I don't think I have to worry about one night of secondhand smoke as much as bullets coming at me in the dark."

"I'll find out who did the shooting. When I do…well let's just say for every action there's an appropriate reaction."

"Sounds a lot like the law of physics."

"I think that would be an opposite and equal reaction. I don't think equal is what I have in mind."

Beth smiled. "I understand."

He lifted a highball glass and said, "To a partnership." He studied her through those ice grey portals, a sly grin forming on his face.

"And what does that mean, exactly?" she asked.

"Full partnership in Giambi Racing. Your lawyers can

draw up the contract. Mine will go over them. I'm not going to play hardball with you. I want to be involved. I want JD back with a ride as soon as possible."

"You move fast," she offered, then took a sip of her martini. It tasted sweet from cranberry juice and the vodka. Perfect, of course.

"Life is short."

"Indeed. It's something of an insult. Just when you start to understand things, it's over. I, too, am in a hurry."

"Then we should work well together." They clinked glasses. "To a great relationship."

"So," Giambi said, "what the hell really happened? JD gave me his version, but I still have questions. I have a hard time seeing how you two managed to get out of it alive."

She knew she had to be cool and calm, but these were exactly the situations she had been trained for at the Athena Academy. She could walk through this conversation half-asleep. "How many casings did they find?"

"Seven or eight. Can't remember. Must have been a nasty situation."

"It was. I thought we were dead." The art of lying is to confess. And fit the facts in the most logical way possible without revealing the truth. That required an alternate story that rationalized the situation. JD had to be the fall guy in this. It was the only way.

"The story JD told you is essentially true."

"Essentially?"

"Yes. From a certain point. I think he might have failed to mention something that happened earlier in the night that may, or may not, be connected. He didn't think it had anything to do with the incident, so he told me he wasn't going to tell you. I disagreed, but I really don't want to cause any trouble between you two."

"Depends on what it was."

"Nothing really serious, just that he got into an argument at a bar."

"Over what?"

"Me."

"That's understandable."

"Some guy made a drunken pass. JD said something the guy didn't like. He found us outside. He and a friend. They were really wasted. I have to say, JD was protecting my honor. He's fast with his mouth and his fists. It came to a quick end. He knocked the one guy down and then a bouncer intervened. That was the end of it. He just thought if he told you that, you'd be all over him about getting in bar fights. Especially with me along. You two seem to have this father-son thing going on between you."

"Was JD drunk when he drove you around in my Bugatti?"

"He was fine. I had more to drink than he did. And I took the car for a short spin."

"Who was driving when you crashed?"

"JD."

"You think it was them, the guys from the bar that shot up the car and chased you?"

"Perhaps, but JD really didn't think so and that's why he didn't want to tell you."

"So these guys may have followed you to my garage. But how did you get away from there? They had you trapped for sure."

"I'm a runner, for one thing. And I work out all the time, obsessively. So when they came at us, we just ran like hell."

She gave him her version of the story, careful not to throw in any new details or anything that could be construed as a lie. "They would never have caught us, but we crashed. Hit something in the road. We survived the crash with some cuts and bruises, but it allowed our pursuers to catch up. So we just took off across the hills on foot. I have to say that it was both the scariest thing that's ever happened to me and the most exhilarating."

"Why no police?"

"Neither of us wanted that. JD was scared of the French police but he was even more scared of you. He didn't think you'd be real happy with him getting into a fight at some bar with me along, then crashing his car. Not too good for his career if the press got wind of it. And besides, underneath all the bravado and macho driver stuff he's just a kid in many ways."

Giambi acknowledged that last statement with a look and a nod. But then, in a stern paternal voice, he said, "He's going to learn real fast that I don't mind fun, but when it comes to business, he's going to have to keep his act together. It'll be in the contract."

Giambi seemed to relax a little. He was buying the story and buying her.

They moved on now. They talked easily about business, racing and his woes in Monaco with the crackdown. He was serious about building a casino in Eastern Europe. And he brought up the idea of a Vegas venue for Formula One. She jumped in on that with full-throttle enthusiasm. She had to admit, a man with dreams was her favorite kind of man, old or young.

Giambi, an old gambling warrior, was someone she could talk to with ease. They understood one another and the world they both came from.

She decided, in spite of the fact that they came from opposite sides of the gaming table, her father and Giambi would have liked one another. She could see them out all night trading war stories, drinking 'til dawn, smoking cigars.

Beth could tell he liked her a lot and wanted to keep talking. That would give JD plenty of time to get into his room, find his keys and make the impression.

They got to talking about the party. Dinner first, dancing and then the movie. She was even a little excited to see what movie stars were going to show.

He said she'd probably see some people she knew. A lot of wealthy jet-setters belonged to his private club and would bring friends.

"I'm sure I'll see a few familiar faces," she agreed. In the corner of her eye she caught a brief glimpse of JD. Giambi didn't.

They had another drink. She tried to remember how many she'd had in the past twenty-four hours and what the caloric effect might be. But then, remembering the night of running, she figured she wasn't about to gain any weight.

They were getting along fine, laughing at each other's jokes. She reached over and touched Giambi's arm from time to time to make a point or when he said something particularly funny.

Seducing him. Developing intimacy.

And, from time to time, making friendly fun of JD.

JD appeared and said he had some things to do in town. That he'd be back in an hour or so. "Anyone need anything?" He gave her the look and smile of success.

"I'm fine," she said.

Giambi declined as well. "You need somebody from security to go with you?"

"I'll be all right, thanks. Even if I was the target last night, I doubt anybody will try anything in Monaco. They have more police on the street than just about anywhere in the world."

About an hour after JD left, she said she was finally

coming down off of last night and needed some sleep. "I hear you're quite the tango dancer and I definitely want a dance tomorrow night."

"It's a date," Giambi said. "You like to tango?"

"Love it."

Giambi smiled. "Me, too."

They got out of the grotto pool and before they parted she took his arm. "Don't be too hard on JD. He is really upset about the Bugatti. He knows what that car meant to you."

She could tell how much Giambi liked that she touched him and was so open and friendly. A couple of tangos and she figured she could get him to think exactly what she wanted.

As she returned to JD's suite she realized she liked Giambi and found him to be an interesting character. She was, in different ways, seducing two men who couldn't be more different.

Or maybe they were seducing her?

Chapter 20

When Beth awoke the next day, she'd been lying on her face in one position for so long that it was red and lined, her hair matted and her arm was numb from lack of circulation.

It took her a long time to completely wake up. She walked out to the kitchen and fixed a pot of coffee. It was already a quarter past two in the afternoon. She couldn't believe she'd slept that long. Almost twelve hours. Her body felt like a lump of lead, and the bottoms of her feet actually ached.

She looked in JD's room and he was sound asleep.

When she came back out into the kitchen and poured her coffee she found the newly cut key on the counter.

The first step to victory.

JD came stumbling out about twenty minutes later when she was on her second cup, grumbling about how his whole body ached. "If this is how you feel when you're old, kill me now so I won't ever have to go through this again."

He stretched and walked toward her wearing only white boxers.

"You don't look old. Matter of fact, you look really good."

He gazed at her for a moment. "Don't tease me when I'm in a weakened state. It's not fair."

She smiled. "Naughty me. There's fresh coffee in the pot."

"Just add milk and give me a straw." He wandered over to the pot, pulled out a cup the size of a bowl, poured in most of the coffee, added milk and several spoonfuls of sugar, limped over to the sofa and collapsed, stretching his long legs across the coffee table.

"You did some good work last night. Thanks." She held up the key.

He nodded. "How'd you do with the old man?"

"I think I have him eating out of my hand."

She told him about her "confession" about what really happened the other night. With her slight embellishment. "I think he bought it."

"The paranoid never completely buy anything," JD said, resting his cup on his stomach.

"The writer William Burroughs said that paranoia is the highest form of consciousness. Whether or not that's true, it is a big weapon in the survival game."

"I think I've heard of the guy, but I don't know why."

"A beat generation writer," Beth told him. "He wrote a book called *Naked Lunch*. He was a gay drug addict, among other things. Had a famous obscenity trial."

"Yeah, I don't know too many gay drug addicts, but his name's familiar. So you got the old man eating out of your hand. Good."

"I have to be careful when I'm talking to him. I let Vegas stuff slip out sometimes."

"Yeah, right. You told me about Vegas. So what's your

real name? I think I've now earned the right to know your real name."

"You don't like Anne?"

"That's a fine name. But you don't look like an Anne."

"Then how about Cathy?"

He turned and studied her. "No. I knew a Cathy once, and she wasn't anything like you. She couldn't shoot a gun."

"How does Laura strike you?"

"The only Laura I knew had freckles and red hair."

"Then, what? What should my name be?"

"Something mysterious, like Monique or Natashya."

She went over and poured herself another cup of coffee, and sat down next to JD. "I've always been partial to Bethany."

He slipped his fingers under her chin and gazed into her eyes. "I really don't care what your name is as long as there's no more guns involved. I don't want you getting hurt."

"I'll try to remember that."

"Anne," he muttered right before he kissed her. It was sweet and gentle and honest.

"I'll tell you when the time is right, I promise," she said when they pulled apart.

"What does a guy have to do to win your full confidence?"

"Just keep kissing me like that, and—"

He kissed her again. This time she didn't want it to stop, but she had business to take care of. She pulled back and rested her head on his chest. He stroked her hair.

"The people who tried to kill us the other night, how do they fit into this, or don't you really know?" he asked.

"I really don't know. There are several possibilities. Patience is a virtue."

"Not my strong suit."

"That shows in your races. To your detriment. Dinner's at nine. I need to start getting ready."

"Now?"

"You obviously don't know much about women."

"I know all the important stuff," he teased.

She stood up, threw a pillow at him and headed for her bedroom.

"That incident with the car is causing additional problems," he yelled after her.

She turned to face him. "How? What's going on?"

"Giambi thinks the police are getting ready for a raid. It gives Prince Albert the excuse he's been looking for. He'd love to check out Giambi's books. See if there's any money-laundering or other illegal activity going on. A prelude to getting the boot."

"How soon could this happen?"

"Real soon. Could be tonight. All those people here, it would send a message."

Beth was concerned now. The police could destroy any chance she might have of getting to Giambi's secrets. "Then I need to get in to his office as soon as possible."

"I still think your best chance is when he shows the movie. It's a collage of my racing history. I'm the big sell. They'll be some dancing after dinner, then the movie. Then more dancing until dawn. Some of the special guests will move up to the grotto for a swim with whatever significant other they've run into. But during the movie, nobody will be up here."

"Okay, I'll stick with that, and figure out a way not to be missed when he's showing it."

"Hey, there's something I want to ask you." He followed her back to her room. "There's been this persistent story floating around about a mob boss back in Boston, where

Giambi is from. How he died. I don't know if any of it is true or not, but I know rumors like that keep people in line. Maybe he starts them himself. If you want to scare people away from trying to do bad things to you, get them to believe you're connected."

"I'm sure it helps," Beth said. She opened the closet and looked at her dresses, deciding which one would be the best "tango" dress. "And the thing about rumors ..."

"If you knew the truth, would you confirm the rumor?"

"Probably not."

"You are a hard bargain."

JD walked back to his room. He knew he had a case on this lady now. She had the right attitude, and just about everything else. It unnerved him that he had no say over anything. That whatever was going to go down, whatever the endgame was, it would be a surprise and very possibly an unpleasant one.

A year ago Giambi had walked in and said, "Boy, you're gonna drive for me and we're gonna win races. Lots of races 'cause you got the talent and I got the money."

It was a rope to grab on to and he'd needed one at the time. He was thinking maybe he should have looked into the situation a little deeper. When a man's name is Salvatore and he's running a casino in Monaco, a place where the *Cosa Nostra*, among others, have been doing business for years, second thoughts should have been in order.

All JD wanted was to drive a damn race car. Instead he was deep in some international intrigue bullshit.

JD walked over to the window and stared out at the day. One of the things he prided himself on was the way he handled women. He let them know up front he was not the long-term kind. He was committed to racing and little more. When the girls understood that, he was fine. Sometimes one would come along who thought she was so special she could change his mind. He disabused that type quickly. He didn't like lying to girls, or playing games. He was straightforward about how it had to be. And most of the rich playgirls he messed with had exactly the same attitude. Everybody just had a good time.

The last thing in the world he needed was to have somebody come along who wasn't after him, who didn't have any long-term situation in mind, who wasn't even giving him her real name and for him to get emotionally involved. That was definitely not a smart move.

The problem was, usually he had to keep the women from getting hung up on him. He had never had to worry about getting hung up on any one girl in his entire life.

Dime a dozen, as his father used to say.

But this girl was different and it threw his game off. Threw his mind into a spin every time he saw her, held her, kissed her.

That's what was getting him. He had never actually believed there was a real deal. Chicks like you see on TV and in the movies were fantasies. Now he was seeing one in the flesh.

And therein lay yet another problem. Sex. Plenty of girls he'd been with liked sex. Some liked it a whole lot. But this lady had a whole other thing going on. She made love on a level akin to how she fought. Hard core. Just thinking about her got him aroused again.

I got to cool this down, he thought. I'm going to get chucked big time at the end of this deal.

He laughed at himself. And at Giambi. This lady comes rolling in here about to blow their world to hell and they both fall in love with her.

Chapter 21

"The rumors will be flying tonight," JD said as he and Beth walked into Giambi's glittering ballroom. She'd outfitted JD with a sophisticated, very tiny earpiece so they could communicate with one another when she made her play to get upstairs and into Giambi's office.

For the party, Beth wore a sexy, black lace top, open midriff and cut pantaloons that showed her legs from ankle to hip when she moved. It was a tango outfit that displayed her lithe body in killer style. She wore Mina tango shoes that were handmade in Buenos Aires, Argentina. If her foot held up she was ready to go. She knew she looked hot and when she spotted Giambi talking to some men at his private table, every man there turned to look at her.

"I think you've got his attention," JD whispered as he ran his hand down her back.

"That was my intention."

"Do you always get what you want?"

She didn't think she should answer that. Instead she looked up at him and smiled.

Nearly two hundred well-heeled guests filled the great ballroom. A fifteen-piece band filled the air with Frank Sinatra hits. Waiters and waitresses in tailored black-and-white outfits cruised like hunting birds offering flutes of champagne.

The last big bash before the roof falls in, Beth thought.

Giambi's face lit up when she approached him. His eyes took her in as if he wanted to remember the moment forever. He cordially introduced both her and JD to his friends. Beth recognized a guy from a poker game in Aruba, but he didn't appear to recognize her.

She and JD took their seats at Giambi's round table and made small talk with Giambi's guests. Sitting between JD and Giambi during dinner, she sensed Giambi was seriously distracted. Several times he took calls, leaving the table each time, and when he returned he looked just a little tighter.

She had no opportunity to chat with him until dinner was over and the dancing began.

"Are you able to dance?" he asked, taking her hand in his.

"Yes, I think so."

"I'll skip the complicated moves and keep it simple."

"Nothing in my life is simple, especially not the tango."

He laughed.

Giambi whirled her on to the floor careful of her foot, but she had it securely bandaged and indicated that it was not a problem. They got into a more vigorous mode, and for a moment she forgot about everything else in her life and concentrated on the art of the dance.

Giambi held her and guided her with grace and style. She moved with him, close to his body, tangled in the heat of the tango.

She saw JD watching them from the table. The scene reminded her of Al Pacino's dance in *Scent of a Woman*. Or, if Giambi had his way, it might be more like *Last Tango in Paris*.

Beth was astounded at his energy. She was beginning to believe him when he said he had fifteen good years left.

He whirled her to the Argentine Nuevo tango.

"How did you become such a good dancer?"

"One of my wives was from Argentina," Giambi said. "She insisted I learn. Once I did, I became so popular with the ladies it made me bad husband material. She divorced me."

Beth laughed as she spun through space, the aches and pains in her feet, legs and arms making their presence known, but she ignored them.

Finally after a complicated move, her battered body won out. "I have to take a break," she pleaded. "I'm still suffering the overall effects of the car crash."

He apologized profusely, with a gallant bow, and they walked off the dance floor.

"I want you and JD to come with me tomorrow to meet Feodras on his yacht," he ordered while they walked back to his table.

"The Greek?"

"Yes."

"I take it he's a potential investor in Giambi Enterprises. Does that also include your racing team."

"We'll see."

He wanted her to meet a few of his guests, but she pleaded a need to sit. She really feared that he would introduce her to someone who might recognize her beneath her disguise. Like the guy from Aruba.

"It's worse than I thought," JD said when she was able to free herself from Giambi, who was once again on the dance floor with one of the many beautiful women at the party.

"Worse how?"

"Giambi's not going to survive in Monaco very much longer. We're talking days, maybe hours. He's talking about getting out before they kick him out."

"Doesn't it take a lot to even start the process?"

"Not when you think you could be raided. Last thing in the world he wants is a bunch of detectives lugging all his records, computers and stuff out of here. Believe me, you don't have much time."

"When is the movie scheduled?"

"It's supposed to happen pretty soon."

"He says he wants us to meet the Greek tomorrow."

"Yeah. The man is worth a billion or more. Big Formula One fan. And a poker player."

Beth was curious why she'd never heard of him on the circuit, but she didn't pose the question to JD.

JD continued, "If the cops make a show, maybe I can delay them and give you time. I know how to shut the whole place down. There was an incident about four months ago when the TV cameras went down."

"What happened?"

"It was like panic city. Giambi and half the security crew were in the power room. Giambi thought the shut down was the prelude to some big heist. He had the money rooms locked down, every guard in the place ready for battle. It was all caused by a rat."

"A rat, in a hotel like this?"

"It came up through somewhere. Was living in the

power room. Ate through a bunch of cables. I guess it liked the taste. Got electrocuted and caused a momentary malfunction in the camera system, which operates independently of the rest of the systems. It has a backup and is never supposed to fail. That night, for about forty minutes or so, it did. If you can't get your thing done during the movie, shutting down the camera is a possibility."

"You can make it go down?"

"I was there. I watched what they did to fix it. I could bring it down again. If I had to."

"I don't think you will. I just need about twenty or thirty minutes to dump his files."

They started back to Giambi's table.

"Can you do anything to get this film going? I'm getting nervous."

"I'll get some people to get on him about it. Otherwise he'll dance until dawn."

Giambi was talking to a group of men when he spotted her. She saw a man she recognized and she would have just as soon avoided the situation, but Giambi was enthusiastic about showing her off.

He brought her over and introduced her around. One of the men she'd met before, under different circumstances, in a poker game in Martinique.

Her chameleonlike transformation was so effective the man, like the one from Aruba, showed no signs of recognizing her as far as she could tell. But she was itching to get out of there.

Giambi made some announcements about upcoming events in his life. The building of a casino in Kestonia. "Las Vegas in Eastern Europe is the future," he announced to great applause.

And then he waxed poetic about the future of Formula

One, the royalty of racing. He sounded like a man who was not on the verge of losing, but one on the verge of making his greatest deals.

Then he announced the film, a compilation of the greatest moments in Formula One racing from the beginning up to JD Hawke's brilliant, if turbulent, career. "A career that will be resuming very soon." That to another robust round of applause.

He came back to the table as the giant screen rose from the back of the stage. "Very impressive," Beth said.

"I know when I like something, or someone, very quickly. It's an instinct developed over a lifetime."

"I like a man with good instincts."

"Ah, what I'd give to be thirty years younger."

She smiled. "JD wouldn't have a chance."

"You have that exactly right."

When Giambi was whisked away by someone wanting to introduce him to another guest, JD made his way over to Beth.

"Good conversation?" he asked her.

"He said if he were younger, you wouldn't have a chance."

"What I hear about his youth, he might be right," JD said. "Fortunately, he's old."

"I have a sweet spot for older guys."

"I'm thinking it ain't that sweet."

Tango eventually gave way to some forties music and then to younger music.

The old bull and the young stud vying for her attentions might have made the night more enjoyable if she wasn't obsessed with getting upstairs.

Finally, at one in the morning, the movie was set to roll. Giambi returned to the microphone to narrate the action with his humorous running commentary.

"I'm going up. If he misses me, I have a little headache and I'm taking a nap. I'll be down later. I'll have my earpiece in, so let me know what's going on about every fifteen minutes or so."

JD watched Anne leave. Watching her dance he'd had a foreign idea enter his mind—this was the kind of woman he could get serious about. Not too serious. He didn't want anything or anyone getting in the way of his ambition to rise to the top of Formula One. Still, if it came down to it, this was definitely the type of lady he really could get with.

If she succeeded, what would that mean? If she failed, then what?

Good luck, girl, he thought as she disappeared.

He turned to the montage of his racing career and reality sunk in.

This would have a bad ending, he thought. He wouldn't survive without her if Giambi came tumbling down. She had seduced him into becoming an agent of his own destruction, and he could only shake his head at how this had happened.

Chapter 22

Fearing a raid at any minute, Beth cursed the slow private elevator to Giambi's suite, knowing this could be the moment she'd been waiting for ever since her father was killed. She had no desire to see it ripped from her by politics.

The list of the men behind the major cheating crews would be a great start, but what she really wanted was enough information on Giambi's illegal activities, and his blackmail situation, to force information out of him directly. She wanted just one name. And she'd come to believe that Giambi had that name.

If she found the key to the identity of his blackmailer *and* the name of her father's killer, she would have her win-win. Her stomach knotted, the memories so intense she was hardly breathing and had to force herself to calm down.

The night had been like any other. She was playing cards and listening to music. It was hot and the air conditioner was broken and she had a fan on. It kept blowing the cards all over the place. She was waiting for her father to come home. To tell her if he won and they were rich, or if he'd lost and they were going to have to figure out how to pay the rent and get food. That's how it was. And somehow, she had adjusted to it. And then the knock on the door. The cop. The look on his face. Never, never, never would she forget that. The look on his face. Later she would know him. And he would be the person who would help her. But that night he was the bearer of the worst news she could ever have imagined.

Now, as the elevator finally let her into the small alcove of the great room, she breathed.

She walked out in the middle of the great room and yelled, "Is anyone here?"

Silence.

"Hello! Anyone home?"

She walked to the kitchen. "Anybody here?"

When she was sure the place was empty, she hurried down the hall past the grotto pool into Giambi's quarters and then his office.

Using the key JD had made for her, she went to the desk. The possibility that the laptop might not be there, that he'd moved it to keep it out of the hands of authorities who might raid the place, was her biggest fear.

"Be there," she said quietly. "Please be there."

She inserted the key into the lock and turned. Half a dozen clicks opening all the desk drawers greeted her effort.

At least that went well.

She pulled the middle drawer and a sleek HP Pavilion zd8000 emerged and rose on its typing platform. She quickly inserted her CD and a flash drive.

On the tiny radio she asked JD how things were going.

"Movie has a long way to go. Giambi is still with the same group. They're having a good time by the sound of the laughter."

"Keep me informed. I'm in."

"Okay."

While the program went to work she began searching through cabinets, opening desk drawers, looking for files, notebooks, records of any kind.

He had plenty of everything. Cash, guns, passports. But no cheaters list.

C'mon, Salvatore, where is your list of bad people. I know you have it. If it's not on the computer, it's got to be somewhere else.

She found the safe and that was where it might be, but she had no way to open it. She'd need a master safe-cracker for that.

It won't matter, she thought, just as long as I get enough leverage from the computer.

She read through a few notebooks but found nothing of specific interest.

Then, with the program still working hard to break down the code, she went into the bedroom to see what was there.

Giambi was very neat. And everything was of the highest quality—from the dozens of handmade suits, shirts and shoes in the closet and a room big enough to be its own apartment, to the silk sheets that covered his bed.

When JD informed her that the movie was nearing the end, she told him she needed just a little more time. The program had broken through the codes and she was downloading his entire file base.

Time was pressing on her now.

She got constant updates on what was going on in the ballroom and where Jason, Giambi and Vincenzio were.

The whole time she stared at the download process.

JD said, "You need to wrap up and get out of there."

"Okay. Another minute."

"I think Jason is coming up. Get out now."

"I can't. Not yet. Delay him."

"I'll try."

JD got her ten more minutes and that's all she needed. She dumped everything onto a flash drive and got out of there.

She went back to JD's apartment certain she had Giambi's secrets and she couldn't wait to see what they were.

When JD came up to his apartment she was already running files on her computer.

"Anything?"

"I don't know yet. But it looks good. The party over?"

"Pretty much. Some of the guests are having breakfast with Giambi. Some are in the pool. He sent me up to see how you're doing and to see if you want to join them."

"Tell him thanks but no thanks. I'm in bed and I'm staying there."

"Man's in love with you."

"You aren't jealous of a seventy-eight-year-old man are you?"

"Hell, yes, I am. He owns the world, and he owns me. At the moment."

"Yes, that all may be true. But you are very lucky."

"Why is that?"

"He doesn't own me. Go on back, before he decides to come up and check on me himself."

It took her another hour to understand Giambi's system and to track down what appeared to be a second and third set of "books." The man had payments going to a lot of numbered accounts and she assumed most of them, because of their regularity and the sums, were money-laundering activities.

The regular casino books were separate and showed all the standard stuff from the casino's supposed outlay to its take and overhead and the profit margins for every single facet of the operation, from the gaming tables, slots, shows, restaurants and bars. Normal balance sheets. Not much profit by the looks of things over the past few years.

She couldn't find a cheaters file and that irritated her a great deal.

But what she did find were two isolated streams of payments. One monthly payment to a bank in Puerto Isla. Another to a bank in France. That one was always for the same amount and had been going on for fifteen years. The one to Puerto Isla had been going on for decades and it was increased every single year. That was the one Oracle wanted.

Beth sent an e-mail to Delphi recounting her success. The payments to Puerto Isla and the communications from someone who signed with an *A* indicated they were zeroing in Arachne.

When JD checked back at seven she told him what she'd found.

"These are blackmail payments?"

"Yes, it looks that way."

"Now what? You've gotten what you came for, do you just leave?"

"I didn't get everything I came for. I'll be around until I do."

"And then?"

"First things first. The thing I need right now is a few hours sleep. We're going to see the rich Greek."

"Feodras. I hope he comes through. Giambi said there was a possibility that the Greek would get me into the

BMW team a friend of his owns. I could be driving in the Montreal Grand Prix in June."

Beth ran through the notes in her memory. "The block party on Crescent Street is like no other."

"You've been to party city?"

"No."

"Oh, you need to go. No fans like Montreal fans. Giambi loves it. The race runs around a casino no less."

"What is Giambi doing?"

"Right now, arguing whether Fernando Alonso is replacing Michael Schumacher as king of Formula One. I had to get away from that."

"You want to be the one they're arguing about, not Alonso."

"That's right."

"Well, I'm going to bed."

"Sounds like a great idea."

She saw the look he was giving her. "Alone. I'm tired. Cranky. Distressed. Sore. Irritable. You want some of that?"

He chuckled. "Good night, then."

He leaned over and she gave him a quick, but decisive kiss in retreat. "See you in the morning."

"The morning is gone."

"See you in the early afternoon. We have to be on the roof and in the chopper by ten to one."

She watched him go. He listened. He was very good. He must have had a good mother or grandmother.

She was exhausted and needed sleep. And she wasn't finished yet. Giambi's lists of cheating crews were somewhere and she had to find them, but not knowing how they would be listed, she had no idea what to look for. He had files on everything. The man obviously spent a lot of those sleepless nights with his laptop.

Finally, too exhausted to continue, she crawled into bed and didn't even remember, several hours later, having fallen asleep.

She glanced at the clock. It was eleven forty-five. *Oh, god, I should get up.*

She closed her eyes—*just a few more minutes*—and bad things immediately came to her. Her bodyguard getting shot. If that wasn't bad enough, she began thinking about the night the police told her that her father was dead. Only to find out he was found in the garbage.

The day that changed her forever.

She forced herself back to the present. Allison had to be right about Giambi. He, of all people, would know all the crews. She was not leaving until she got that information.

Giambi woke. For a time, after a few hours sleep, Giambi ignored his bladder and his reality and just lay there for a long moment thinking about a young woman in a black tango suit. A vision.

He didn't, as he usually did, congratulate himself that he was alive another day, or that his party had been a success. He was imagining a black top and long, slit pantaloons and the fluid, tight, beautiful body it clothed. He was remembering the deep-throated laugh, the slope of her head, the alabaster white of her neck, the extraordinary eyes, the swell of her young breasts.

He decided that it was okay that JD was keeping the lady happy. She wasn't going to let a seventy-eight-year-old man do it. Even if he could. But it would help keep her close and if that's the best he could do, so be it. You can't have everything.

But he couldn't hold reality off forever. Not even for ten minutes. And with it came the anger.

It got his blood hot in a hurry. They can't get me, he thought. They can steal this place, but they won't stop me. I'll have casinos up and running in Eastern Europe within months. And I'll have a racing team in less time than that. They can't stop me, damn them to hell.

His "friends" in the police department would give him warning if and when a raid was imminent. Time to move his things. That was part of the deal. He had enough on people in the power structure to ensure a certain discretion. They could get him out, but they couldn't make a public fool out of him.

Age is a damn number, he reminded himself when he finally got up and staggered into the bathroom.

And, of course, as he stood naked in front of his bathroom mirror, he knew age was also a deterioration. An insult to body and mind.

Giambi flexed his muscles. Not too bad. But not great, either. You could work out all you wanted, take DHEA and testosterone and a million vitamins, but they could only hold time back for so long.

He wondered if Jack LaLanne was still alive. He was the beginning of it all as far as staying in shape and staying alive was concerned. What was the guy now, ninety-four, ninety-five?

Morning was rough on old men. It was nice to have another day, he would never turn that down, but he'd give a lot to get one day of being a young man again. Same mind, better body. The day was coming when you would be able to do that. Maybe fifty years. Maybe less. He would miss it.

Jason had his coffee, juice, protein bar and vitamins on the bathroom counter when he came out of the shower. Being old and rich was doable. He didn't see how the poor could stand it. If you end up poor you're really screwed. 'Course, most of the poor didn't live all that long to start with.

I'm gonna be poor one of these days if I don't get that blackmailing, murdering bitch, he thought.

Now that was who could really get him going. Goddamn her to hell. For so long he'd tried to track down that bitch so he could personally kill her.

He stared at his bloodshot eyes and wondered how she could have survived this long.

Had to be the damn CIA protecting her. No other explanation. She must have them by the short hairs. She's got something so nasty they won't let anybody touch her.

Probably knows who set up Oswald on Kennedy or something like that.

I'm not gonna die before she does, he thought with a sense of deep frustration.

Then he tried to calm down. Morning is when you're gonna have your heart attack and die, the little carping doctor had told him about a hundred times. You get worked up, get that blood surging through those tight, hard veins, see you later, alligator.

In his experience doctors with great bedside manners were usually incompetent. They covered up their incompetence with pleasantries. All good doctors—actually, all people really good at what they do—were a bit prickly. You had to be, all the fools and bloodsuckers you had to deal with.

And right away, just the term *bloodsuckers* got Giambi's thoughts back to all the years he'd been paying, and raging.

He was supposed to take out his blood pressure monitor when he got enraged just to see what he was doing to himself.

To hell with that, he thought.

Why is it other men grow calmer and less stressed with age and I just get angrier?

He shaved, put on the face lotions, the Retin-A cream, the hair tonic and got himself together. Today he was taking his future wife—what the hell, he could think of her that way for the fun of it—to meet the Greek. Had to watch that guy as well, cockhound that he was.

The man joked that when he started on Viagra, his wife immediately divorced him. Didn't mind spending his money, but sure as hell wasn't gonna be fucking him every day and night. That always brought down the house. He was a funny guy, the Greek. And richer than God.

Giambi had to get out to the yacht by one. He finished dressing, then went up to the heliport. JD and Anne were to meet him there at fifteen to the hour.

The Greek had a great appreciation for fine, intelligent women. Giambi figured she'd be a real asset in the negotiations.

Chapter 23

A bad dream shocked Beth awake. She lay there, heart pounding. It took a moment for her to realize what had awakened her wasn't just the dream, somebody was knocking on her door.

JD stuck his head in. "Wake up, sleepyhead."

She'd been dreaming she was running through downtown Vegas, the lights and music in a crazy kaleidoscope splashing all over the street, the "Fremont Street Experience" gone crazy, exploding all around and she was trying to catch up with the man she thought was her father. It turned out to be Curtis and he was bleeding from his wounds.

"Bad dream?"

"Closer to a nightmare."

JD came in with a tray. "A little caffeine and a croissant might help."

"Lifeblood. Thank you. Put them on the table. You're too good to be true. What time is it?"

"It's flying time. You only have forty-five minutes. If you need any help taking a shower—"

She checked his wicked grin with a, "No way, Jose. Get out of here."

He chuckled and retreated.

She crawled out of bed, body parts still reflecting the effects of the car rollover, and stumbled to the bathroom and then into the shower. The water removed the cobwebs from her brain, awakened her blood and brought her back to life.

This is half over, she thought. I've got leverage on Giambi now. He's going to have to cooperate with me.

She felt good about everything. Getting into his files with JD's help had been much easier than she'd anticipated.

Once Giambi realized his entire secret world had been opened up and delivered into the hands of Delphi, he would have little choice but to accept whatever terms were presented to him. That would give her the upper hand.

She dressed in shorts and a halter top for the trip out to the Greek's yacht. He was, in the world of the rich, very rich. She'd played poker with several Greeks and they were a lot of fun. The Greeks she'd met carried their deep and long history well.

She stretched to see how her body was working. Her legs were feeling much better. The right foot was solid in spite of the dancing.

She was almost out the door when a call came through from Delphi. Beth hesitated, considered letting it go to message, but then relented.

The digitally transformed voice that hid Delphi's identity said, "Beth, we have discovered a problem with the information you've forwarded. It appears, in the process of hacking into the computers, you've been compromised."

"What?" Beth felt an icy stab in her gut. Everything had been going so well.

"Spyware embedded in the codes is active. Whoever monitors it is aware that you've hacked into Giambi's files. We're sending your computer a special program that you need to monitor. It will assess the damage and origin of the compromise. Everything sent to you will have a special encryption. I will text the codes to you so that you can run the programs. Whoever was in Giambi's system left a back door open for their regular return. It is almost certain they are aware of your presence."

"I'll do it now."

Beth swore under her breath. If somebody knew she'd hacked into Giambi's system it would turn the situation critical for Giambi. His files, if known by the wrong people to have been compromised—people who didn't want his connections to money laundering and blackmail payoffs leaked to the authorities or anyone else—would put him in a very precarious situation.

Who was it? Probably the one blackmailing him. If that was the case, then Arachne knew he'd been compromised.

That was bad for everyone, including Giambi.

Then again, it could be mob people keeping an eye on what he was up to. But then they'd know about his blackmail payments. Maybe they were behind them. Maybe they were somehow connected to this Arachne.

Maybe it was Prince Albert's people.

Whoever it was, she had to track it down.

She found JD waiting for her in his living room.

"I have a big problem. I can't go."

"What happened?"

She went back into her room, JD trailing. As she entered the code to access the program, she quickly told him about the situation. "This is critical and can't wait."

"He's going to be pissed."

"Can't be helped."

"When he says one, he means one. Man is never late."

"He can go. I'm not going. Actually, if you stay as well, we can talk about an exit strategy."

"Now?"

"JD, this is going to reach critical real quick."

"Anne, you don't know him. He doesn't take no for an answer. He's already promised the Greek he's bringing us along. He's gonna do the whole Monaco tour thing, then wine and dine the guy. Later we'll all go back to the yacht for a party."

"Sorry. Tell him I'm really sick. Throwing up. That you're going to babysit me. Get me better for later. I can't be riding around in a chopper. Go tell him. Then come back down. I don't want anyone coming in here."

JD's cell went off. "That's him."

"Hurry up. I don't want him running down here all worked up. I'll go up just about the time he's supposed to take off."

"He's not going to like this at all. When it comes to dealing with the rich and powerful, he's careful. Like he says, you step on a big man's toes, you're liable to find them in your butt. I think that also includes Giambi. Are you sure—"

"I'm sure, JD. Get up there. Don't tell him on the cell. He's liable to come down to argue."

"If he decides to do that?"

"Give me a heads-up. I'll jump in bed."

* * *

When Giambi saw JD walk out on the roof without Anne, he snapped his phone shut and cursed under his breath. "Where the hell is she?"

He hated to be late. Especially now. He glanced at his watch. Behind him his pilot had the bird warmed up, the warm air blowing Giambi's carefully coiffed hair.

"What the hell, JD, it's damn near one. Where is she? Why do all women have to be late? You said she was up."

"She's up, but she's down again."

"What does that mean?"

"She can't go."

Giambi swore angrily. Then he said, "Look, dammit, I told Feodras we'd be there at one. It's two minutes to one right now."

"She's sick."

"How sick?"

"Throwing-up sick. She's got some kind of allergy to something and I have to get her some prescription medicine. Look, go on out and take care of this guy. I'll get her better. We'll do the tour a little later. If you want her to meet him today, let me get her back on her feet."

"I'll call my doctor—"

"I already suggested that and she said it wasn't necessary. She says this happens a lot and that once she takes her pills, which she left back at her villa, she'll be fine. She wants me to stick around because sometimes she gets it bad and might need some help."

Giambi sighed, heavily conflicted. He was more than a little fond of her and he didn't want to see her sick or leave her behind, either. But right now the Greek was waiting.

On the other hand, shit, JD could deal with it. "Okay,

damn. Go take care of her. Get her well. I'll go meet the Greek. He can meet her later."

JD nodded and left.

Giambi watched him disappear through the roof door, then turned to board the chopper.

He stopped. He thought for a moment. What if she really has a serious problem? Last night she was down. That damn accident. She could have internal injuries she doesn't even know about. The woman needs to go to a hospital and get some X rays or something.

Giambi realized how much he cared for this woman. Those dances had stayed with him all night. She was great fun and made him feel like a young man again. JD wouldn't know what to do. She needed to be looked at.

He considered calling the Greek, but decided against it. He went over and told his pilot to go pick up the Greek and bring him right back. "Tell him I have a problem with my lady. She's ill and may have to go to the hospital. I'll meet him when he gets here. Just get out there and bring him back."

Giambi was amazed at how much impact Anne Hurley had on him. I'm worse than a damn teenager, he thought.

As he was thinking that he watched his chopper head out toward the fifty-million-dollar yacht that resembled a floating hotel.

Then he scrolled to his doctor's number and hit the speed dial.

The truth was, he liked having a beautiful, sophisticated young woman around him. Liked it a lot. There was something about her that he connected to. She had a toughness underneath all that class and refinement that told him she was a real player.

He didn't know what kind of relationship he'd ultimately end up with. That hardly mattered at this stage of his life. He could deal with a close friendship if that's all it became. What mattered was that he wanted a relationship of some kind.

Giambi was staring at the chopper as it crossed open water, heading out past the flocks of sailboats that swarmed the shoreline on this perfect day, when he suddenly felt a wave of unusual happiness. He felt a lot like some kid in puppy love. Things he didn't pay that much attention to, the deep blue of the sky, the greenish blue of the water, the gulls and sailboats, he was aware of these things.

For a moment, thinking about Anne Hurley, he forgot about his troubles. About the people he wanted dead. People who had done things to him that had yet to be avenged. The goddamn prince and his purification shit. They would be taken care of. All the usual litany of negative thoughts slipped away from him on this pristine day as he waited for the doctor to answer his cell. Giambi had fallen in love for the first time in many years. The dancing had done it. She'd ignored whatever lingering pains she'd had from the accident and had flowed with him across that floor.

That was his mood, maybe the best one he'd been in in a very long time, when the chopper turned into a ball of fire, followed by a loud boom that was like a clap of thunder from summer lightning.

Giambi didn't react right away.

He couldn't react, or believe, what he was seeing. What the hell?

The bits and pieces of the chopper flew out in a vast umbrella. They seemed to hang for a few seconds before finally falling like the detritus of a spectacular piece of fireworks, the pieces dropping into the water.

Giambi was supposed to be on that chopper, was supposed to be part of that falling debris.

And in that moment thoughts came into his mind like small explosions of their own. Bad, dark thoughts wiping out the nice bright ones he'd had a moment ago: *Bullet holes in the car...the shoes...JD and Anne Hurley staying behind...her getting ill when she did last night...Vincenzio's suspicions...lies and more lies...*

"Son of a bitch," Giambi said softly, a stabbing realization cutting through him— he'd been set up to be blown up.

And just that quickly, joyful reflection became bitter realization. Love fermented into hate.

He was shaking as he called his security chief. "Get up to JD's apartment. Now! Take some men with you."

"What happened?"

"Somebody just blew my chopper to smithereens, that's what happened."

Giambi headed for the roof door.

I'm a damn fool, he thought. *She pulled me into something. She and JD are working for somebody.*

He pulled out his small, j-framed snub .38 with it's concealed hammer. All the glory and happiness of his day had been replaced by that bleak landscape of rage that was always lingering, waiting to emerge.

Somebody's going to die besides my pilot, he thought, *but first I want answers.*

His blood was racing, his breathing getting shallow as the idea sunk in that he could have been in a million pieces right now, fish food.

He opened the door and headed into his suite ready to hurt people, ready to do some serious damage.

Betrayal was the one single sin that Giambi could not

abide. It was the only reason he'd ever killed because of emotion and not just in the cold calculations of business.

That JD looked to be part of this betrayal stung him deeply.

I saved him, he does this? I treat him like a son, he tries to murder me? Blow me to pieces?

As for Anne Hurley, the concept of her betrayal brought with it deep pain as well as rage. No betrayal could ever equal that of a woman one loves.

Chapter 24

Beth had her laptop on the coffee table in JD's living room, elevated by three heavy books, when JD walked in.

She said, without looking up from the screen, "He okay with it?"

"Wasn't happy."

"But he bought it?"

"Yeah. He's going to give the Greek a quick tour, then bring him back here."

"I need time. They come back, you have to keep him out of here."

He leaned over her shoulder. "How long will this take?"

"Depends on what sort of nasty little Bot spider I might be up against. And what it's programmed to do when located. These things can be problems."

"Who did it?"

"Well, that's the million-dollar question. Giambi's mob

associates or his blackmailer. Someone's hitched a ride into a search engine, jumped on the information highway and snuck over Giambi's firewall into his system. It's feeding information back to the source. It now knows I was also doing a little spying and, worse, copying the entire contents of his computer."

"What's your program doing?"

"It's a seek mission. I'm trying to latch on to the intruder to ride it back down its trail."

"How's it work?"

"Don't ask me. I'm a card player with good math skills, but the people who created this program are software geniuses right at the top of the programming universe. There's nothing we can do but let it run."

"You haven't told me what the endgame is," JD said. "Maybe now's a good time."

"Depends on what I find. I know you've been patient, but you're going to have to hold on for a little bit more."

"Once you find it, and it's bad, then what?"

"It's what kind of 'bad' it turns out to be."

They were both staring at the computer screen on the living room coffee table when the door burst open and Vincenzio charged in, followed by two of his men.

JD jumped up. "You don't barge into my place—"

Vincinzio went right for JD. "You have some questions to answer, boy." He reached for JD and received a forearm to the jaw.

It happened so fast, Beth barely had time to catch the computer when the table was bumped.

JD and Vincenzio fought toe-to-toe; the other men attempted to help their boss but JD moved with great agility and speed as he traded punches with Vincenzio.

The fight ended when guns were drawn.

Vincenzio said, "You'll pay for that," as he wiped blood from his mouth and nose.

Moments later Giambi charged through the open door, gun in hand. He looked like a man in shock, his eyes narrow with rage.

He came at JD and it was all JD could do to ward off the blow from the pistol.

"Stop it!" Beth yelled. "What is going on here?"

"You go to hell," Giambi snapped back. "You're going to tell *me* what is going on, lady."

His face was mottled with rage. "I don't know which one of you betraying bastards I should shoot first."

"Either would be a pitifully stupid mistake on your part if you do it before you have any idea what is really going on," Beth said calmly. "I don't take you for a man who acts on emotion and not reason. Your entire world is at stake here, so if I were you, I'd get ahold of myself and find out what's going on before you lash out in all directions."

Giambi reacted to her demanding, aggressive rebuke by calming down. He said, "All right, then you better start talking and it better be good."

"Clear the room of your goons and I will."

Vincenzio started to object, but Giambi waved him off. "Take JD to my office and ask him some questions. I'll talk to this little lady."

"JD stays," Beth said.

"You're giving the orders? I don't think so."

"What happened?"

"What happened! I'll tell you what happened. I didn't get on the chopper. My pilot's dead, but I'm not."

"How did your pilot die?"

"Don't give me that innocent crap. I've had enough. You

aren't sick. You weren't sick last night. My pilot is feeding the sharks just like I was supposed to."

"Your chopper crashed?"

"Blew up into a million pieces. And now what's going to happen is I'm going to find out who you are. What you and JD are up to and who's behind it all. I don't care how I have to do it. The old ways work pretty well. A finger at a time."

"First, you're going to listen," Beth said. "And then we'll see about fingers and toes. Your entire world has been hacked by someone other than me. You're completely compromised. So I'd get your boys out of here, sit down and listen to what I have to tell you. Because everything you are, everything you have, is on the line."

Giambi turned to JD. "All I did for you. You got no right to betray me like this. What kind of man are you?"

Beth said, "JD's got nothing to do with this."

"He can speak for himself."

"You'd best listen to her," JD said. "I don't really know what's going on myself. But I had nothing to do with what happened to the chopper."

Giambi turned to Beth. "Who the hell are you?"

"Salvatore, I asked you to get your men out of here. Then we'll talk."

Vincenzio had her bag. He pulled out the cloner, port connectors, CD programs and displayed it on the desk. "This bitch has been getting into your office with this. And I bet she's been in your computer."

"That right?" Giambi demanded.

"He's right. I've been in your office and in your computer. And it's not good news for you, so get these men out of here, because I'm not the problem. Right now I'm the solution."

JD said, "Salvatore, put that gun away. Your life and

your future depend on what she has to say, just as mine does. Like you are so fond of saying, a smart man knows how to listen."

After giving her his best Godfather stare, Salvatore lowered his gun. He told his men to leave.

As he went out, Giambi's security chief glanced back at her malevolently before closing the door, as if letting her know he was right outside.

Beth remained in her chair and Giambi sat in one of the two matching leather chairs on the other side of the desk.

"Let's start by understanding something up front. I'm not after you," Beth said. "And I had nothing to do with blowing up that chopper. JD didn't, either."

"I'm listening."

"Salvatore, I know all about you. Your money laundering, blackmail payments, the location of your numbered accounts, your past and what your future is going to look like."

"You a federal agent?"

"No."

"Then who the hell—"

"I'm an agent with another organization and that's not really important. I'm after the identity of the woman who's been blackmailing you for decades."

His face paled. "What do you know about that?"

"Everything," Beth said. "She's of great interest to the people I work for. I'm here to confirm some things."

"Who do you work for? Don't I have a right to know?"

"Let's just say I work for an agency with interests that intersect with yours at the moment. As to my true identity, I keep that to myself. What you need to know is what you've already seen. You're in big trouble. You have a past. It has finally caught up with you. Your blackmailer, the one who signs off with an *A*, is my primary interest."

Giambi swore softly under his breath, his anger deflated, as if he was relieved that this information, so long known only to him, was finally out in the open. "Why would you be interested in who's blackmailing me?"

"When you were involved in the firebombing of the jail in Phoenix, you missed your target. Like I said, that target is of great interest to us. Names such as Weaver, Madame Web, Arachne. The Queen of Hearts. I'm sure you're familiar with them."

"You know all of this?"

"Yes."

"So what is it you want?"

"I want to connect the dots. And, in the process, protect you."

"You want to protect me. Why?"

"It's all I can offer you for your cooperation."

"And if I refuse?"

"You won't. Once you realize you've now become the target of what might be the most dangerous assassin on this planet, and, simultaneously, the target of some mob folks who might not like what you can reveal about them, you're going to need protection. More than you can provide for yourself. They can get to you, as you've seen. Even if you were allowed to stay in Monaco, which you won't be, you wouldn't be safe."

A knock at the door interrupted them.

"What?" Giambi yelled.

Vincenzio opened the door and stuck his head in. "*Officier de police judiciaire*. They want to see you about the chopper crash."

"Where are they?"

"In the security office."

"I'll be right down."

Giambi rose. "Damn OPJ. You two are under my house arrest. You won't be leaving here. When I'm done with the police, I'll be back. And I'm taking this with me."

He grabbed the computer and she grabbed his wrists. "No. There's a program running and I don't want it messed with. It's critical. Whoever has been watching your activities, whoever is trying to kill you, I might be able to find them with that program. They already know they aren't alone. The more we can find out, the better."

Their eyes locked at about a foot distance, both of them with their hands on the laptop.

She said, "You mess this up, we might lose one of the most important means we have to find *A*. Go deal with the police, let me do my thing, then come back here and we'll talk. Trust me when I say I'm way ahead of you."

Giambi released the computer. He straightened up and glared at her. Then he turned and walked out, slamming the door behind him.

JD said, "I hope you know what you're doing or we aren't getting out of this hotel in anything but a body bag."

"Giambi's in big trouble and he knows it."

"Before we were so rudely interrupted, you were about to tell me how this is going to end. Apparently that has changed."

"I'll get cooperation from Giambi. After that, I'll see to it that he goes into the U.S. witness protection program."

"You're deluding yourself if you think that man will ever go into a witness protection program. Not in a million years. You can't be serious."

"He might not have much of a choice."

"You don't know him like I do. He won't do it. I know he won't."

"We'll see."

"And when you do, I'm on my way down the drain."

"No. You don't go down the drain. You don't think all those people that were here the other night were really interested in Giambi? My guess is your exile is just about over. A year or two off for bad behavior and suddenly you're on everybody's mind. When's JD coming back? Who will get him? How will he do?"

"Won't there be some guilt by association because of my relationship to him?"

"No. I'll take care of it. Just like I promised."

Chapter 25

Beth was convinced Giambi had no choice but to cooperate. She made contact with Delphi to discuss the end game. Delphi told her that federal protection would be in place and that agents in France, involved with other situations, would be available to take Giambi back to the States. The federal agent who would be in charge was in Nice. Beth was given a contact number and an ID code.

Four hours after he left, Giambi returned to JD's apartment.

Beth and JD heard him beyond the door arguing heatedly with his security chief, the ever present Vincenzio.

"We need to get that man the hell out of here," Beth said under her breath.

Giambi came in alone. He was shaken and Beth thought he was now beginning to show his real age. Whatever was going on with the police, it wasn't good.

"What happened?"

"You mean other than somebody trying to kill me? The authorities in Monaco are not going to protect me, they want me the hell out of here. There's been some deal behind my back. A conspiracy to turn everything I've built here over to that lying, swindling rat-fink bastard sitting out there on his fifty-million-dollar yacht."

"The Greek."

"Damn right, the Greek. He's coming over here with a bunch of lawyers. They already have documents drawn up. He was, no doubt, expecting to see me blown to bits."

"Do you have some evidence that he knew what was coming? Or are you making an assumption?"

Giambi went over to JD's bar and poured himself a drink. "I don't know anything. You tell me what the hell is going on. You seem to be the key to it all."

"I'll tell you what you need to know. First, get Vincenzio out of here. He's probably standing right outside the door. Get him off your floor. I don't want any of your staff up here. That includes Jason. Everybody out. Now."

"Jason stays." Giambi opened the door and told Vincenzio to go back to the security office.

When Giambi shut the door and came back Beth told him to sit down. She asked JD to make sure everyone was off the floor and to give her some time alone with Giambi. "Have Jason lock off the elevator for now."

When JD was gone, she sat across from Giambi. "I didn't come here to destroy you. I came here to find out two things. One of them, the primary one, has to do with the person who's been blackmailing you. Unfortunately, the blackmailer, and/or some of the people involved with you in your money-laundering business, know you're in trouble. And a man in trouble might just start selling out his friends and associates. I don't know where the hits are coming from. But it's over for you, not only here, but everywhere. You need to understand that."

Giambi stared at her. After a few seconds, as if processing what she was telling him, he said, "Go on."

"We believe the person blackmailing you, the one that leaves her calling card…the *A*…is the someone we're after. And, this someone is after us. We're trying to connect the dots. Help me. Tell me everything you know about her. How this all happened."

With heavy reluctance he opened up his past. He told her about the Queen of Hearts, the assassin from Boston, and confirmed she was a former CIA agent known as Weaver. He said he tried to take her out when she was in jail in Phoenix and confirmed that the blackmail accounts in Puerto Isla were hers. Then he said, "Who are *you* working for?"

"I'm with an intelligence agency that few people know exists. I can tell you nothing about it. It's of no importance to you."

"Of no importance to me? You're destroying me. You've invaded my privacy, forced me into a no-win situation, sold me out to the highest bidder and it's of no importance? Let me ask you something. Since you mentioned how far back all of this goes, is Marian Gracelyn—"

"She's dead."

"Yes, I know. But she was Weaver's lawyer. And I know about the school for girls that she helped found. Athena Academy. Maybe I know more about a lot of things than you might think."

"I'm sure you do. Unfortunately, I'm not at liberty to corroborate your notions. Just know this, under the present circumstances, if you cooperate with me, I'll give you the one chance you might have to survive."

"Which is?"

"The obvious, considering the people who might want you dead. Federal protection."

"To hell with you," he exploded, jumping to his feet. "If you think a man like me would go into some witness protection program, you're nuts!"

"Salvatore, sit down. You can go where you'll be protected, or you can go to your funeral. That'll be your choice. But we need to lay the cards out on the table first."

"You mean my cards."

"I'm going to reciprocate as much as I can."

When he calmed down enough to sit, she repeated the simple and hard truth. He was now a threat to two proficient killing machines, the mob and the assassin known to him as the Queen of Hearts. His chances of surviving one of them, let alone both, were not good. And wouldn't improve.

"No matter how good you think your security is, or how good you think you can make it, I assure you it won't be enough. You know that as well as I do. Somebody had to shoot at your car. Somebody had to put the explosives in your chopper. Somebody knew you were going to fly. That's coming from inside. That's how close the people who want you dead are. They missed twice. Maybe they won't miss the next time. And the next time could be very soon. You're out of options. So let's talk more about the Queen of Hearts, Boston, the bombing of the jail in Phoenix."

He stared at her like a man who couldn't believe what was happening to him, but couldn't deny it, either. He shook his head. He finished his drink and she got him another.

Part of him knew it was over, it was just difficult for him to believe it, really accept it. She waited.

Finally, he started to talk and once he started, he unburdened himself of the whole mess. From the moment he ordered the killing of a mob boss in Boston, a job done by the Queen of Hearts, to his failed attempt to get rid of her once she became a threat to him. He talked about not only about how much money he'd paid the killer-turned-black-mailer over the years, but how much he'd paid other hit men to find her and finish the job. None had succeeded. All had died in the process. The CIA had trained her well.

"For all I know, you could be working for her. Or the CIA. Or any one of a dozen other intelligence agencies. You have my files, my secrets, so now you own me. You tell me what my fate is but I don't know if you're telling me the truth or not."

"Listen to me. Your future is federal protection. You can pick some nice town, go in with a new identity and live out your years playing golf or writing your memoir or whatever."

"You said there were two reasons why you're here destroying what's left of my life. What's the second one?"

"My father was murdered. He was part of a cheating crew. I was twelve when it happened. I think you can help me find his killer."

His eyes widened and she took that as a sign he did know something. "I take it you aren't the rich widow Anne Hurley and never were?"

"I'm neither rich nor a widow."

"CIA?"

"Stick to the discussion."

"How did you get JD? I send him to find out about you, instead you flip him and he betrays me. How did that happen? Are you that good?"

"I'm good at what I do. It helped that we were ambushed and nearly killed."

"Who is your father and why would I know who killed him?"

"He was part of a card-cheating crew out of Vegas. The kind of crews you keep out of Monaco. I know that one of the reasons you were allowed to put a casino here, something outsiders don't get to do, is because of that. You have connections and interests in Vegas. You probably know who I really am."

Giambi's whole demeanor made a subtle change, as if now she was touching on things he really didn't think she could know.

"My father was a man with serious addictions, but trying desperately to break free of them for my sake. And that's what got him killed. I knew in the week before it happened he was scared. He'd angered somebody he was working for and he was thinking maybe we should get out of Vegas. He worked for a cheating crew that's still around. You know the crews better than anyone. I want the name of the man who ran the most successful crew in Vegas at that time. You give me that and I'll give you protection out of Monaco to the States and into the witness protection program. The feds will want to know all about your mob ties. But the rest of it, where the Queen of Hearts is concerned, others will deal with that."

Giambi, highly agitated, got up and walked over to the window to ponder his situation.

"Talk to me," Beth said.

"There's not much, apparently, that you don't already know. There's no real quid pro quo here."

"I've told you all you need to know. I'm after your blackmailer. She's a threat to me and to the people I work for. We're going to hunt her down."

"And your father's killer?"

"I know you have information on him as well. That's why I'm here and not someone else."

His voice grew somber. "Two birds with one shot. Tell me about your father, what happened to him."

"Like I said, it happened when I was twelve. One minute my world was just fine as I knew it, and the next it was wiped out like a bomb hit it. Boom, gone. He was a gambler and worked for a cheating crew. He wanted out. That, apparently, wasn't acceptable. Too big a threat to the crew's anonymity."

Giambi turned around and walked back to her, eyes tight, shoulders drawn in. "Let's say I decide that you're right about my options. And it appears you may well be. But you don't know everything. If I give you the name you're looking for, assuming you tell me some more about your father and I can check and see what crew he was working for, then you have to do something for me before you hand me over to the feds."

"What?"

He sat down across from Beth. In a confessional voice, a man revealing a secret that pained him, he said, "I have a daughter, a daughter I didn't know I had until fifteen years ago. I did everything I could to keep her out of my world. I thought it was the right thing to do. That my world wasn't good for her. But things change. I changed, and I wanted to get to know her. I sent her a note several times suggesting we meet. She would have nothing to do with me. She's here in France and I want to see her before I go anywhere. Her mother was a dancer. In Paris. I met her many years ago. She's from Africa. She had a daughter that I didn't… Well, circumstances… I was in my fifties and, well, it doesn't matter."

"Your daughter lives in Paris?"

"No. Actually she lives in the countryside. About forty miles from here in a small French village. Her mother passed away some years ago. I want to see her one more time. And I want to be certain when I leave Europe that she's not going to want for anything. She was doing well up until recently. I want to help her financially. And I want to talk to her."

"Why did you keep her such a the big secret."

Giambi smiled sadly. "Circumstances, and enemies. It's better for her not to be connected to me. Safer."

He was silent for a time. Nowhere in any of Beth's investigation of him was a daughter mentioned.

She waited. In some ways she felt sorry for him. Not that, given the life he lived, he deserved sympathy, but she liked the guy. He was, after all, from her world. Casinos and casino operators were the same everywhere. Disguise them with glitter, entertainment and great restaurants, but underneath the disguises, it was all about extracting money from fools and protecting that money from skilled highwaymen. It's about robbing without being robbed. Nothing was "produced" in a casino but illusions. It was all about the flow of money. How much comes in and how much gets away. The rest was bait.

Giambi said, "I'm being forced to sell the casino, give it away actually, to the Greek. Within hours. Once I'm out of here I'm fair game. You are right. I'm a target and I need protection. But there are other things more important than that. You get me to her before you bring the feds in, I'll help you if I can with this other thing. But I have to know more about exactly who your father was. Starting with his name."

"All right," Beth said. "Make your deal with your Greek friend, and we'll visit your daughter. I'll make arrangements with the feds to come here and take you back to the states. My real name is Bethany James. My father was Lew 'Jesse' James."

Chapter 26

Giambi studied her intently for a moment, his eyes narrowed almost to a squint. "Your father, he's the one they called the gunslinger for his style of play?"

"Yes."

"Lew *Jesse* James."

"Yes. You knew of him?"

"I never met the man, but various pictures of him were in every casino's file, you can be sure of that. When he stayed sober, he was one of the best. He played against guys like Amarillo Slim Preston, Doyle Brunson, Stu Ungar, maybe the greatest of the great, along with Johnny Moss."

Beth said, "You know how Hollywood brats, the sons and daughters of movie stars, grow up around all the great stars of the day and just take that as normal. That's how I grew up in the poker world. Stuey and my dad played some poker together, drank and did some drugs together. I knew all of them."

"A poker brat. Yes, that is definitely a different kind of childhood."

"Binion died in ninety-eight. Stu died the next November and in some ways an era ended. He was forty-five. He had cocaine, meth and Percodan in his system. Died in a lousy adult motel on Las Vegas Boulevard. This was the same guy who won the World Series of Poker three times. In ninety-seven he won over a million in that tournament alone. My dad was killed five years earlier. Do you know anything about why he was killed and who was behind it?"

Giambi frowned, a look of surprise and shock on his face. "I can't believe that I'm looking at the daughter of Lew Jesse James. I heard about you. The rumor had it you were playing poker in your highchair."

"That is, in fact, true. You know something about what happened?"

"Yes, I do know something about his death. A man in his business had plenty of enemies. The crew he worked for not only hit casinos, they hit private games. I know the name of the man behind that crew. If Lew was killed because he was trying to get out, that would be the man you're looking for. He would give the order."

Beth tried to control the beat of her heart. Fifteen years she'd been waiting for this moment. "This man, is he still alive?"

"He's still alive the last I heard."

JD, having returned but gone into his room so as not to interrupt them, walked out at that moment.

Giambi glanced up at him. "She turned you easily enough." He shook his head. "I knew setting you up with him was a damn mistake. In the end, no matter how hard you work, what you accomplish, how much wealth you accumulate, it all goes to the young."

"Would you take it with you if you could?" JD asked.

"No. I got a kid can make use of it. She's fighting the French government over this policy of destroying small vineyards to keep the prices up. Kills the little growers and helps the big boys."

"The way of the world," JD said.

"Yeah, well with some serious money she can put up a fight."

"I'll take you to your daughter," Beth said. "But we're going to have to get out of here very soon."

"All I have to do is sign some papers."

Beth followed Giambi back to his office, where he said he had something he wanted her to see.

She was excited. This man had her in the palm of his hand and she would do everything in her power to protect him. He was the most important person in the world to her right now.

Giambi opened his safe and took out a large red leather case. He sat it on the desk.

"I have had, for almost as long as I've been in this business, what I call my relocation package."

Beth remembered a similar package. Only her father called it their getaway pack. He'd had pictures, cash, a few gold coins, birth certificates, other papers. He'd never used it. Never had the chance, as Giambi did now.

He showed her bearer bonds, jewelry, cash, and fake IDs. "My daughter gets the bonds, jewelry, cash. I'll keep the fake IDs."

He'd pulled out an envelope from his red leather case and was looking at some photos.

"This is my daughter. Kaya. Somebody told me that in one of the African dialects is means 'don't go back,' or 'don't die.'"

"It's a beautiful name," Beth said as she took the picture. The girl had those great African features, high cheekbones, broad, exquisite face. "She's stunning. How old is she now?"

"She would be thirty-four now. That was taken when she was twenty-four. I didn't even know she existed until her mother got sick and sent me a letter and these pictures. I didn't believe it at first. I sent some men to get a sample of her DNA."

"You sent some men?"

He shrugged. "I guess that wasn't the best way to do things. They got some hair samples. They didn't do anything to her, just got in the house in Paris and took some from her hairbrush."

"Broke in to her house."

"Well, yes. Anyway, they proved out. I tried to help her mother but it was too late for that. She died from cancer. I wrote a letter to Kaya with money in it to cover the expenses. I told her who I was and that I'd make sure she didn't have financial problems. I've been sending money every month for the past fifteen years. But she doesn't take it. She sends it to some foundation for kids with AIDS in Africa. Now she's in a fight to keep her small vineyard and she needs help herself. I just don't want her to continue to reject me."

"She can't reject what she never knew."

Giambi glanced over at her. That seemed to sting him.

"You're a stranger," Beth said. "Nothing more than the sperm donor."

He nodded. "You're right. She owes me nothing."

"Is Kaya married?"

"She was married for a while to this Frenchman who ran a restaurant in Paris. He died in a small plane crash two years before the mother died."

"You call her 'the mother.' That's kind of cold. She didn't have a name?"

"Iniko. It's Nigerian. She was a beautiful woman. I only knew her over a couple of weeks in Paris. She was a singer and dancer. One of those flings."

Giambi put the picture of his daughter in his case.

"You've never seen your daughter in person?"

"Once. From a distance. She owns land worked by a vintner. She sells their wines in a shop in town. One day I drove into town, stopped and had breakfast at this restaurant across the street from her shop. She came outside once to talk to a woman. Very tall girl. Beautiful."

"You didn't try and talk to her?"

"No."

"So, why now?"

"I may not get a chance again. I guess I just want to give her a chance to ask me whatever she might want to ask. Or not. I want to see who she is, for her to know I wanted to make a connection even if she doesn't want to know me. No reason she would, except to see her genes are good."

Beth thought he looked a little nervous just talking about it, like a man facing the guilt of having made a big—and at the time, self-serving—mistake.

He had a pile of pill bottles on the table. When he saw her looking at them he said, "My fountain of youth. Vitamins, testosterone, DHEA. You name it, I take it. My joie de vivre."

"Seems to be working."

"So far."

He packed his pills in the case along with jewelry, several stacks of hundred-dollar bills, personal papers. He cleaned out his office, shredding paperwork he didn't want to go with him. He had some notebooks in the safe that he put in his case.

She said, "As a precaution, it's best that nobody on your staff knows what you're doing, or where you're going. Especially anyone who might have had access to your office and computer."

"Nobody had access when I wasn't there. Until you came along."

"That's not true. JD knew what to do and if he'd had motive he would've had access. How about Vincenzio? If I got in here as easily as I did, he could have as well. And he knows the business of security even better than I do."

Giambi bit his lip as he considered that. Then he shrugged. He seemed ready to believe the worst about everyone at this point.

He began going through the drawers of his desk, taking out things that mattered to him. "I made the stupid assumption that it's a lot easier to keep secrets from the outside than from the inside, that I could control those around me by what I knew about them. I may have been wrong."

"You may have been outbid in that department."

He gave her a look, and a knowing nod. "I knew you were somebody special, but I didn't know what that meant. Now I do. It's funny, but you, the stranger with the agenda, the one who destroyed my world when you broke in to it, are the one I'm forced to trust."

"I'm sorry it has to work out like that. I had no way of knowing that my penetration of your computer files would be picked up by somebody else lurking on your system, watching your every move."

"If you had known you'd be detected, would that have stopped you?"

"No. But I would have approached it differently. In the end, I had to track down your blackmailer and if there was no way to avoid detection, then it had to be."

"You think that's where the attacks are coming from?"

"I don't know. Could be from any of your three biggest enemies. Or, as you suggested, from someone who is going to take over your little empire. You've lived a long life. Plenty of time to produce a plethora of benefactors to your demise."

He laughed. "You're right about that. Have a drink with me."

They walked out onto the balcony. Beth glanced around at any buildings that might have a view.

Giambi said, "What are you looking for? Snipers?"

"Certainly. People want you dead. If they're willing to go after you in your car or your chopper, they'll do it here. Maybe we should stand over there where nobody has a shot. You're in a good spot. The prince could probably get you from his place, but I don't think he'd use a sniper."

"My keeper."

"That's what *I* am now. I'm not leaving you alone for a minute. From this point on, they'll have to go through me to get to you."

Giambi made drinks at the small bar.

He sat down and they clinked glasses. "To better days," she said.

"I think my better days are back there in the dust. I'll drink to you finding your father's killer and getting on with your life."

She thanked him for that, then said, "Where exactly does your daughter live?"

"Between Lorgues and Draguignan. Really pretty country there."

"I'll tell you one thing," Beth said, "I'm going to take you to see her, no matter what."

They drank in silence for a few minutes, just looking at the view.

"I was in Vegas a lot in the sixties," Giambi said, breaking the quiet. "I knew Benny Binion when he regained control of the Horseshoe Casino. Had to have his kids run it because he was a convicted criminal. Tax evasion. Strange to think that the poker tournament he started is what it is today. Your father was involved in the Horseshoe's poker tournaments before you were born."

"He loved those days. He talked about them a lot."

"It was basic and real then. Ted ran things. Math genius. But he got into women and drugs and let it all slip away. Got himself barred from the casino forever. You go to the trial?"

"No. It was all over the news at the time, though. You couldn't avoid it."

"Yeah. When Ted Binion died, like Stu, they put it down as an overdose. In his case, Xanax and heroin. Of course that was before the police caught his partner trying to dig up Binion's buried treasure, something like six tons of silver Horseshoe casino chips."

"And rare coins."

"Stacks of money and over a hundred grand in rare coins."

She remembered it had kicked off one of the most famous murder trials in Vegas history. It involved Binion's girlfriend and her lover, the former partner. They were convicted. Then the conviction for murder was overturned and they got sent up on burglary charges. It went on for years.

She enjoyed listening to Salvatore talk about those early years and the great poker tournaments long before the rest of the country knew about Texas Hold 'Em. It had been a more innocent time for her dad as well.

"About the only guy from that time still playing on the world tour is Doyle Brunson."

"My dad called him the Babe Ruth of the game. He

made a table with him once and got beat by him. He said it was the best loss he ever had."

Giambi laughed. "If you're gonna get beat, get beat by the best."

"That was the year he won the tournament with the Brunson ten two."

Giambi studied her. "So, when you're not out here doing whatever you're doing, you still a rounder?"

"Absolutely. I'll be going the rounds 'til I can't get around. It's my passion. And I intend to see the ladies rise to the top."

"Maybe you."

"No. I stay out of the limelight. I'll leave that up to Annie Duke and Lynette Chan."

They were silent for a long moment. It occurred to her that he might not know anything and was just using that as a means to guarantee that he would get to see his daughter. She needed to probe a little deeper, find out if he was actually trying to bluff her.

"Look. I don't like being disappointed. I know the information I want is your hole card, but I'm good to my word. You can lie, but you have to look me in the eye when you do. I'm really good at being able to find the truth. I know you didn't come out of Vegas, and haven't been there much. Maybe you don't really know anything."

He looked directly at her. "Of course I do. That crew didn't just work Vegas. And I'd know even if that was their only stomping ground. I have some interests and friends there as well. I know who it is. He's actually behind several crews. I know all the crews and I know when something happens."

"Like when one of them gets murdered."

"Yes."

"Then you absolutely do know who killed him?"

"I know who ordered it."

She sat forward.

"Back then there were only a half-dozen crews that were any good. We had to know them all. They were so good they could kill you if you didn't get them banned. Sometimes, it went beyond that. Everyone thinks the Mint and Horseshoe that took things over in downtown Vegas were ripped off by the owners. It's more complicated than that. A crew got into the big games. Very smart. They took a ton of money out of there."

"I used to hear about the scores."

"Everybody heard about them. In those days, you hurt a casino badly enough, you might want to watch your back. You could end up buried in the desert."

"Or dumped in the garbage."

"That, too."

Chapter 27

Beth was fascinated by how Giambi lit a cigar, the preparation, snipping the end, rolling the cigar in the fire of his lighter. All so ceremonious.

But in her mind, all the misery of that day so many years ago came flooding back. The sheer horror of it. How do you live through something like that, she thought. But she had. She'd found a way to live through it. She fought to keep back tears.

Giambi nodded at some thought going on in his mind. Then, after a moment of drawing on his cigar he let the smoke go deep, then stream out. "You won't have to look beyond him. It's common knowledge that he ordered your father killed. He may have done the killing personally. They had a major falling out and when that happened, your father became a big liability. He knew way too much about how the operation worked and who was part of it.

"There were a number of very good crews working. MIT types," Giambi said. His voice had an absent, almost hollow quality. He was thinking beyond his words. "Switchers so bold it was amazing. Before electronics played a big role, some of these crews were seriously talented magicians. They could cheat you while you were staring at every move they made. Even the eye-in-the-sky had a hard time because of how clever they could be. In the end, knowing who they were and going after them outside of the casino became part of the action that is rarely ever seen or reported. But, believe me, when a casino, or a private party, took a big enough hit, all bets were off and the game got nasty.

"For the crews, the biggest problem, besides watching over their shoulders, was the same as it was for all illegal organizations. Someone on the inside getting flipped by the feds or deciding to hang it up and go straight. Your father's mistake was letting anyone know that's what he had in mind, and not having a place to run and hide for a few years until the people he worked for decided he wasn't going to rat them out."

She told him about the "getaway" backpack and his plans to go back to his hometown in the North Carolina area. In the telling, she felt a little sick to her stomach. Sixteen years seemed to have erased nothing.

Giambi said, "He should have told no one and just went on and did it. He went down just at the time when the poker craze was getting going. Maybe, like you say, your father had decided, as a father, he needed to get his act together. But he hung around because he loved the game and the game was going ballistic. Got himself caught between his two great loves. You and the game. That was his tragedy. I understand it well."

Beth stared blindly off toward the sea, and into the past. Giambi was exactly right. Her father had wanted to get out, but couldn't. She remembered her father's gaunt face, the stubble, the graying in his hair, the emerging bald spot, how thin he was at that time. The way, when sober, when not on anything, he would stare at her, grimacing, lips tight, and say things like, "This is not the way a young girl should grow up." And she'd say she was fine. Happy. Don't worry about it. But he did. He worried. She knew it more each year. His struggle was great. He wanted to do the right thing. He desperately wanted to change course. And he would have. She had no doubt about that.

"He actually thought they'd let him play it straight," she said. "He wanted to get into legitimate tournament play. Have a more normal life. Get himself together."

"Hardly ever happens for a guy in his situation," Giambi said. "All the big money, TV money. A scandal, a hint of cheaters involved, it's too great a risk for the powers that be. He could never have gotten into the big game with his rap."

"Sometimes I feel guilty. If it weren't for me—"

"No. Don't do that," Giambi said adamantly. "You were the innocent victim of circumstance. Your father made his own bed. Just like I made mine. You had no more to do with his mistakes than my daughter has with mine. It's a waste thinking like that. Guilt requires action and intention. You did nothing. He made the mistakes that he, and you, paid a high price for. That's just how it is. Let the guilty carry their own burden. Not the innocent. *You* didn't even cause your father to decide to go straight. His desire to be a better person was the right thing for him to do regardless. But the bottom line is, in spite of his mistakes, somebody murdered him. His death was a decision, not an accident. There is where the real guilt lies."

Giambi was a wise man with a lot of experience in the field of crime and punishment, guilt and revenge. And he had perspective. She said, "I know. You're right. And that's what I want from you. A name."

Giambi pulled his cigar from his mouth, looked at her and said, "Justice and revenge are two different animals. As the Chinese proverb says, 'he who seeks revenge digs two graves.' There's a lot of truth to that."

He was very serious and it made her think hard about the situation. Focus on what she wanted. The weight of Giambi's influence on her at the moment was considerable. She said, "You think it really matters *who* brings him down?"

"I think it matters whether you decide to kill him yourself, or bring him down using the law."

"That sounds strange coming from you."

"I'm sure. But look at where I'm headed. And look at the burden I've carried all these years. You don't need that. Your father wouldn't want that. If you kill this guy in self-defense, that's one thing. But if you set out to assassinate him, that's different. I don't think that's who you are."

After a moment's reflection, she said, "I agree."

Being consumed by revenge, as she had been for so long, wasn't something she'd wanted. Nor did she want to be consumed with guilt over having assassinated someone in cold blood in an act of revenge. She told Giambi how she felt, and what it had done to her over the years.

"I understand. I've spent my life doing it the wrong way. Because of that, I lost my freedom a long time ago. Guys like me are always looking over their shoulder."

In spite of who he was, what he'd done in his life, Beth couldn't help but feel some compassion for the man. No one had stopped him from his course early enough in his life. And it made her understand what her father had wanted to do. He'd wanted to stop her before it was too late. He'd seen signs of trouble, and there had been plenty of them.

"My father didn't want to save himself," she said. "He wanted to save me. And as terrible as it was, he did just that."

Giambi nodded. "You're absolutely right. I can see that you are somebody he would be very proud of."

A few minutes later, Giambi got a phone call.

When he hung up he said, "The Greek, that bastard with the Midas touch, is going to steal my casino, my race shop and probably my driver." Then he called JD, and told him to meet the Greek in the Cypress Bar.

Giambi turned to Beth. "You believe this guy? He's ready to jump ship before it's taken on any water."

"He's got to find a ride somewhere."

Beth followed Giambi across the floor of his great room. He glanced toward a room where the lawyers were working.

The Greek's lawyers, four of them, had arrived ahead of their boss to begin working on the papers. The Greek was with Prince Albert at the moment, explaining the situation and getting his okay.

"I should burn this place to the ground."

"Wouldn't be worth much then."

The lawyers filed into the conference room.

"But this is my baby. I built this. It's what I am. If it weren't that my daughter needs the money I wouldn't sell to him. I'd give it to the city."

Beth said, "Tell me more about your daughter's financial problems."

"The damn French government is going to make her dig up her vines."

"Why?"

"French wine isn't in demand. American and Australian

wines are popular. The EU thinks if there's less French wine, the lack of supply will support the price for the big growers. But it will kill the small vintners."

"Then you are sacrificing for a good cause."

The Greek arrived with his security retinue, entering like a professional boxer, tall men on either side, another behind, all of them moving smartly to his pace. JD was at the back of the pack.

Beth had the thought that most of the really rich men in the world were either short or nerds.

The Greek was an inch or two shorter than she was, but aggressively handsome in a roguish way, with wavy white hair and a sun-leathered face. He had bright eyes that glistened with anticipation of the bounty that was about to fall into his grasp. He kissed Beth's hand with old-world elegance, bowing slightly.

"It is my pleasure to meet the famous Anne Hurley."

"I wasn't aware of my fame."

"Such charm and beauty does not long go unrecognized."

"You're too kind."

"You bring the best out in any man, I'm sure."

Giambi looked like a man on his way to his execution as she watched him follow the Greek into the conference room.

Then his lawyers, four of them, came in and sat at the table with the Greek's lawyers.

"How long will this take?" she asked JD. "You have any idea?"

"I think it's a deal that's already been approved by the prince. And what he wants, he gets. It's not a negotiation at this point. Apparently, the prince is actually protecting Giambi. Other authorities here would like to make an example out of him. The prince wants him the hell out of here."

Beth shook her head. She remembered Allison's discussion of Giambi's problems.

"The Greek told me that the prince is having him over for dinner tonight. He suggested you and I go along. I said I didn't know if that was possible."

Getting rid of Giambi as quickly as possible, especially after the shooting up of his car and the explosion of his chopper, suddenly took on a different light. Beth had been looking at only two possibilities. Now there were more.

Once the deal was complete, Beth wanted to get Giambi out of there as quickly as possible. Meeting Prince Albert might be interesting, but it wasn't going to happen.

"We need to talk," she said.

They went back to JD's apartment.

"What?"

"The Greek."

"What about him?"

"Did he make you any promises?"

"He mentioned the idea of my getting a ride. Soon. It looks like I might be part of the deal."

"Like how soon?"

"Toronto."

Beth studied JD for a moment. "How many conversations have you had with him?"

"Two. Well, one with him and one with one of his associates. They wanted to know what my plans were."

"Both after the explosion?"

"Yes. Why?"

"Timelines. I just like to know who knew what, when. I need you to get us a vehicle. We're getting the hell out of here."

"You think—"

"I don't know what to think. Anything is possible at the

moment. Maybe the Greek is carrying out orders. Maybe the CIA is involved. Maybe the Pope for all I know right now. I just want to get moving and fast. Get a van. He's got things he wants to give his daughter—"

"He's got a daughter?"

"I'll explain later. And tell nobody anything. If you want to make a deal with the Greek, do it after we take Giambi to see his daughter and then hand him over to the feds. That is, if you want to come with us."

"What does that mean?"

"Well, if necessary, I can take it from here. You don't have to get in any deeper. You can stay here, go meet the prince—"

"Now you're pissing me off. I'm going to get a van."

"Park it where we can get to it without being seen. We're leaving in the middle of the night. Are there blind spots in the executive parking lot?"

"No. I'll leave in my car, come back in the van and be wearing a hat and different jacket. Nobody will think I'm anything but a customer. I know how to get into the private garage without being picked up by the cameras. Nobody needs to know I'm back. Where's the daughter live?"

"He said it's between Lorgues and Draguignan. You know where that is?"

JD nodded. "I've been through there."

An hour later Giambi returned to his suite alone. She met him in the great room. He looked thoroughly miserable.

"The deal done?"

"Yes."

"He take you to the cleaners?"

"When you're the only game in town you get things the way you want them." He looked around. "Well, I'm just a guest here now."

"They gone?"

"Yes. And the sooner I get out of here, the better. When are we leaving?"

"A few hours. JD will put a van out in the back parking lot and move it up to your garage entrance when we're ready to leave. Pack one suitcase and one travel bag. Destroy what you want to destroy, bring your laptop and any material you have to have. Clothes you can replace."

"I can't replace my shoes."

"I understand, but you only get a couple pair. You can have everything else shipped to an address the feds will give you and they'll make sure you get it later, when you're settled."

Giambi said, "You've done this sort of thing before? Come in and clean house?"

"Actually, no. You're my first."

Beth went into her room and sent a message to Delphi about her plans. She hoped to have the operation completely wrapped up in the next twenty-four hours and to be on her way home.

Delphi told her she was very pleased with her work. The feds had been contacted and would have a team waiting in Nice. When she was ready to hand Giambi over she simply needed to call the agent in charge.

JD called her a few minutes later and said he had the van and was on his way to the casino.

Beth found Giambi in the master bedroom to let him know they were getting ready to leave. He was laying out suits.

"You're taking all those with you?"

"No. I wish I could. I'm giving these to Jason. He's always loved my clothes. Man like that could never afford handcrafted Italian suits, shirts and shoes. But he always appreciated them. I have different tastes in clothes than I did back in my Vegas days."

"I still keep thinking you probably met my father at one time or another back in those days."

He brought another suit out of the walk-in closet. "Maybe."

"Did you play poker yourself?"

"Not much. I was more of a house guy. I preferred taking a cut of the action. You never lose money. I'm a big believer in the steady incoming stream rather than the big hit."

He laid the suit out with loving care. It was, he said, one of his favorites. All the cutting and stitching was, of course, done by hand. This was an Ermenegildo Zegna. Linings and accessories made of either cotton, horsehair or silk. "Feel how soft."

She touched the cloth and it was indeed very soft. Everything he had was handcrafted. Even the soles and linings of his shoes were personalized. He had, of course, half a dozen suits from the great couturier, Valentino. They were made by an atelier in Naples.

He showed her a Luciano Barbera, pointing out the gambero stitching, hand-sewn seams that covered the edges of the sleeves and cuffs. The dozen suits he laid out for Jason each had its own fabric-covered hanger and garment cover with Giambi's initials.

He then laid out some Truzzi shirts and four pairs of Moreschi handmade shoes and a pair of loafers. "These might be the finest shoes in the world," Giambi said. He pulled out the shoe kit with it's nutrient-rich shoe creams and horsehair brushes and protective glazes.

"I think Jason is going to be a happy man," Beth said.

"He has been the best houseman I've ever had. He is the ultimate butler. It's the very least I can do for him."

He called Jason in and told him to pack up the suits, shirts and shoes and take them somewhere out of the hotel. He handed the man a packet of money as well. Jason seemed more stunned than happy to be getting presents of suits and money. Giambi went off with him for a few minutes.

When he came back he said Jason was packing and would be gone in an hour.

"How about having a last drink to the Sapphire Star with me?"

"Make mine water. I've had enough alcohol in the past couple of days."

Chapter 28

Beth and Giambi again went out on his balcony.

"I guess this is goodbye to my baby, my home."

"You know, I'm sorry it ends this way for you."

"Everything ends somehow. I've had a good run. A man gets to where I am, and stays there for as long as I have, can't really get away with complaining. You want it to go on forever, but age teaches you to let go. It does that by weakening you, step by step. You fight it, but you know you're fighting a losing battle."

He got her a bottle of Perrier, then lit a cigar and filled his glass with whiskey as he turned and leveled an open look at her. Then he stared out at the night, finally turning back to Beth. "You're one of the finest young women I've ever met. Time and circumstance, as has been said, spare no man. You can't understand the regrets of an old man like me. Unlike Sinatra, I've had many. I wish I'd met you under different circumstances."

"I'm sure you would have swept me off my feet."

"That's nice of you to say."

"I'm serious. You're very charming now. I tremble to think of what you must have been like as a young man."

He smiled, and grimaced at the same time. "Yes, I guess I was a handful. But the thing is, most of the women I met were in my world. Casinos here and in Vegas. I met some good women, but you, you're a cut or two above, believe me. Or maybe it's just how much things have changed in the world. When I was young they didn't have many young women like you running around kicking butt and taking names."

"You better stop now or I'm going to forget how old you are and where you're headed."

He smiled, yet he looked deeply sad. Then, with a hint of anger, he said, "JD's made a deal with the Greek. Maybe he's been making deals all along."

"You say that like you meant to say he's making a deal with the devil. But I don't think so."

"Don't let him fool you. He comes off as this simple Tennessee mountain boy, but he's a very shrewd operator. He fools people. Maybe he's got you fooled a little. Maybe he's got us all fooled."

Maybe he does, Beth thought. She faced the balmy breeze coming off the Mediterranean, the waters ruffled by the wind. It was a magnificent evening. "I make mistakes. I don't think so this time."

But it did cause her to rethink her relationship with JD. Their affair may have compromised and clouded her judgment. Still, she defended him. "No, I don't think you have to worry about JD. I'm sure he's looking out for his own interests once he realized what kind of trouble you were in. He was going to get on that chopper and I stopped him. And somebody tried to kill him at the shop. If he's playing a game, he's on the wrong side."

"You're probably right," Giambi said. "I hope you are." After a long pause, he said, "Your father must have been quite a guy to have a daughter like you. This world just isn't fair. It really isn't."

"All he wanted was to have a more normal life. One without the addictions. He wanted to be a better father. Hard drinking and heavy gambling are lethal to family. He used to say that cocktail waitresses were like leukocyte, white blood cells. They float around the casino with trays full of infection fighters. Alcohol wears down resistance, encourages excess and stupidity. It keeps the blood of the casino flowing, the cash coming in. He knew it and he couldn't escape it. When he finally had the courage to walk away, they didn't let him."

Giambi wanted to know little details about her life with her father and she told him because she knew he had missed that in his life with his daughter. She told him about when they were living with a lady friend of her father's, a dancer, after getting kicked out of a hotel for nonpayment of rent. It was one of the worst times for her because she'd heard her father talking to the lady friend about what to do with Beth because he had no money and couldn't take care of her.

She told him how, when her father knew he'd gone past the point of no return, and was on the verge of running away, he used his last dollars to rent the movie *Paper Moon*, with Ryan O'Neal and Tatum O'Neal.

"It was, for me, like watching a movie about my father and me. The only difference was what he did for a living. He said that's how it would be with us. He'd get his act together and change some things. That we'd stay together no matter what. 'I won't give you away. I won't leave you.

I'm your father and I'm going to be your father.' He tried. But they wouldn't let him. And in the end, they took him away from me."

"What happened after that?"

"I was discovered by the woman who ran an academy for girls. She saved me."

"My daughter's not much older than you," Giambi said wistfully. "Strong like you are. I wish I could say I had something to do with that. It's one of my big regrets."

"Just help her now. That won't change the past, but all we have is now and the future."

"If she'll let me help her. You two are both independent types. Maybe you can talk to her."

"I'll do what I can."

They fell silent, a red glow on the horizon and the sailboats swarming, nightlife starting. He said he loved this view, that he'd miss it terribly.

She felt sorry for Salvatore Giambi. He might be a bad man on some levels, but he wasn't evil. He was what he grew up to be in the tough streets of Boston. And she was pretty sure the men he'd killed in his life were men who'd earned it one way or another. She wasn't going to judge the man who was going to give up her father's killer.

She knew she more than liked Salvatore Giambi. She felt she understood him on some deep level. That she had a connection with him.

"Now that we've gotten to know each other," she said, "I'm going to be sorry to lose you as a friend."

He nodded. "Me, as well," he said. He squeezed her hand. "Me, as well."

When JD returned, she met him out in the great room. "The van?"

"It's ready to go."

"Good. Let me make the call."

"How soon we leaving?"

"Couple hours."

She made the call to Nice to let them know they'd be ready sometime tomorrow.

Then she sat down with JD and told him as much as she could about herself, her real name, the operation and her father. None of it seemed to shock him as much as the news had shocked him that Giambi had a daughter.

"So this will all be over by tomorrow."

"Yes."

"And you're going back to Vegas to take care of your situation."

"Yes."

He frowned.

"Unless you want to take me to Paris for a couple days before we have to go our separate ways. Show me the town."

"You've never done Paris?"

"Not with a Formula One driver. But if that's going to interfere with your schedule—"

"Paris, it is."

She smiled. "Then let's get Salvatore on his way."

At two-thirty in the morning, like three people escaping a prison, they went down to the garage in Giambi's private elevator. They slipped out through the garage side door, JD leading the way with two suitcases and a dress bag, Beth with her three bags and Giambi with one suitcase and two smaller travel bags.

JD dropped his bags, went out and brought the van over to the side of the building. He pulled up with the van and they piled their bags and themselves inside.

Giambi sat in the back, JD drove, Beth was in the front

passenger seat. They pulled out of the private back gate and left the Sapphire Star behind.

Beth turned to Giambi. "It's not all bad."

"How is that?"

"You get to meet your daughter and, eventually, we're going to get your nemesis."

"Half the intelligence agencies in the world have tried, and failed."

"We're very good and we only have to succeed once."

They drove quickly out of Monaco and headed toward Nice, the traffic very light on the French country roads.

After a half hour or so into the quiet escape, the distinctive lights of a French motorcycle cop flashed behind them.

"Shit. No, I'm not speeding," JD said, anticipating her question.

"Get the hell out of here," Giambi snapped. "Run the bastard off the road and get moving."

"No. Pull over," Beth said. "Maybe there's a taillight out or something. We don't want a major incident."

"Maybe it's not a cop," Giambi argued. "Maybe this is a set-up."

"Keep it in gear," Beth said, all too familiar with getting caught in an ambush. "Be ready to move in a hurry if that's the case."

She glanced back at Giambi. He had a gun out. He tucked it alongside his right leg as the cop approached from the driver's side. This could get ugly in a flash.

Beth didn't see any other signs of a set-up. No other vehicles. Just this lone motorcycle cop. And he didn't look like he was going to make a move.

The cop took a good look inside the van with his flashlight, then asked JD to turn off the engine and produce his license and the van registration.

He went back to his bike to make a call.

"What the hell is this?" Giambi grumbled.

"Everybody just relax," Beth said. She glanced at JD. "You said you've had some run-ins with the French police before. How bad were they?"

"He shouldn't have been driving," Giambi said.

Beth decided it was a good time to make another call. The federal contact in Nice. She called the number and after a half-dozen rings a groggy agent answered.

She gave him her contact code, then told him the situation and that they needed to get hold of the prefecture in Nice in a hurry.

"Have they arrested you?"

"No. But we need to avoid that."

"Where are you?"

She told him their location. He said he'd be out to pick up Giambi.

"No. That has to come later. We have something to do first."

"We're taking him now, before something else goes wrong."

"That wasn't the deal."

"It is now."

"All right. We'll talk about it when you get here. Just get this cop off of us."

"Just sit tight."

They waited while the cop talked to somebody on his radio. When he finished, he walked to the car.

He gestured for them to get out.

"We are on a mission that you cannot interfere with," Beth said. *"Nous sommes sur une mission que vous ne pouvez pas interferer."*

The cop took half a step back and his hand dropped to loosen his sidearm.

Beth sensed Giambi making a move in the back and she reached back and grabbed him. "No."

She leaned over JD so that the cop could see her hands and her face. "We are American agents."

He ordered them out. "*Sortir! Garder vos mains où je peux les voir!*"

He had one hand on his sidearm, the other working his collar mike.

"You know what," Beth said, whispering in JD's ear. "Maybe we need to get the hell out of here. I'll call my contacts and see if they can do something about this, but in the meantime, take out his motorcycle and get out of here."

"He's got my license and the van's registration."

"The feds will sort it out and clean it up for you later," Beth said.

"I don't want to end up with Giambi in some witness protection program."

"Shut up and get the hell out of here," Giambi said. "I want to see my daughter."

Beth leaned over and apologized to the cop, but they really had to go. "*Désolé, gendarme. Nous devons aller.*"

"Maybe the feds are behind this," Giambi said. "Or the prince. That damn Greek. I'm telling you this is a set-up."

JD turned the engine over and took off so fast the cop hardly had time to react.

He took out the motorcycle and sent it off the road and into the ditch, they swerved violently back up on the main tarmac and screamed off down the road.

Chapter 29

"This is bad," Beth said, as she turned to see what the cop was doing. He didn't fire at them, instead he was busy on his radio. She turned to JD. "I think we need to get the hell off the main road and get very lost."

"There'll be a hundred cops and a half-dozen choppers looking for us," Giambi said. "I'm not letting them take me in. I'd rather die right here than spend one day in a French jail. They'd never let me out."

"The FBI would get you out."

"To hell with the feds. They'd let the French soften me up first. I'm not getting caught."

JD glanced in the rearview mirror. "Maybe we need to change vehicles."

"Whatever we do," Giambi said, "it better be quick."

Beth took out her cell phone. "Just get off the main road and into the hills. I'll see what I can do to take the heat off of us."

Getting tangled up with the French police was the worst of all possible situations at this moment. The feds in Nice had better have a solution.

Beth called her contact and rattled off the predicament and told the man to get the police to back off or they might never see Giambi. "You want what he's got, you better have some clout with the French police or you can kiss Salvatore Giambi goodbye."

When he tried to argue with her, she cut him off. "Look, this is an emergency situation and it's going downhill very fast. Get the hell out of bed and deal with this or forget you ever even came close to the man who knows everything about who is moving what money in and out of Europe."

She didn't wait for any counterarguments.

"I hope he comes through," JD said as they cut up a narrow lane through a grove of poplars. "I'm no more interested in quality time in a French jail than Salvatore is."

Beth just sighed and shook her head. She didn't want to lose this operation when she was so close. "I don't know who that agent is," Beth said, "but he better have some juice."

Giambi expressed his doubt. "I don't know of any American agent who has juice with the French police. Unless they have something on a high minister who can pull the plug."

"I'm sure they do," Beth said.

They tore up a narrow, tree-lined road. There were shrubs every so often cut in the form of giant candy kisses.

"Take a right at the next road," Giambi said. "I think it'll eventually take us to Draguignan."

"Runnin' from the feds is in my bloodline," JD said in an affected, twangy drawl, maybe trying to lighten things up a little.

Giambi just scowled. "So, what did you and the Greek have to talk about?"

"My future. Not that it looks like I have much of one at the moment."

In a testy voice, Giambi asked, "And just how long have you been talking about your future with him?"

"One day," JD shot back.

Beth listened to their banter, but her mind was on the federal agents and what it would mean if they whisked Giambi out of the country before he got a chance to see his daughter. He said he wouldn't give her the name if he didn't get this opportunity and she had no reason not to believe him.

For the next hour they wound through the foothills, taking a roundabout way through the French countryside, before turning toward Lorgues.

Then they pushed northeast toward wine country, swinging along narrow country roads, hiding in the trees for periods of time to see if they were being hunted in the area, coming out again and maneuvering their way toward the rolling hills and old farms in the vicinity of Draguignan.

The agent finally called Beth and told her that the French police were not in a good mood, but that they had until noon to turn Giambi over to the feds. If that happened, there would be no further action.

Beth hung up with the agent and told Giambi.

"Could be a ruse," he suggested.

"Not a lot we can do about it if that's true," Beth said.

When they reached the outskirts of Draguignan, Giambi said it was too early to go to her house. "She opens her shop in town around eight-thirty, so we should show up at her house around seven-thirty. She's only a few minutes from town."

They had time and decided to eat breakfast in town.

Beth thought Giambi looked nervous. It seemed to her that he shouldn't have any expectations. Kaya didn't know him any more than he knew her. They had no personal history. Yet he seemed to have some idea that this was going to be a powerful moment.

Beth wondered if the fact that he had a daughter of color was the overriding factor. She had no doubt it played some role. Giambi had grown up in a different era when having a black in the family was probably unthinkable. He probably had some other reasons as well. A man with his lifestyle might find kids an interference, although even the ultimate playboy, Hefner, had a daughter who now ran his empire.

"Your daughter's half-black. Is that bothering you? A man your age, from your generation…"

"Maybe it did once. I got past that after a while. But when you don't know you even have a kid, black or green or whatever, and they're already older and you show up in their lives…"

Beth let it drop. The man had never even said hello to his own daughter, and now he was saying goodbye. Not to have known her own father would have been too tragic to imagine. But why should Giambi's daughter even want to talk to the man who had lived so close by, yet never ventured to introduce himself?

She said, "You should have let her know who you were. Tried to connect with her."

"I know. It was a big mistake."

At least he acknowledged it. Not that it would make a bit of difference to his daughter.

They found a breakfast place on the edge of Draguignan, in a medieval-looking area of town, so old that it was obviously trendy. It was more like eating in someone's house than in a restaurant.

While they were waiting for their eggs, sausage and croissants, Giambi, tempting fate and the police, took his coffee and a cigar and went outside to walk around, leaving JD and Beth alone.

JD, looking out to the street where Giambi stood, said, "I still can't see him staying in some witness protection program. Maybe he wants the cops to challenge him. Do some O.K. Corral shit right there on Draguignan's main street."

Beth glanced out the window. "Well, he's at that stage of his life where he might think that is the best way to go. A guy like that spending his last years in hiding or in jail would be tough. But I won't let him die without telling me what I want to know."

"If you get what you want, and your other situation is taken care of, then what?"

"I'll resume my normal life."

"Always in the dark. Wouldn't you like to just be yourself, maybe play in the big open tournaments like the World Series of Poker?"

She shrugged. "I like the intimacy of the small, rich games. And I like being other people. Transforming."

"You're not like anyone I've met before, that's for sure."

"That good or bad?"

"It's good. But it doesn't bode well for a long-term relationship."

"And you think you're ready for one?"

"Shit, I don't know."

She chuckled. "Believe me, you aren't. Not at this point in your life. Maybe later, when you've achieved some of your goals, you'll look beyond just racing. But that doesn't mean I can't become a real Formula One fan. Show up for a race now and then."

She saw Giambi coming back. "He looks miserable."

"That's gotta be tough at his age," JD said. "Man like that, no family but a daughter who wants nothing to do with him. Loses everything he's built. Nothing to look forward to but the feds. Makes you want to tie yourself to a fifty-gallon drum full of cement and throw it into the ocean."

"So, did you and the Greek make a deal?"

"It's in the discussion stage. If not him, there are still a couple of the Hollywood people who are interested. But I'd go with the Greek first. He's got the experience, the money, and he can get me a ride sooner."

Giambi came in and they ate their breakfast in relative quiet. He looked really tense and she found that interesting. A man who dealt with the mob, professional killers, authorities, and all the things that a casino in Monaco throws at him, and the thing he seems most nervous about is some young woman he's never met.

They were back on the road at seven-fifteen. When they turned up the country road and drove about a mile, Giambi pointed out a house sitting back off the narrow road about a hundred yards, surrounded by trees.

"Keep going."

JD drove down through a long tunnel of old trees until Giambi told him to stop, pull over and park.

"What's wrong?" Beth asked. "You didn't like the car we passed that was parked off the road, hidden in the trees?"

Giambi nodded.

It had been visible only because a shaft of morning light cutting through the trees glinted off it's windshield. Otherwise Beth doubted they would have noticed it.

A farmer on his tractor was working the field, moving their way.

"If she has visitors," Beth said, "the farmer would probably know." She left JD and Giambi in the car and walked through the trees to the edge of the field.

JD watched Beth until she reached the fence, then he turned to Giambi. "Maybe she's got a boyfriend and that's all it is."

"A boyfriend hides his car in the trees? Doesn't park out in front of the house?"

"Maybe she just doesn't want nosey neighbors knowing she has a visitor."

Giambi got a look on his face. When his eyes narrowed JD knew something was coming. Suddenly Giambi pulled his gun, grabbed JD by the shoulder and pointed the gun at his head. "You're the only one who could have given her access to my office and my computers."

"That's right. I did."

"You called off the ride on the chopper and told me to go on ahead."

"I told you what was going on."

"Hell you did. You knew it was going to blow up."

"You're crazy. I had no idea. What's wrong with you?"

"You and that goddamn Greek. How did anybody know I had a daughter who lives here? You sorry son of a bitch."

"You're out of your mind," JD said. "You want to point that somewhere else?"

"Maybe I don't know what the hell is really going on and maybe you don't, either. You think she's been talking to the FBI, but how do we know that?"

JD stared at Giambi. "You're letting your paranoia get to you. If we were involved in some conspiracy, why in hell go through all this? You make no sense. Back off and get that gun away from me, old man. Whoever was in your computer before her would already know you were sending money here. Face it, if Beth and I were in it together, we'd be digging your damn grave in one of these fields by now."

JD pushed the gun away and got out of the van, pacing along the side of it. He was growing tired of the man's endless finger-pointing. He walked back to the window, looking in at Giambi. "You need to get yourself straight. Next thing you'll be thinking this was all orchestrated by Prince Albert and we're all part of the great conspiracy to get you. Which would make you about the most important person in the universe. Maybe the President of the United States, the mob and the European Union are all involved.

"The conspiracy against you is there. But it's none of the above. You know who it is. If somebody has your daughter and is waiting for you, then you'll finally have somebody you can shoot instead of me."

Giambi sank back in the seat. JD had never seen him this confused and weary. The man always seemed to know what was going on and what he had to do. Suddenly he was just this old guy who didn't know what the hell had happened to him. JD felt sorry for him. The man was losing everything, all at once. That would be enough to make you crazy.

JD turned and watched Beth waving at the tractor driver, but the farmer had yet to see her.

He turned back to Giambi and said, "Look, I would never try to kill you. All that you did for me—what the hell's wrong with you? I'm gonna betray the guy who saved my ass and got me straightened out and was trying his best to get me a seat in the show? C'mon, you've got to give me more credit than that."

Giambi glanced up toward Beth, then back to JD. "It's a hell of a thing."

"What?"

"The way things happen in this world. How things have a nasty way of coming back to bite you long after something should have gone away."

JD nodded. How a man like him could be blackmailed for that long and not be able to find a way to track down the blackmailer was amazing. He wondered what all the blackmailer had on Giambi. It had to be really bad.

"You didn't get a good look at that car in the trees, did you?" Giambi asked.

"It looked like a BMW to me. There are a million of them running around. You want to go take a look?"

Giambi nodded, then got out of the van. They walked through the trees to the car. They didn't have to get very close when the old man whispered, "Son of a bitch."

The car had a decal on it for the executive parking area. And there was only one person who had that particular model. A model neither of them liked. 2006 BMW X5 SUV.

Vincenzio.

Giambi was beside himself. "I'll kill that bastard. I'll rip him apart and bury him out in that fucking field."

"I take it you don't want to bring the police into this?"

"No police. They'll just get her killed."

"You have any ideas?"

Giambi glanced over at Beth, who was still trying to wave down the tractor.

"Yeah, that tractor would be one way to get close to the house. If somebody was out front causing a distraction, somebody hiding on the other side of the tractor could jump off and get up to the back with nobody seeing him. Go get Beth and tell her what the situation is."

Chapter 30

Beth turned as JD ran through the trees toward her. She could tell something had happened and she ran to meet him.

"What's wrong?"

He told her about Vincenzio's car.

"The tractor could drive right past the back of the house. No one would question it. A distraction out front would provide additional cover. Giambi is going to do this one way or another, Beth. Without the police. The man wants a fight and now he has one. You can argue with him if you want, but it won't do any good. I know him. When he makes up his mind how things are going to go, that's how they go. Vincenzio is the one who's been betraying him. Probably to the *Cosa Nostra*. He's probably the one who set off the bomb in the chopper."

"What about the attack on us?"

"I don't know. Maybe the hit team did think it was

Giambi. Not even Vincenzio knew who was coming and going from Giambi's private quarters."

In the distance, Beth could see Giambi checking his weapon. She had no doubt JD was right. "Let me deal with the farmer," she said. "Keep Giambi under control until I can arrange something. If we're going to do this, let's do it with some chance of success. He may want to die in a shoot-out, but I don't."

JD nodded and walked back into the trees toward Giambi.

Beth waited until the farmer turned again, maneuvering the tractor along the rows.

Finally, when the farmer drove close to the fence line, he saw her waving him to come over. He slowed, then turned and drove over to the fence and cut the engine.

"Bonjour."

"Bonjour, madame."

"I need to talk to you. It's important."

He dismounted, walked over and asked her what was the matter, taking off his wide-brimmed hat, running his hand through his graying hair.

Beth told him they were worried about the woman who lived in the house and owned the land he was working. She had not come into town to open her store and she might be in trouble. "The man with her is dangerous."

"There is more than one man," the farmer said. "I saw two, maybe three."

The farmer stood with his hands in his pockets. He was a solid-shouldered man, ruddy, his face heavily lined from years outdoors.

As Beth explained what she wanted from him, he kept glancing toward the house that was just on the other side of the knoll. They could only see the top of the roof from where they were.

"There is no time to call the police," she told him. "These men probably have a lookout on the highway. They will kill her and get away. They're professionals."

"You don't expect me to get involved with killers, do you?"

He looked up when Giambi and JD walked over to join them.

Beth said, nodding to Giambi, "This man is her father."

Giambi said, "You know the Sapphire Star Casino in Monaco?"

"Of course."

"I am Salvatore Giambi. I built that casino. Kaya is my daughter."

He told the farmer what he wanted to do, but the farmer wasn't showing any signs of compliance. He looked both skeptical and more than a little nervous.

It was a hard decision for him, he said. He didn't want any trouble. He kept saying the best thing was to call the police. "They will be here in just a few minutes," he argued.

"Police would only complicate matters," Giambi said. "And it might get her killed."

The farmer said he was Kaya's friend and he worked for her whenever she needed plowing or other tasks. He was plowing up some of her vineyards now on directives from Paris. It was a terrible thing, he said. But this? No, he couldn't get involved. He had a family of his own to think about.

"We must do this quickly," she said. "We have no time. You only have to drive by. Two of us—"

"No. That is impossible. I will become an accessory to whatever happens. This is a police matter."

"You said you think there are two or three men?"

"I did hear more than one man talking when I went up

on the porch to deliver Kaya eggs and milk. You must listen to me. This is something for the police."

Giambi walked over to the fence. It had three split wood rails. He insinuated himself through the top two and walked over to the tractor.

"We can fit here in back of the seat. Nobody will see us."

"I can't help you. I'm sorry. This is not possible."

Giambi pulled a gun. "You're going to drive the tractor with us in it over to the back of the house."

"Wait. I can drive it," JD said. "I'll put his hat on, they won't know who it is."

"No," Giambi insisted. "We need you to drive up to the front of the house and make some kind of diversion. Get their attention directed to you so we can get in the back. My daughter's life is at stake here and I'll do what I have to. And that includes," he said pointedly to the farmer, "putting a bullet in you if you jeopardize her."

"I'm sorry," Beth said. "We have to do this. If the men in there are the professionals we think they are they probably have the means to listen to police calls."

"Get on the tractor and let's go," Giambi demanded. The farmer's face paled and he nodded, finally realizing Giambi was in charge. "She could be dead already. JD, get going. Whatever you do, make sure you get their attention."

"Don't worry about that," JD said. "Soon as the tractor gets near the back of the house, I'll do a few donuts in the front yard. Raise holy hell."

"The longer you divert them, the better our chances of getting in without being seen."

"I can act like some crazy country boy who's coming back from an all-night drunk and wants to see his girl."

"Just don't get yourself shot," Beth said.

"Don't worry, I'm not gonna be an easy target."

Then Giambi took out a small handgun and gave it to Beth. She hefted the piece and said, "I think I'll go back to being an analyst."

"What?"

"Nothing. Just talking to myself."

They went over the plan one more time. The farmer would drive them along the edge of the field, to the rear of the house, then tinker with something in the engine.

They would lie in the box behind the seat out of sight. When the tractor made one pass, then came back, that's when they'd go in. When JD saw them coming back for the second pass he'd do his thing.

Beth grabbed Giambi's arm. "We don't know for certain who those men are. Maybe they're relatives, friends. Don't shoot innocent people. And if the shooting starts, your daughter might be in the way."

He gave her a look that said he didn't appreciate being treated like a fool. "Friends and relatives don't show up in the middle of the night," he said. "And they don't hide their car in the weeds and prevent somebody from opening their shop. Somebody knew I was coming here." He glanced back at JD.

"I know but I don't want to be part of a real mistake." She nodded to JD and he went back to the van.

She and Giambi climbed onto the tractor and settled down in the tiny compartment behind the seat, squeezed in tight as sardines.

"Wouldn't want to go far in this," Giambi said. "Even with you practically on top of me."

It got a little worse when the tractor kicked to life and started along the field.

"You didn't think the feds would let you keep your guns, did you?"

"I need them for protection. Isn't that the meaning of the witness protection program?"

The tractor had a canvas roof but it didn't cover the box and they had the sun beating down on them as they headed out across the furrows. Beth couldn't remember ever in her life being on a tractor out in a field. Vegas didn't have farms.

Beth leaned toward the farmer. "How many doors in the back of the house?"

"One in the middle. There's a porch. Around to the left side there's another that leads into the kitchen. That's where I put the milk and eggs."

"Does she usually keep doors locked during the day?"

"No. This isn't America."

"What was the reason we saved these people? I forgot," Giambi said dryly.

They settled in while the tractor paused and the farmer acted like he was checking something. Giambi warned him as he was getting down not to run or he'd end up with a couple bullets in him.

The farmer got back in and they continued on for another hundred yards or so before turning. This time he would be going right by the house.

"All right, JD," Giambi whispered, "You better be ready to do your thing." Giambi turned to Beth. "You ready?"

"As I'm going to be. You okay?"

"If I can walk after being cramped up in this thing. Last time I was being pulled by a tractor it was when I was in high school on a Christmas hay wagon with Margie Huff."

"You remember her name after what…sixty years?"

"That's the thing. I can remember that better than I can remember last week."

"I think it had something to do with Margie Huff."

He made a sound that resembled a chuckle. "She was a

lot of fun, that's for sure. Back in those days, or as the young would say, back in the day, girls weren't as charitable as they are these days."

"We're getting close," the farmer said.

Giambi asked if he saw any signs of anyone. He didn't.

"Okay, JD," Giambi said on the cell. "Do your thing."

JD turned the van down the feeder road toward the house. "I'm about to make some noise."

He watched as the tractor approached the rear of the stone house.

He didn't know how French country guys behaved after a night of drinking, but he knew how a good ol' Tennessee, Thunder Road, dog in love would behave.

He hit the horn three blasts. Then he gassed the van, turned down across the lawn taking out a fence on the way. He leaned out the window and began yelling at the top of his lungs in his bastardized French accent about his love.

He spun his wheels in the grass, did a three-sixty that almost turned the van over.

Leaning out the window, he screamed, *"Belle fille! Belle fille!"*

Faces appeared at the windows.

The tractor was behind the house now, out of sight.

He crashed through the garden and took out some bushes.

A girl's face appeared as the door opened. It was her and somebody had a hold of her arm.

"Allez-vous en! Allenz-vous en!" She was yelling for him to go away.

"I love you," he yelled back. *"Je t'aime! Je t'aime!"*

He tore directly at the house, then at the last second did another wild turn, ripping up lawn and anything in his path, whooping it up and hoping no bullets came flying at him.

Chapter 31

Beth angled toward a side door, leaving Giambi to the back.

The racket out front continued. When JD said he was going to raise hell, she didn't realize how far he would take it. The van was running down everything in sight, horn blasting, JD yelling out the window.

Behind her the tractor was making its own noise.

She ducked under the line of sight of the windows, then straightened up at the screen door. It was old, desperately in need of paint and she wondered how loud it would screech when she pulled it opened.

She hit the screen with the gun hard enough to tear it away from the wood. She reached in and undid the latch. The main door wasn't locked.

When she opened it, a cat squirted out, startling her and sending her heart racing. The cat scampered off into the field.

Beth stepped into the kitchen. The knot in her stomach tightened. She smelled the stale aroma of coffee and bacon.

Dishes in the sink.

How many were there?

Four plates. Maybe one for Kaya?

She hoped so. Jesus, four of them would not be good.

She heard the chaos out front, the men inside talking angrily to Giambi's daughter.

Don't shake. Hold the damn gun steady. What do I do? Just tell them to surrender? And then if they don't?

Where's Giambi?

I don't like this, Beth thought.

Beth, her gun in front of her, gripped in both hands, moved forward toward the hall.

Grandfather clock, pendulum swinging. Ticktock, ticktock. So loud now that her senses had heightened.

Then she saw something in her peripheral vision. Someone moving from the center room. Giambi was now ahead of her.

She was wondering exactly what he would do, when it all just came apart. She couldn't tell who shot first.

The crash of gunfire enveloped the room. Screams. Yelling. Men going this way and that.

Giambi just standing there shooting.

His daughter, being held by one of the men in front of the window, screamed and jumped to the side and down.

Outside, passing the window, she saw the van continuing it's mad dash, tearing the place up, with JD whooping and beeping the horn.

One of the two men she could see turned. Vincenzio. Then he and Giambi exchanged fire. Both went down.

Then the other man, the one who'd been holding Kaya, swung toward Beth and she shot him before he could even bring his weapon to bare.

But then Vincenzio, wounded but still in the fight,

grabbed Kaya and screamed for Beth to throw her gun down or he would kill Kaya.

Before Beth could react, Giambi's daughter made a violent attempt to pull away, exposing him. Giambi, still down on the floor, shot Vincenzio in the chest three times.

Suddenly it was quiet.

Even JD had stopped his antics. A weird stillness filled the house. The smell of cordite stung Beth's nostrils. Her heart was beating like crazy and she could hear the blood rushing past her ears.

Giambi, bleeding from the shoulder, used the chair nearest him to get to his feet. He kicked the gun on the floor away from the man Beth had shot, then went over to check on Vincenzio.

Four plates. Not for serving, but at places. Four.

Beth turned and there he was coming down the staircase with a shotgun. The third man.

The barrel turned through a shaft of sunlight, the grease on the stock giving off a bright flash.

He had on a white T-shirt. He seemed slow.

Beth aimed to fire.

Something's wrong. Something's wrong.

In that split second she thought maybe this was a relative. An uncle or someone come to help them and that made her hesitate.

He wasn't looking at her, he was looking at Giambi, who had his back to the man.

He seemed ready to pull the trigger when he saw her out of the corner of his eye and jerked the shotgun toward her. She pulled the trigger.

The man fired as he fell, the deafening blast hitting the ceiling. Pieces fell in a tiny cloud of dust.

Beth turned to Kaya, fearful of learning who she'd

shot. "Is he one of them?" She hoped for the right answer.

"Yes. He … he has a problem with his bowels. He's been on the *toilette* all morning. He's the leader. Who are you?"

Beth didn't answer. She turned to Giambi. "You're hit."

"Minor scratch."

JD came in the door with a tire iron in his hand. He looked around at the carnage. "Jesus!"

"The men are dead. I don't know if they have somebody else out there. Go up to the road and watch, make sure nobody comes."

"Everybody okay?"

"Giambi got nicked in the arm. You did a great job distracting them. They were looking out that way when we came in behind them."

"I'm nothing if not a prime-time distracter," JD said as he headed back outside.

"Take a gun with you," Giambi yelled.

JD looked around at the weapons on the floor and picked the one closest to him.

Then he retreated back to the van.

Beth turned to Kaya. "Salvatore will explain it to you. I'll leave you two alone."

Beth went out the back door. She started to shake in a delayed reaction to the violence. She took a couple of deep breaths as she stepped out on the porch and went down the steps.

The farmer had moved some distance away but had stopped and was staring at the house. She walked out to meet him.

"I thought you'd all be dead," he said. "Every one of you."

"You have it about right, just the wrong group."

"Kaya is okay?"

"Yes, she's fine. Her father is slightly wounded. The others are dead." She told him the situation was under control and the authorities were on their way.

"If you don't want to get involved, maybe you should just go home."

"Yes, I think I will do that."

"I appreciate what you did even if it was against your will."

"I'm happy she's not hurt. She's a good neighbor. A good woman. Who were they?"

"We don't know yet. Maybe we won't know. Giambi has many enemies."

His eyes turned to the house and he seemed to be wondering what that would mean for Kaya sometime down the road. "The Germans once occupied that house during World War Two. I was three then, so I don't have memories of it the way my father does. It has a history. In World War One it was the English."

Now she turned and looked at the house, but with a different perspective. She imagined it in the hands of the English. Then the Germans. It always astounded her that World War II, with all the incredible and horrific things that had happened, was not very far back in history. That a man who was now only in his sixties could have been born then. In the middle of it.

"*Au revoir.*"

"*Au revoir.*"

He started his tractor up and headed across the field toward his own farmhouse, at least a quarter mile away.

She watched him for a time, admiring the life he was living, the nature of the man and his machine.

As she was returning she received a call from the federal agent. They were airborne in a chopper coming from Nice and wanted to know what had happened. She told them Giambi's condition and the situation on the ground.

When she went back into the house, Giambi and his daughter were in the kitchen talking intensely. Kaya had his shirt cut away and was looking at the wound.

She glanced up at Beth. "He says you're some kind of CIA agent."

"He's wrong about that. But it doesn't matter." Beth turned to Giambi. "The feds are on their way. I want that name before you go."

"You'll have it."

Kaya finished wrapping the wound on his left arm. She looked at Beth. "What are the American FBI doing here?"

"They're coming for your father."

"Arresting him?"

"No. To protect him."

"They're a little late."

Beth nodded. "He's got other problems. This was just one of them."

She went back outside to talk to JD.

Beth felt the weight of the silence. The fields were still. Even the air and the dust hanging in the sunlight seemed frozen in the aftermath of the violence.

She felt like she had come upon some great and terrible accident and was looking now at the dead, trying to make sense of the carnage.

JD was leaning against the van watching her as she approached. "He give you the name?"

"Not yet. He's talking with his daughter."

The chopper showed up about fifteen minutes later, *whoomping* across the sky.

Giambi and Kaya came out of the house. Then he

went to the van and took out a small suitcase and gave it to his daughter.

Beth could really see the resemblance in them, not so much in their faces, but in the cut of their bodies and the style of their walking.

The chopper settled on the edge of the nearby field, throwing dirt and weeds up in a storm. When it calmed down, three FBI agents got out, ducking their heads as people instinctively do when leaving a chopper whose blades are still swirling, even if very slow and a safe distance above them.

Beth shook hands with the agent in charge and explained the situation. The AIC said not to worry, that they had an arrangement with the French. The men in the house would be removed and this would become a nonevent as far as Giambi's daughter was concerned.

"It would be a good idea for you and JD Hawke to disappear."

"We're on our way."

"Good."

Beth didn't ask what the arrangement was, but assumed there were all kinds of such arrangements going on between intelligence agencies.

Giambi said goodbye to his daughter. She was very matter-of-fact about it. Beth didn't know what she might be feeling inside. Kaya had to be seriously traumatized by the entire affair.

Giambi then went over to JD and shook his hand and patted him on the shoulder. "Good luck with your career. I expect to see you win a lot of races."

Then he came over to Beth. He took out a small envelope and handed it to her. "As promised."

She took the envelope from him, stared at it for a moment, then put in it her purse. "Thank you."

"Remember what I said."

"I will. I'm sorry it comes to this for you, Salvatore. I hope they take good care of you."

"I'll be seventy-nine in a month. Maybe I should just be happy I got this far. Nothing is guaranteed in this life except the end. I'm happy that I met you. You're an extraordinary lady and I will think about you often."

"I won't forget the tango. Take care of yourself. Remember, you still have fifteen good years left."

He smiled sadly. "The last tango in Monaco. Old casino guys like me, as General MacArthur said of old soldiers, we don't die, we just fade away. Have a great life. I mean that from the bottom of my heart. Don't let anything stop you from getting what you want. And don't let the past hold you back. You have real quality. You deserve it all. Go get it."

She was shocked to see how wide his eyes opened, how clear they were, and that they had moisture in them as he stared at her. He looked at her not from cold gray gun turrets now, but from some other, highly emotional place.

He bent in his elegant way and kissed her lightly on the cheek, held her in his moist gaze, and then he walked away, a tall, proud, well-appointed man who wore his clothes as few men she'd ever met. He gathered his bags, then joined the agents in the helicopter. He flew away with them to whatever life he had left.

She stood for a long time staring at the chopper until it vanished over the hills in the direction of Nice.

"He was something else," JD said. "Not many like Salvatore Giambi."

They said goodbye to Kaya. JD apologized for messing up her lawn and she said it had saved her life and not to worry about it. They left her there waiting for the French authorities to show up.

"You aren't going to look in the envelope, see who it is you're going after next?" JD asked.

"No hurry now. I'll do it later. I want to wind down, relax, have some fun. The minute I know who I'm after, the hunt begins. I need some rest and recuperation first."

Plenty of time, she thought.

The man whose name was on the piece of paper would be there when she got back. Plenty of time. After sixteen years a few more days wouldn't matter.

The only thing she wanted to do right now was get away from all of it, become somebody else for a couple days, and not think about anything. Go to clubs, bars, cafés. Sleep all morning. Make love all night.

And forget the name in the envelope until she was on a plane home.

"Paris, here we come," JD said as they got into the van.

"Let's not go to Paris."

"I thought you wanted to do Paris."

"What's that little town we drive through on the way from Nice to Monaco…where Bono lives."

"Côte d'Azur?"

"Yes. Let's go there."

Chapter 32

It was funny. Now the last thing she wanted was glitter and glitz, trendiness and floods of tourists milling about in the great urban hustle of Paris, Cannes or Nice.

She wanted quiet. Old-style, Medieval quiet. With artists wandering about on cobblestone streets in a bohemian atmosphere beneath the shadows of stone citadels with dark passages. After making love she wanted to walk along the quay where the Mediterranean looked as it had for about five hundred years or so. She wanted to eat at the Josy-Jo restaurant in *Haut de-Cagnes* and *Le Cagnard*. Then stroll where Renoir and Nietzsche and a thousand artists and thinkers had walked.

They got a room at the portside Hotel Welcome on the *Villefranche-sur-Mer*.

Before doing anything else, Beth made a complete report to Delphi about her success with Salvatore Giambi.

With the information obtained about the Queen of Hearts assassin from Boston that Giambi tried to kill in Phoenix, Beth knew Delphi would send an agent to Boston to probe deeper into the Queen of Hearts's background, now able to connect the dots.

Another agent would no doubt be dispensed to Puerto Isla where Giambi's blackmail payments had been sent over the years. From his financial records they knew no one had made a withdrawal in the past three years since the dictator of Puerto Isla had been overthrown. What did that mean?

Madame Web, Arachne, Weaver, the Queen of Hearts. One and the same? No matter the answer, the deadly game of tracking the woman was now going to be easier thanks to Beth's work.

As much as she wanted to open that envelope, she refused. Once she saw the name she knew it would be almost impossible for her to enjoy this quaint spot.

JD didn't understand how she could do it. "What if the hotel burns down? What if there's no name and he was just playing games with you? How can you sleep knowing the secret is right there?"

"I've been waiting sixteen years. I can wait a couple of days," she repeated. But she did keep the envelope in the hotel safe, just in case.

It took a bath, making love, then a dinner, a few drinks, and finally a long walk along the quay to begin to escape the long day. By morning the past and future had all been dissolved. Now they were just there, in this beautiful place on the Mediterranean.

Slowly the tension drained out of them. They began to have some serious here-and-now-and-nothing-else fun and that's precisely what she needed.

JD told her a dozen times that he loved her chameleon-

like changes. She was a new woman for him every day.
Sometimes twice a day. He said he felt like he was with five
hot young women. Men like variety and she was the defi-
nition of variety. He couldn't decide which one he liked
best, the feisty redhead or the wild blonde, or maybe the
intellectual with the glasses, bobbed hair, severe suit and a
passion for making love in secret places outside their room.

It was mad sex, crazy fun. And then it was over and time
for them to return to their respective realities. Still, both of
them knew this wasn't the end.

"I want you to come to Toronto if I have a seat by then,"
he said. She promised that she would. He told her to be
careful with her hunt. He didn't want to see her get killed.
She promised to be careful. It was all very civilized.

Then he was gone and she was on board the flight out
of Nice and on her way home, the envelope still unopened
in her shoulder bag. It had been a week like no other.

Only when she was on the final leg of her journey, many
long hours and two plane changes later, the America West
aircraft beginning its descent to McCarran International in
Vegas, only then did she finally decide it was time.

Beth reached into her purse and pulled out the envelope.
She hoped she would take Giambi's advice and seek justice
rather than personal revenge. That would depend, she
imagined, on how things played out.

She held the envelope and thought about it for a
moment. There were choices here. She could just not open
it. That was an option. Just let it go.

But that thought lasted only until she remembered again
what had been done to her father.

So she did it. She opened the envelope.

There were two pieces of folded paper. On the first was

a note from Salvatore Giambi. A confession of love for her. An old man's passion for a young woman.

You have broken my heart, beautiful lady. I will suffer every moment of every day for the rest of my life.

How sweet. Pushing eighty and still an incurable romantic. She opened the second piece of folded paper.

On it was the name of the man whose identity she'd been seeking all her adult life. The man who had ordered the death of her father sixteen years ago.

Salvatore Giambi.

She stared at it, stunned.

How could this be? Was it some horrible joke?

But she knew it was no joke. All the pieces were right there, she just hadn't put them together.

Her emotions were struggling to reverse themselves.

Beneath his name was another short note apologizing for the attack on her in Las Vegas, assuring her that it wasn't on his orders and that she had nothing further to fear in Vegas. He'd made some calls.

With shaking hands, Beth folded the paper and put them both back into the envelope, then put the envelope in her purse. It was like an out-of-body experience.

She put her head on the headrest and stared into space. She thought back to her conversation with Allison and wondered if Allison had known more than she'd let on about Giambi and her father. More than anyone else, Allison knew what having a murdered parent was all about and how important it was to Beth to solve the murder.

Questions filled her head.

Was Salvatore Giambi really the mastermind behind some of the world's most successful cheating crews? Had he played both sides of the street? Protecting his own casinos and at the same time wreaking havoc on the bottom line of the competition? Was that where a lot of the laundered money was originating? Was the crew that tried to kill her one of Giambi's?

Beth pulled the note out once again to make sure. She, like any shocked card player who gets a big pair in the hole, had to look again.

Nothing had changed. She wasn't seeing things.

And now she understood Giambi's profound sadness. His regrets. How strange and ironic that Giambi had fallen in love with the daughter of the man he had ordered killed.

Life is anything but rational, Beth thought.

The worst part about it was how much she'd come to like the man.

She closed her eyes and waited for something to come to her about what she was going to do about this. She remembered again how he'd advised her to ask for justice, not revenge.

It was over. She'd found the killer. And he would, as he said, suffer every day for the rest of his life, however long that was, for he'd fallen in love with his victim's daughter. He'd lost everything. His own daughter, his casino, his dreams and Beth. Everything he valued.

Her next thought surprised her: Justice had been served.

It was really over. It was time for her to get past her sixteen-year obsession and move forward.

She remembered the tears in his eyes and she knew now they were tears of sorrow for what he'd done. And she realized that now there were tears in her own eyes for both men, her father and Giambi. Her father had been killed because he wanted to leave the business to become a good father. And the man who had killed him lived long enough to realize what that meant. And he would die with the knowledge.

As the plane turned and the brightest city on earth came

into view, Bethany James understood that she was now free to live the rest of her life.

Free to look forward and not back, forward to more rendezvouses with that Tennessee bad boy who definitely knew where the victory lane was. She smiled through her tears.

Thirty minutes after landing, she took a cab and headed to Sunrise Hospital to see how Curtis was doing. On the way she made a call to some friends to see if there were any big games in town. Tomorrow she would visit her father's grave and tell him that she was free.

* * * * *

*Don't miss the next exciting book in
the Athena Force adventure
MOVING TARGET
by Lori A. May
Available January 2008
Turn the page for a sneak preview.*

Chapter 1

He pulled tight around her throat, choking her.

He didn't say anything. He didn't have to.

Francesca Thorne was accustomed to gathering information from criminals in what wasn't said, whether it was through a look, a nervous tick, or simply the change in vocal pitch.

It was what an opponent did not say that aided in the patchwork of piecing together a personality. Her role was simply to watch. Observe. Filter the subtleties of the subconscious into her puzzle-solving mind.

Whereas she would normally calculate facial expressions and measure the pupil dilation of her suspect, waiting for a flinch to reveal so much more than well-selected words, the opportunity had not been given with this particular hunt.

Instead, she had to count on the sound of his breath, the weight of his grasp as he held one arm tightly around her neck.

He had snuck up on her.

Though she had returned to the scene to analyze its meaning, determine why the killer had chosen this location for his last victim, Francesca had not been counting on his presence. Not yet.

The killer had demonstrated an odd pattern of returning to the scene of his crimes only to enact another, but in between he always committed a murder at a much different location.

One location, then another, then back again.

By their calculations, he should have been somewhere else preparing to commit the sixth murder. She had chosen to come here with the hope she could piece together something about his selection process, quickly enough to determine where the next crime would take place.

But his M.O. had changed.

"You like taking risks," she said, holding her own voice steady, not allowing even a shred of fear to show as the pressure of his grip grooved over her esophagus. "Yet you refuse to show your face. Slightly passive-aggressive, don't you think?"

When in close contact with a serial killer, Francesca Thorne—lauded forensic psychologist for the FBI—pulled no punches in calling it as she saw fit. That included tempting fate by asking somewhat dangerous questions, or igniting a suspect's volatile nature. It was a trait for which she was known.

In this case, mocking her captor only made sense. Her action would cause a telling reaction on his part.

It was the nonvisual clues, such as his scent, his body temperature, that would matter most. And with what little headway they had made with this case, these variables would not only help her plan a maneuver away from his grasp, they would also lend a hand in discovering the identity of their prey.

He scoffed at her. "What—you some kind of shrink?"

Francesca registered the curve in vocal pitch, his agitation showing fluctuation in the short response. She had hit a nerve, without trying much at all.

"I don't need a shrink." His voice, increasingly harsh, told her she needed to make a move. Fast. His agitation would escalate and there was only so much fire she wanted to tempt within him. He was, after all, a serial killer.

Though she wanted to put an end to his existence when he said, "Maybe you have something else I want."

Killing was what she studied, not what she did. There had to be something she could do to not only end her captivity, but also ensure he was stopped from ever committing another crime again.

And then she spoke.

"Maybe you have something I need," she said, carefully reaching her hand around to settle into the small groove of space between her behind and his crotch.

Under the guise of giving him what he wanted, Francesca began to move her hand over the small bulge in his pants, twisting her gesture until her palm faced the small of her back, and while she listened to his breathing accelerate under her touch, she slowly moved one finger, then the next, into the gap between her flesh and her jeans until she felt it.

"I do, don't I?" he asked of her.

"You most certainly do," she cooed to egg him on, as she cautiously slid out the small knife from the sheath buried in the back of her pants. Within a heartbeat, she twisted its edge into him, stabbing the blade into his left hip as she said, "Your DNA."

ATHENA FORCE

Heart-pounding romance and thrilling adventure.

CAUGHT IN THE CROSS FIRE

Francesca Thorn is the FBI's best profiler…and she's
needed to target Athena Academy's most dangerous
foe. But as she gets dangerously close to revealing the
identity of her alma mater's greatest threat, someone
will stop at nothing to ensure she remains dead silent.
Her only choice is to accept all the help her
irritatingly sexy U.S. Army bodyguard can provide.

ATHENA FORCE

Will the women of Athena unravel Arachne's
powerful web of blackmail and death…or succumb
to their enemies' deadly secrets?

Look for

MOVING TARGET
by *Lori A. May,*

available January wherever you buy books.

Visit Silhouette Books at www.eHarlequin.com AF38977

nocturne™

Jachin Black always knew he was an outcast.
Not only was he a vampire, he was a vampire
banished from the Sanguinas society. Jachin, forced
to survive among mortals, is determined to buy
his way back into the clan one day.

Ariel Swanson, debut author of a vampire novel, could
be the ticket he needs to get revenge and take his
rightful place among the Sanguinas again. However,
the unsuspecting mortal woman has no idea of the
dark and sensual path she will be forced to travel.

Look for

RESURRECTION: THE BEGINNING

by

PATRICE MICHELLE

Available January 2008 wherever you buy books.

REQUEST YOUR FREE BOOKS!

2 FREE NOVELS PLUS 2 FREE GIFTS!

Silhouette® Romantic

SUSPENSE

Sparked by Danger, Fueled by Passion!

YES! Please send me 2 FREE Silhouette® Romantic Suspense novels and my 2 FREE gifts. After receiving them, if I don't wish to receive any more books, I can return the shipping statement marked "cancel." If I don't cancel, I will receive 4 brand-new novels every month and be billed just $4.24 per book in the U.S., or $4.99 per book in Canada, plus 25¢ shipping and handling per book plus applicable taxes, if any*. That's a savings of at least 15% off the cover price! I understand that accepting the 2 free books and gifts places me under no obligation to buy anything. I can always return a shipment and cancel at any time. Even if I never buy another book from Silhouette, the two free books and gifts are mine to keep forever.

240 SDN EEX6   340 SDN EEYJ

Name _____ (PLEASE PRINT) _____

Address _____ Apt. # _____

City _____ State/Prov. _____ Zip/Postal Code _____

Signature (if under 18, a parent or guardian must sign) _____

Mail to the **Silhouette Reader Service**™:
IN U.S.A.: P.O. Box 1867, Buffalo, NY 14240-1867
IN CANADA: P.O. Box 609, Fort Erie, Ontario L2A 5X3

Not valid to current Silhouette Intimate Moments subscribers.

Want to try two free books from another line?
Call 1-800-873-8635 or visit www.morefreebooks.com.

* Terms and prices subject to change without notice. NY residents add applicable sales tax. Canadian residents will be charged applicable provincial taxes and GST. This offer is limited to one order per household. All orders subject to approval. Credit or debit balances in a customer's account(s) may be offset by any other outstanding balance owed by or to the customer. Please allow 4 to 6 weeks for delivery.

Your Privacy: Silhouette is committed to protecting your privacy. Our Privacy Policy is available online at www.eHarlequin.com or upon request from the Reader Service. From time to time we make our lists of customers available to reputable firms who may have a product or service of interest to you. If you would prefer we not share your name and address, please check here. ☐

SRS07

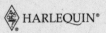

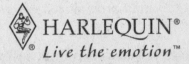